PEN PAL

PEN PAL

J.T. GEISSINGER

BRAMBLE

TOR PUBLISHING GROUP

NEW YORK

PEN PAL

Copyright © 2022 by J.T. Geissinger, Inc.

A Bramble Book
Published by Tom Doherty Associates / Tor Publishing Group
120 Broadway
New York, NY 10271

www.brambleromance.com

Bramble™ is a trademark of Macmillan Publishing Group, LLC.

The Library of Congress Cataloging-in-Publication Data is available upon request.

ISBN 978-1-250-35891-2 (trade paperback)
ISBN 978-1-250-34669-8 (ebook)

Our books may be purchased in bulk for promotional, educational, or business use. Please contact your local bookseller or the Macmillan Corporate and Premium Sales Department at 1-800-221-7945, extension 5442, or by email at MacmillanSpecialMarkets@macmillan.com.

Previously self-published by the author in August 2022

First Tor Trade Paperback Edition: 2024

Printed in the United States of America

0 9 8 7 6 5 4 3 2 1

To Jay, who knows how to find me in the dark

I

INFERNO

The path to paradise begins in hell.

~ *The Divine Comedy*

1

It's raining as my husband's casket is lowered into the hole in the ground. Raining hard, as if the sky itself is about to rip in half like my heart has.

I stand motionless under an umbrella with the other mourners, listening to the priest drone on about resurrection and glory, blessings and suffering, redemption and the holy love of God. So many words, and all so meaningless.

Everything is meaningless. There's a Michael-shaped hole in my chest, and nothing matters anymore.

That must be why I feel so numb. I'm empty. Grief has blown me apart, scattering my bones into a desert wasteland where they'll bake in silence under a merciless sun for a thousand years.

A woman behind me quietly weeps into her handkerchief. Sharon? Karen? A colleague of Michael's who I met at a long-ago faculty party. One of those awful holiday work parties in a school auditorium where they serve cheap wine in plastic cups and people stand around making awkward small talk until they're drunk enough to say what they really think about each other.

Sharon or Karen behind me told Michael he was a prick at that party. I can't remember why, but that's probably why she's crying now.

When someone dies, you start counting all the ways you failed them.

The priest makes the sign of the cross over his chest. He closes his Bible and steps back. I walk slowly forward, bend down to grasp a handful of soil from the pile to one side, then toss it onto the closed casket.

The wet clump of dirt makes an ugly hollow sound when it lands on the gray lid of the coffin, an uncaring splat of finality. Then it slides off, leaving a smear of brown behind like a shit stain.

Abruptly, I'm shaking with anger. I taste ashes and bitterness in my mouth.

What a stupid ritual this is. Why do we even bother? It's not like the dead can see us mourning them. They're gone.

A sudden gust of cold wind rattles the leaves in the trees. I turn and walk away through the rain, not looking back when someone softly sobs my name.

I need to be alone with my grief. I'm not one of those people who likes to commiserate over a tragedy. Especially when the tragedy is my own.

When I open the front door of the house, it takes a moment for me to register that I'm home. I have no recollection of the drive from the gravesite to here, though the blank spot in time doesn't surprise me. Since the accident, I've been in a fog. It's as if my brain is blanketed in thick clouds.

I read somewhere that grief is more than an emotion. It's a physical experience, too. All kinds of nasty stress chemicals get released into the bloodstream when a person is grieving. Fatigue, nausea, headaches, dizziness, food aversion, insomnia . . . The list of side effects is long.

I've got them all.

I kick off my shoes and leave them under the console table in the foyer. Tossing my wool coat onto the back of a kitchen chair, I head to the fridge. I open the door and stand looking inside as rain drums against the windowpanes and I try to convince myself I'm hungry.

I'm not. I know I should eat to keep my strength up, but I have no appetite for anything. I let the door swing shut and press my fingers against my throbbing temples.

Another headache. That's the fifth one this week.

When I turn around, I notice the envelope on the table next to the fruit bowl. It sits by itself, a white rectangle with neat handwriting and a stamp that reads "LOVE" in red letters.

I know for a fact it wasn't there when I left.

My first thought is that Fiona must've brought in the mail. Then I remember she cleans the house on Mondays. Today's Sunday.

So how did it get there?

As I cross to the table and pick up the letter, a rumble of thunder rattles the windows. A sudden gust of wind whistles through the trees outside. The eerie feeling intensifies when I read the return address.

Washington State Penitentiary.

Frowning, I tear open the edge of the envelope and pull out the single sheet of white unlined paper inside. I unfold it and read aloud.

"I'll wait forever if I have to."

That's it. There's nothing else, except a signature scratched below the words.

Dante.

I flip the page over, but it's blank on the other side.

For a fleeting moment, I think the letter must be intended for Michael. That idea gets tossed aside when I realize it's addressed to me. That's my name right there on the front of the envelope, printed in neat block letters with blue pen. This Dante person, whoever he is, meant for me to receive this.

But why?

And what is he waiting for?

Unsettled, I fold the letter into thirds, stuff it back into the envelope, and drop it on the table. Then I make sure all the doors and windows are locked. I draw the drapes and blinds against the wet, gray afternoon, pour myself a glass of wine, then sit at the kitchen table, staring at the envelope with a strange feeling of foreboding.

A feeling that something's coming. And that whatever it is, it isn't good.

⁓

When I drag myself from bed in the morning, the headache is still with me, but the oppressive sense of dread is gone. It's gray and blustery outside, but the rain has stopped. For now, at least. It's wet and cloudy year-round in Washington, and January is especially dreary.

I try to work, but give up after only an hour. I can't concentrate. Everything I draw looks depressed. The children's book I'm illustrating is about a shy boy who befriends a rabbit that can speak, but today, my rabbit looks like he'd rather take an overdose of Percocet than eat the carrots the boy tries to feed him.

Abandoning my desk, I head to the kitchen. The first thing my gaze lands on is the letter on the table. The next thing I notice is the water all over the floor.

Overnight, the ceiling has sprung a leak. Two of them, to be specific.

I knew we should've bought something newer.

But Michael didn't want a new home. He preferred older homes with "character." When we moved into this Queen Anne Victorian six years ago, we were newlyweds with more energy than money. We spent weekends painting and hammering, pulling up old carpet and patching holes in drywall.

It was fun for about three months. Then it became exhausting. Then it became a battle of wills. Us against a house that seemed determined to remain in a state of decay no matter how much we tried to update it.

We'd replace a broken water pipe, then the heater would go out. We'd upgrade the ancient kitchen appliances, then we'd find toxic mold in the basement. It was a never-ending merry-go-round of repairs and replacements that drained our finances and our patience.

Michael had planned to replace the leaky roof this year.

I sometimes wonder what will be left on my to-do list when I die.

But then I force myself to think about something else, because I'm sad enough already.

I bring two plastic buckets from the garage into the kitchen and set them on the floor under the places the ceiling is dripping, then get out the mop. It takes almost an hour to get all the water up and the floor dry. Just as I'm finishing, I hear the front door open and shut. I glance up at the clock on the microwave.

Ten o'clock. Right on time.

My housekeeper, Fiona, walks into the kitchen. She takes one look at me, drops the plastic bags of cleaning supplies she's holding, and lets out a bloodcurdling scream.

It's a testament to how exhausted I am that I don't even jump at the sound.

"Do I really look that bad? Remind me to put on some makeup before you come next week."

Breathing hard, her face white, she braces an arm against the doorframe and makes the sign of the cross over her chest. "Christ on a cracker! You gave me a proper fright!"

I frown at her. "Who were you expecting? Santa Claus?"

Unlike the rest of Fiona, her laugh is small and weak.

Of Scottish descent, she's plump and attractive, with bright blue eyes, rosy cheeks, and stout legs. Her hands are red and rough from years of work cleaning houses. Though somewhere north of sixty, she's got the energy of a woman half her age.

Having her help me keep the place up is an expensive luxury, but with two stories, over five thousand square feet, and what seems like a million nooks and crannies that gather dust, the house needs constant cleaning.

She shakes her head, fanning herself. "Hoo! You got the old ticker pumping, my dear!" She chuckles. "It's been a while."

Then she turns serious and looks at me closely, peering at me as if she hasn't seen me in a hundred years.

"How are you, Kayla?"

I glance away. I can't lie while gazing right into those piercing blue eyes. "I'm okay. Just trying to stay occupied."

She hesitates, as if unsure of what to say. Then she exhales in a gust and makes a helpless gesture toward the window and the cloudy view of Puget Sound beyond. "I'm so sorry about what happened. I read about it in the paper. Such a shock. Is there anything I can do?"

"No. But thank you." I clear my throat. *Don't cry. Don't cry. Pull yourself together.* "So don't bother with the kitchen today, obviously. I'll find someone to come out and take a look at the leak, but in the meantime, there's no sense cleaning up in here if it's only going to get wet all over again. My office doesn't need to get cleaned this week, and also . . ."

I swallow around the lump in my throat. "Also maybe skip Michael's office. I think I'd like to leave it as is for a while."

"I understand," she says softly. "So you'll be staying?"

"Yes. I'll be here all day."

"No, I meant you'll be staying in the house?"

There's something odd in her tone, a subtext I'm not getting, but then I understand. She's worried about her job security.

"Oh, I couldn't sell now. It's too soon to make such a major decision. Maybe in a year or two, when things feel more settled. I don't know. Honestly, I'm just taking it one day at a time."

She nods. We stand in awkward silence for a moment until she points over her shoulder.

"I'll get to work now."

"Okay. Thank you."

She picks up the bags from where she dropped them on the

floor, then turns to go. But she turns back suddenly and blurts, "I'll pray for you, dear."

I don't bother telling her not to waste her breath.

I know I'm a lost cause, that no amount of prayer in the universe can help me, but that doesn't mean I have to be rude about it. I simply bite my lip, nod, and swallow my tears.

When she walks out, my gaze lands on the letter on the table. I can't say what compels me to do it, but before I know it, I'm sitting down to write a reply. I scribble it on the back of the letter Dante sent me.

What are you waiting for?

I mail it before I lose my nerve. It takes a week before I get a response, and it's even shorter than mine. In fact, it's only one word.

You.

On the bottom right-hand corner of the paper, there's a smudge of something dried and rust-colored that looks like blood.

2

I put the letter in the back of my underwear drawer and leave it there, determined to forget about it. If another one comes, I might call the nice detective who interviewed me after the accident and see what he thinks about it. Maybe I'll get him to look into this Dante character and see what he can find out.

In the meantime, I've got other things to worry about.

Aside from the new roof leak, the house has also decided it has electrical problems.

The dining room chandelier flickers. I hear popping and crackling noises when I hit the light switch in the master bedroom. Every once in a while, the doorbell rings when no one is there.

I tried calling three different local roofers, but nobody called me back. So now I'm waiting for a handyman, some guy named Ed. I came across his business card in the bottom of my kitchen junk drawer when I was looking for a pen.

I don't know why, but I'm expecting an older man with a balding head and a beer belly wearing a tool belt slung around his hips. Instead, what I get when I open the front door to his knock is a smiling, slender young man with long brown hair held off his face with a braided leather headband. He's wearing a John Lennon T-shirt, faded bell-bottom jeans, and sandals, and holds a rusty metal toolbox in one hand.

He reeks of pot.

"Hey. You Kayla?"

"That's me."

Grinning, he extends his hand. "I'm Eddie."

I return his smile, and we shake hands. He seems sweet and harmless, two things I appreciate in any man I allow into my home while I'm here alone.

"Come in. I'll show you around."

He follows me into the kitchen, commenting on how cool he thinks the house is.

"Cool, but falling apart a little more every day." I gesture to the two brown water-stain rings on the kitchen ceiling.

"Yeah, these old houses need lots of TLC." He cranes his neck to stare up at the stains. "Especially with the humidity here. You got mold problems?"

"Not anymore. Took care of that a few years back. Right now, it's the roof leak and the electrical." I give him an over-view of what's been happening with the lights and the doorbell. "Plus, I smell something burning when I run the dryer. And the TV sometimes turns itself off. Oh, and a couple of light bulbs have exploded recently."

A sudden cold draft lifts the hairs on my arms and the back of my neck and sends a tingle down my spine. Shivering, I rub my hands over the goose bumps on my arms.

I should ask him to have a look at the weather stripping around the windows while he's here. But first things first. "Let me show you where the electrical panel is."

Eddie follows me to the utility room at the back of the house next to the garage. The washer and dryer are there, along with cabinets containing a hodgepodge of household supplies.

Setting his toolbox on the floor, Eddie flips open the metal door on the electrical panel and does a quick visual scan of the switches.

"I'll check the voltage first, see if the breaker's running at the right capacity. Then I'll look at the integrity of the wiring. You might have water damage or fraying that could cause problems. Then I'll check all your outlets, make sure they're not compromised. Where's the meter?"

"Right outside the garage door."

He nods. "Dig it. I'll take a look at that, too. Should take me an hour or so to get through everything, then I'll give you an estimate for the repairs. Sound good?"

"Sounds great, thanks. To get into the attic, the access is on the second floor through the master bedroom closet. The ladder's in the garage."

"Cool."

"Holler if you need me. I'll be around."

"Will do."

I leave him to it and head into my office. I'm able to work for a while before the headache starts. It's a dull throbbing around my temples and pressure behind my eyes so strong, it makes them water. I lie on the small sofa with the shades drawn and the lights off until Eddie appears in the doorway with his toolbox.

"Oh, sorry, man. Didn't know you were sleeping. I was just gonna check the outlets in here."

Disoriented, I sit up. "I wasn't asleep. Just resting my eyes. I have a terrible headache."

He nods in sympathy. "I used to get crazy migraines."

Used to, past tense. I feel a weird pang of hope. "Did you find something that helped them? Nothing I take makes a dent."

"You'll laugh. Mind if I turn the lights on?"

"Go ahead. And I won't laugh, I promise. I'm too desperate." When Eddie hits the switch and light floods the room, I wince. I try to stand, but discover I'm too dizzy. So I sink back onto the sofa, close my eyes, and gingerly pinch the bridge of my nose.

When did I last eat? I can't remember.

Eddie ambles around, hunting for outlets. He's so slim, his footsteps are silent on the floor. I've known cats who made more noise.

"After I started seeing a therapist, the headaches went away. Poof, man. Just gone. Turns out, I had lots of emotions bottled up."

I open my eyes to find him crouched under my desk with a small power meter in his hand. He sticks it into the electrical outlet, waits a moment as he reads whatever it's telling him, then stands and moves to the next outlet, where he repeats the process.

"Psychosomatic illness, they call it. Your brain literally makes you sick. Stress is *that* toxic. Far out, isn't it?"

"Far out," I agree, wondering if he lives in a commune or co-op. They're all over Washington and the Seattle area, communal-living groups started in the free-love sixties where people share housing and resources and eschew modern things like cell phones and GMO foods.

I'm much too private to live in such close quarters with

people I'm not having sex with, but I don't judge anybody's life choices.

Standing, he turns to look at me. "I can give you my doc's name if you want. Unless you don't think stress could be a problem for you."

"Does losing my husband count as stress?"

I don't know why I said that. Or why I said it in the biting way I did. I don't normally wear my heart on my sleeve, and I'm not sarcastic like Michael was. He dealt with depressing or morbid things with black humor that sometimes came off as insensitivity, but I knew was just a coping mechanism. The man was a marshmallow.

Confused, Eddie stares at me. "You lost him?"

No one can possibly be this dumb. "He died."

Now he looks stricken. "Oh, dude. I'm so sorry."

"Thank you."

"Was it recent?"

"New Year's Eve."

"Holy shit! That's only a couple weeks ago!"

I should stop talking now. Every word out of my mouth makes poor Eddie more and more upset.

I've always had a problem over-empathizing with other people, which is one of the reasons I tend to keep to myself. Everyone else's emotions piled on top of my own can get suffocating sometimes.

"Yes. Anyway." I manage to stand this time, then avoid Eddie's eyes as I say, "So what's the verdict?"

In his pause, I feel him looking me over. Reading the stiffness in my body and the artificially bright tone of my voice.

Maybe he's empathetic too, because he takes pity on me and changes the subject.

"Well, that leak in the roof is a bummer. It's coming from the roof deck by the turret, which means you're gonna have to remove the shingles and cut away the wood to repair the leak. Between the gables, the turret, and the steep pitch of the roof itself, it's gonna be a major job, I'm sorry to say. You're definitely gonna have to bring in a specialist."

My heart sinks. Anytime a specialist gets involved, the price goes up. "I tried calling three different roofers before I found you, but couldn't get hold of anybody."

He chuckles, shaking his head. "Yeah, don't know why, but roofer guys are notoriously flaky. I'd give you a recommendation, but I don't know anybody I trust with a job like this."

"Okay. Thanks anyway. I'll just keep trying. I was hoping to avoid calling a firm from Seattle because they're so pricey, but I guess I have to."

After a beat, he says gently, "If you want, I can look at the quote you get. You know, so you don't get ripped off."

Because I'm alone, he means. Because I won't have a man around to negotiate for me.

Because someone in my position—grieving, disoriented, desperate—is a target for scams.

When he smiles, I know he's not trying to flirt with me. He's just a genuinely nice guy trying to help someone out who he can tell is in distress.

If only the whole world were made up of such kind people.

"That's very sweet of you, Eddie. But I can handle it. I come from a long line of ball-busting Jersey girls."

His smile turns into a laugh. He has a crooked front tooth,

which is oddly endearing. "I knew one of those once. She was only four foot ten, but she scared the living shit outta me."

I smile at him. "Even small dragons can still breathe fire."

"True that."

"So how about the electrical? It's bad, isn't it?"

He shrugs. "No. Everything checked out."

I stare at him in disbelief. "What do you mean it checked out?"

"I mean there aren't any problems. The current's strong, breakers aren't tripping, can't find any frays in the wiring, there's no arc faults, hot spots, dead outlets, or loose connections . . ." He shrugs again. "Everything looks groovy."

"That can't be right. What about the flickering lights?"

"Could be a problem with the local power grid. You might want to ask a neighbor if they've got the same thing happening. Parts of the network around here are over a century old. Whatever the cause, it's not coming from inside the house."

"And the exploding light bulbs? That's definitely not normal."

"It's more common than you think. Either the manufacturer didn't put enough insulation in the base so the filament overheated, or there was a loose connection between the bulb and the socket that made the current jump. Just make sure you don't buy cheap bulbs from now on, and also make sure they're screwed in real tight."

I'm getting a little exasperated. Did he even check the wiring, or was he up in the attic smoking pot this whole time?

"Okay, but the doorbell rings when nobody's there. And what about the burning smell when I run the dryer? How do you explain that?"

He hesitates. I sense him carefully choosing his words.

"I mean . . . you have been under a lot of stress lately, man." He adds sheepishly, "What with your husband and all."

For a moment, I don't understand. Then I get it, and I have to take a breath before I speak so I don't bite off his head. "My mind isn't playing tricks on me, Eddie. I'm not hallucinating electrical problems."

Uncomfortable under my stare, he shifts his weight from foot to foot. "I'm not trying to be disrespectful. All I can tell you is that when I was in a bad place, I thought I heard whispering voices and saw shadows move."

"Did any of that happen while you were under the influence of mind-altering substances?"

His expression is pained, which I take as a yes.

Either way, I think our business relationship has reached its conclusion. Maybe whoever I get to do the roof can recommend an electrician who's sober. "Never mind. Thanks for coming out to check. What do I owe you?"

He stuffs the small power meter into the back pocket of his jeans, bends to pick up his toolbox from where he left it on the floor, then straightens and shakes his head. "Nothing."

"No, that's not right. You should be compensated for your time."

His smile is lopsided. He flips his long hair over his shoulder. "I appreciate it, but it's my policy that if I don't find a problem, the visit is free."

I have a sneaking suspicion he just made up that policy on the spot because he feels sorry for me. "Are you sure? I don't want to take advantage."

"Nah, we're cool. But maybe if one of your friends needs a handyman . . . ?"

"I'll recommend you. You bet. Thanks, Eddie, I really appreciate it."

He grins at me, flashing that crooked tooth. "I'm outta here, then. You take care now, okay? And call me if you want my doc's name. He's really the best."

I force a smile and lie. "I will. Thanks again."

"I'll let myself out. See you around."

He leaves. When I hear the front door open and close, I go after him to make sure it's locked. Then I go into the kitchen for a glass of water, but stop short when I see the envelope sitting on the table.

Even from halfway across the room, I can see the "LOVE" stamp in the corner and the neat block printing in blue pen spelling out my name.

My breath catches in my throat. My heart starts pounding. My steady hands begin to tremble.

Then all the overhead lights in the kitchen ceiling grow brighter.

With a sharp buzz of noise, they flicker and go out.

3

Dear Kayla,

You didn't respond to my last letter, which I understand, because you think we've never met. You're wrong. I could bore you with the details, but for now, just trust that I know you.

In every way one person can know another, I know you.

I know the sight, sound, taste, and smell of you.

I know your darkest darks and your lightest lights.

I know your dreams, your nightmares, and every secret you've ever kept hidden, all those nameless desires you never admitted even to yourself.

I know the shape of your soul.

I know your hands tremble as you read these words, and your heart beats as fast as a hummingbird's wings. I know you want to tear this letter up, and I also know you won't.

How I need to touch you. How I need to hear your voice. I can't, of course, because I'm here and you're there, but the distance doesn't make the longing go away.

I can still taste your skin.

Dante

4

I stand next to the kitchen window with the letter in my hands and read it again in the gray afternoon light. Then again. Then once more, because it's so bizarre, my brain refuses to come up with any plausible explanations for it.

Probably because there aren't any.

The overhead lights flicker back on, illuminating the room.

Throwing my arms in the air, I say to the ceiling, "I wish you'd done that when Mr. Everything's Great Eddie was here!"

Then I fold the letter, put it back into its envelope, set it on the table, and pour myself a glass of red wine. I gulp it down, deciding on impulse that I need to make sure the house is secure. I go from room to room, checking window latches and door locks until I'm satisfied that I'm locked in tight.

After that's done, I sit down at the kitchen table and make a list. I always think best with a pen in my hand.

POSSIBLE EXPLANATIONS
- Someone is fucking with you

I immediately cross that out, because obviously someone is fucking with me. The question is why? And why now?

- This Dante person saw the article in the newspaper about the accident
- He smells money
- He's trying to pull a lonely-widow scam

As soon as I write that down, I think I've nailed it.

He's in prison, after all. To get there, he had to do something bad. So the man has what could be politely called compromised morals. He probably trolls the obituary section of the newspapers and sends these letters out to new widows all over the place, hoping one of them will take the bait and write him back so he can strike up a relationship and seduce her into sending him large sums of cash.

But the letter is too weird to be scam bait. And too specific. He should've just said he was a lonely guy looking for a pen pal, not that he could still taste my skin.

Or that he knows the shape of my soul.

What does that even mean, anyway? What does *any* of it mean?

"Nothing," I mutter, glaring at the envelope. "It's a fraud."

I specifically don't address the mystery of how a letter arrived on my kitchen table without me knowing how it got there—again—because I suspect I'm having more lapses in memory and brought it in from the mailbox myself.

I take a little consolation in the fact that the letter from the mysterious Dante had no overtones of hostility. Admittedly creepy, with all the "I know you" business, but at least he isn't threatening me harm.

Though I suppose he wouldn't be able to. I think I read somewhere that prison correspondence is monitored. He'd probably get in trouble if he tried to send a violent threat through the mail.

Not that he'd have a reason to send a threat. Michael didn't have any enemies, and neither do I. We're your average middle-class married couple, both overworked and overtired, so our idea of fun is snuggling together on the sofa to watch a movie on Friday nights.

Was. Our idea of fun *was* watching a movie together.

We'll never do that again.

The sudden tightness in my chest makes it impossible to breathe. Dizzy, I rest my head on my forearms and listen to the rain tapping against the windows like a thousand fingernails.

"He's just a jerk felon who's trying to prey on a vulnerable woman," I tell the tabletop.

It doesn't make me feel any better. In fact, it makes me feel worse.

Who does this guy think he is, sending me this crap?

Whoever he is, he clearly has mental problems.

I sit up abruptly. Maybe *that's* it. Maybe he's not trying to run a scam on me at all.

Maybe the mysterious Dante is simply out of his mind.

I'm not sure which I feel more: empathy or trepidation. I mean, if the poor guy is only locked up because he's got some kind of mental illness that wasn't diagnosed and he should really be medicated, not incarcerated, that's one thing.

On the other hand, he did *something* to land himself in prison. What if it was something violent?

He could be dangerous.

I remove the letter from the envelope and read it again. An odd impulse makes me lift it to my nose and sniff.

A faint whiff of cedar and woodsmoke fills my nostrils. And something else, earthy and musky, like the scent of a man.

Or an animal.

The thought unsettles me. I fold the letter quickly and slide it back into the envelope, then take it upstairs to my bedroom and stuff it in the back of my underwear drawer.

Then I go back downstairs, log on to my computer, and do a search for Seattle roofers.

⌒

When the doorbell rings two days later, I'm in the laundry room, folding towels. I head to the front door, hoping an actual person will be there this time when I open it.

There is.

And he's everything sweet, smiling Eddie is not.

His height and size are immediately intimidating, as is his stony expression. He has dark hair, dark eyes, and a dark beard covering a square jaw. Wearing faded jeans, battered work boots, and a hunter-green button-down shirt rolled up muscular, tattooed forearms, he looks like he just wandered out of the forest after building himself a cabin from trees he cut down with an axe.

To my great surprise, I find him sexy.

It's surprising because he's not my type at all. I like the clean-cut, Wall Street type. A man with an advanced degree or two, excellent hygiene, and a solid understanding of how a 401(k) works.

This guy looks like the founder of an underground fight club.

He stands in the doorway gazing at me in intense silence until I say, "Can I help you?"

"Aidan."

When it becomes apparent that's all he's going to say, I assume he's looking for someone named Aidan who he thinks lives in this house.

"I'm sorry, there's no Aidan here."

His stony expression flickers with what appears to be contempt. "*I'm* Aidan. From Seattle Roofing." He jerks his thumb over his shoulder, indicating the white pickup in the driveway with the company name stenciled on the side in red letters.

Embarrassed, I laugh. "Oh! Sorry, I thought you weren't coming until next week."

"Had an opening in the schedule," he says without a trace of warmth. "Thought I'd drop by. If this is a bad time—"

"No, no, this is great," I interrupt, swinging the door open wider. "Please, come in."

He steps across the threshold. Instantly, the foyer feels smaller. I shut the door behind him and gesture toward the kitchen.

"I'll show you where the leaks are, if you want to start there?"

He answers with a wordless nod.

I feel as if a rabid wolf is following behind me as we make our way into the kitchen. No, not a wolf. Something bigger and even more dangerous. A gorilla, maybe. Or a lion.

"So that's where the water's coming in," I say, pointing to the kitchen ceiling. "I had a handyman out to look at the electrical.

He also looked at the roof and said something about the deck needing to be cut out and replaced near the turret."

Aidan doesn't look at the ceiling. His cool, steady gaze remains fixed on me.

"You get the electrical fixed?"

"No. Not really."

"Which is it? No or not really?"

He doesn't smile when he says it. There's no hint of playfulness in his tone or expression.

He isn't hostile exactly, it's just that I'm getting the impression he'd rather be anywhere else on earth than here.

I take a moment to answer, because I'm not sure if I even want to have this guy in my house. I'm finding him more and more irritating with every passing second.

"The handyman said he couldn't find any problems with the wiring, but I'm still having issues."

Aidan grunts. "I'll take a look at it."

"You do electrical, too?"

His dark eyes meet mine. "I do everything."

He says it flatly, as if I've deeply insulted his manhood. As if he can't believe that I couldn't tell just by looking at him that he's Captain Capable.

I wish someone else were here so I could turn and ask a reasonable person what they think Aidan's problem is, but since I'm alone, I'll have to figure it out by myself.

"Do you do impressions of a person who knows how to be polite? That might come in handy from time to time. Like right now, for instance."

His brows draw down over his eyes. "You want your house fixed or you want to have a tea party, lady?"

His rude tone makes my hackles go up. "I don't have tea parties with wild animals. And yes, I'd like my house fixed, but I don't pay people to be mean to me. Also, my name is Kayla. In case you haven't noticed, women are actual individuals. So are you going to act like a human being now or are you leaving?"

He bites back whatever insult he's got brewing and glowers at me. Then he looks up at the stains on the ceiling and exhales a slow breath.

"Sorry," he says, his voice gruff. "It's been a bad couple of weeks."

When he swallows and a muscle in his jaw clenches, I feel like a jerk.

It's easy to forget that everybody else has problems when you're so caught up in your own.

I say softly, "Yeah, I get that."

He glances at me. Warily, as if he's not sure if I'm about to give him a smack or not, which makes me feel worse.

"Listen, let's start over." I stick out my hand. "Hi. I'm Kayla Reece."

He looks at my hand. Something approximating a smile lifts the corners of his mouth, but disappears before it commits to staying.

He takes my hand and shakes it solemnly. "Nice to meet you, Kayla. Aidan Leighrite."

His hand is huge, rough, and warm. Like the rest of him, except for the warm part.

I smile and drop his hand. "Okay. Now that all that's out of the way, will you please help me with my roof? I'm desperate."

He tilts his head and considers me. "You always get over stuff so quickly?"

An image of Michael's casket being slowly lowered into the ground flashes through my mind. My smile dies. A lump forms in my throat. I say tightly, "No."

Aidan's gaze sharpens. I can't stand to meet his piercing stare. Suddenly, I just need to be alone. I can already feel the hot prick of tears welling in my eyes.

Backing up a step, I cross my arms over my chest and say, "The roof access is in the master bedroom closet. Upstairs, first door on the right. I'll let you take a look around. Please excuse me."

I turn and leave him standing in the middle of my kitchen.

I barely make it into my office and get the door closed behind me before I burst into tears.

5

Dear Dante,

    I don't have any money, so go pick on someone else if that's what you're after. Seriously, I'm broke.

    Who are you? What do you want? Why did you contact me? You said you know me, but you're wrong. I don't know anyone with your name, much less anyone in prison.

    I'm not judging you, so you know. But I'd like to know what you did to get yourself there.

    Actually, forget it. I'm only writing now to ask you to stop contacting me. If you send another letter, I'll give it to my detective friend and let him deal with you.

                           Sincerely,
                           Kayla

6

I take a while to pull myself together, splash water from the bathroom faucet on my face, and dry my eyes. Then I put a stamp on an envelope, slide the letter inside and seal it, and take it out to the mailbox.

When I return to the kitchen, Aidan is nowhere in sight. I go into the laundry room and finish folding the towels, go back to the kitchen and empty the plastic buckets into the sink, replace them on the floor under the drips, then stare into the fridge in search of something I know I won't eat because I have no appetite.

Along with everything else, it died with my husband.

I shut the door, rest my forehead against it, close my eyes, and sigh.

That's how Aidan finds me.

"You okay?"

I look over to find him standing in the kitchen doorway, gazing at me with what might be concern. Or alarm, I can't tell.

"Honestly? I haven't been less okay in probably never." I frown. "Was that a double negative?"

Aidan says, "Doesn't matter. I got it. You're not good."

If he's anything like most men I've known, he'd rather chew his own arm off than hear the details, so I change the subject. "I'll be better if you tell me you can fix my roof."

"I can fix your roof."

"Oh. Really?"

His expression sours. I've insulted his manhood again.

"Sorry. It's just that I haven't had any good news lately, so I'm happy to hear that."

He examines my expression. "You don't look happy."

"I'm not. It was a figure of speech."

We stare at each other in silence until he says, "You're gonna be less happy when I tell you how much it'll cost."

"Should I be sitting down for this?"

"Dunno. You prone to fainting?"

I lift my brows. "I'd ask if you were making a joke, but I'm pretty sure humor isn't in your wheelhouse."

"You don't know me. I could be hilarious."

We gaze at each other. Neither one of us smiles. A skull tattoo on his neck looks as if it's smirking at me.

I ask, "Are you hilarious?"

Without missing a beat, he says, "No."

I can't help it: I laugh. "Great. So I'm not happy, and you're not funny. This project should go extremely well."

"Except I just made you laugh, so maybe I *am* funny and you *are* happy."

When I only stare at him, he says, "You were for a second, anyway."

Is this weird? I can't tell if this is weird or not. Feeling awkward and self-conscious, I clear my throat. "Well. Thanks for that."

"No problem. You're looking at ten thousand."

That's such a sharp right turn it takes my poor brain a moment to figure out that he's talking about the price he'll charge to repair the roof. "Ten . . . *thousand*?"

"Yeah."

"Dollars?"

"No, seashells. Of course dollars."

I make a face at him. "And you claim you're not hilarious."

"I'll write up the quote." Without another word, he turns around and walks out of the house.

I have no idea if he's leaving and will mail me the quote or what, but he comes right back in without knocking and sits down at my kitchen table with a pad of paper. He starts scribbling on it.

He's so big, he makes the table and chairs look like they belong in a kindergarten class.

When he rips the piece of paper off the pad and holds it out to me, I take it and look it over. "Labor is eight thousand, but materials are only two?"

He leans back in the chair and folds his arms over his chest. "If you want, I'll bring all the materials over, and you can do it yourself."

Smart-ass. "What I want is a fair price."

"That is a fair price."

"How can your labor possibly be so much?"

"Are you an expert in construction pricing?"

"No, but I am an expert in BS spotting." I flick my wrist, snapping the paper. "And this is BS."

He glances at my wedding ring. "Ask your husband if you don't believe me. It's a fair quote."

A flush of heat creeps up my neck. My heart starts banging around in my chest. Holding his gaze, I say stiffly, "I'm perfectly capable of making judgments on my own."

His eyes narrow. But not like he's angry, just like he's trying to figure me out.

Then the kitchen lights flicker, reminding me that this boorish beast is the only person who called me back besides Eddie the pot-loving hippie, so maybe I shouldn't throw him out of my kitchen just yet.

I pull up a chair and sit across from him. "I don't have ten thousand dollars."

He says nothing. He simply stares at me.

Oh, how I'd like to take his quote and give him papercuts with it all up and down his arms.

Not that you'd be able to see the cuts through all the tattoos, but still. It would be satisfying.

"I'm not lying to you, Mr. Leighrite. I don't have ten thousand dollars."

"It's Aidan. And how are you living in a house this size if you don't have any money?"

"That's a very personal question that I'm not going to answer. And I never said I didn't have any money. I said I don't have ten thousand dollars."

He leans over, rests those big tattooed forearms on the table, and threads his fingers together. "So we're negotiating."

His intensity is formidable, but I don't want him to think he's intimidating me. I sit up straighter in the chair and lift my chin. "You say that like negotiating is your favorite thing."

"It is."

"Hmm. I would've guessed charming potential clients with your dazzling sense of humor."

"No. That's my second favorite thing."

We're staring at each other again. Once again, neither of us is smiling.

Finally, I say, "Four thousand."

His snort indicates what he thinks of my opening bid.

"It's double your materials cost."

"I'm able to do basic math, thank you. Ten thousand."

"I thought we were negotiating."

"We are."

"Then you can't just keep saying the same number."

"Says who?"

"Says me!"

"Lucky for me, you're not the one with the upper hand here."

I stare at him in outrage with my mouth hanging open. Then a strange thing happens: he smiles.

"I just wanted to see what you'd do when I said that."

I'd like to run him over with my car. I say firmly, "Forty-five hundred."

"Ninety-nine-ninety-nine."

"You've got to be kidding me."

"We've already established I don't have a sense of humor."

"If you're going to come down by one dollar every time we go back and forth, we'll be here until next year."

His gaze is level and his voice is cool. "You got somewhere else to be, Kayla?"

Is he screwing with me? What exactly is going on?

Another rumble of thunder makes the kitchen windows

shiver in their frames. The rain starts to fall harder, pattering against the roof. The drips falling into the buckets on the floor pick up speed, little *ploop ploop ploop*s that seem to mock me.

Like Mr. Personality here is.

"I can't afford ten thousand dollars to fix my roof. Or ninety-nine-ninety-nine, either. So thank you for your time." I leave the quote on the table, stand, and gaze down my nose at him. "I appreciate you coming out."

He looks up at me. His dark eyes are calculating. "What if I throw in the electrical?"

"That's generous, but it won't make money magically appear in my bank account. Nice to meet you. I'll show you out."

I walk away, expecting him to rise and follow me. When he doesn't, I stop and turn around.

He's still sitting there at my kitchen table. He isn't even looking at me, he's just watching the water drip into the buckets on the floor.

"Mr. Leighrite."

Without turning his head, he says, "It's Aidan. And if you can afford five grand, I know a guy who can help you out."

I think about that. "Is he licensed?"

He makes a small motion of his head, a shake that seems to indicate his amazement at my stupidity.

I say crossly, "I'm not letting anybody work on my property who isn't licensed and insured. I'm sure I don't have to go over all the reasons why."

His shoulders rise and fall as he inhales and exhales. He runs a hand through his thick dark hair. Then he shakes his head again and rises.

He walks to where I'm standing and gazes down at me. "It's

me. I'm the guy. I'll be back first thing in the morning. Cash or check, I don't take credit cards."

Then he brushes past me and leaves without asking if we have a deal.

He already knows we have a deal because I'm desperate.

The son of a bitch just checkmated me.

7

At eight o'clock sharp the next morning, Mr. Personality knocks on my door.

Pounds on it, actually, with brutal force. As if he's the leader of a SWAT team, and he's been tasked with taking down a group of crazed hostage-takers to save a hundred people's lives.

I open the door and stare at him. "Good morning, Mr. Leighrite. What's the emergency?"

Frowning, he looks me up and down.

Because the house is freezing, I'm wearing a bulky sweater with a down vest over it along with sweatpants and a scarf, but the man looks at me like I'm wearing a beehive on top of my head paired with assless leather chaps.

He asks, "You okay?"

"Do I look as if I'm not okay? No, don't answer that. Why were you trying to break down my door?"

"I've been standing out here for ten minutes."

"I see your sense of time is as good as your sense of humor."

He holds up his arm. Wrapped around his thick wrist is a chunky black watch. Some kind of sports thing that tracks your steps and spies on you while you sleep. He taps the crystal. The readout shows ten after eight.

"Ten minutes. And for the fourth time, it's Aidan."

Didn't I just look at the clock in the kitchen? It said eight on the nose. Flustered, I say, "Sorry. My clocks must be off."

"Is your hearing off, too?"

Because it seems to be our thing, we stand there and stare at each other in silence.

Until he demands, "Look, are you letting me in or not?"

"I haven't decided yet."

"Well, decide. I'm not getting any younger."

How old is *he? Thirty? Thirty-five? Hard to tell. He's in great shape, whatever his age. God, those biceps are huge. And those thighs could crush a Volkswagen.*

"Yes, come in," I say too loudly, trying to drown out the idiotic voice in my head simpering over his big stupid muscles.

Avoiding his eyes, I leave the door open and turn and walk into the kitchen. I sit down at the table, then stand up again because I don't know what to do with myself.

The front door closes. Heavy footsteps cross through the foyer. He lumbers into the kitchen and stands a few feet away from me.

We commence our silent staring game of Who Will Say Something Strange First.

I break under the strain before he does. "I have your money."

He looks at my empty hands. "Do I have to dig around in your backyard for it, or are you gonna give it to me?"

"You know, I think you lied when you said you don't have a sense of humor. I think you're a big frickin' comedian."

"You can curse in front of me if you want. I won't get of-fended."

I take a moment to massage my pounding forehead before sighing. "That's very generous. Thank you. I was up all night worrying about how not to upset your delicacy."

"You're welcome. And for the record, my delicacy is as solid as my humor."

Either he's trying not to smile, or he's having painful stom-ach cramps. It's hard to tell. The man has a face like a brick wall.

"You said a check was okay, right?"

He inclines his head.

Today he's wearing another version of lumberjack chic, with an untucked, faded black-and-red plaid flannel to go along with the faded jeans. His boots are—

"Oh no."

Following my gaze, he looks down at his feet. "What?"

"You tracked mud all over my floor."

He glances back up at me. "You don't have a doormat. And it's raining outside."

"You make a good point."

"Plus, this floor is pretty dirty anyway."

"Excuse me, but I just mopped it."

"When? A hundred years ago?"

My neck starts to burn with anger. Man, this guy gets under my skin!

Glaring at him, I say flatly, "Yes, Mr. Leighrite. A hundred years ago. I'm going to go get my checkbook. Do I make the check to Godzilla, or should I just leave it blank?"

"Godzilla's fine," he replies, gazing steadily at me. "What should I put on your receipt? Dragon Lady With the Sad Eyes?"

I can't argue with the first thing. But the second one annoys me. "I don't have sad eyes."

He takes a beat to consider me before saying, "It's none of my business, but if you need some help—"

"I don't need any help," I interrupt hotly. "I'm fine. There's nothing wrong with me."

"Didn't say there was," Aidan replies softly.

But his gaze isn't as tranquil as his voice. His eyes are like his fist pounding on my front door, loudly demanding an answer.

With my heart racing, I say, "You know what? I don't think this is going to work. I'm sorry to inconvenience you, but I'm going to ask you to leave now."

Rain thrums against the roof. A gust of wind rattles the windows. Somewhere upstairs, a loose shutter bangs back and forth, rusty hinges groaning.

After a long, tense moment, Aidan says, "Okay." He turns and walks to the front door.

I'm relieved until he turns back and gazes at me. His eyes are dark and penetrating. It feels as if they can see straight down to the bottom of my soul.

"But if you change your mind, Kayla, you've got my number."

I don't know if he means changing my mind about needing help with my roof or something else.

He walks out, closing the front door behind him.

As soon as he's gone, I pull the scarf from around my burning neck and go to the powder room down the hall. I switch on the light, then stand in front of the mirror and look at myself, trying to determine what's so wrong with my eyes.

I gasp in shock when I see the ugly purple splotches encircling my neck.

The one just beneath my left earlobe looks like it was made by a thumb.

⌒

Five days later, the marks on my neck have completely faded. I searched the internet for causes of unexplained bruising and found everything from diabetes to vitamin deficiencies.

Considering my poor diet and the amount of stress I've been under lately, I'm betting it has to do with that. I'm probably anemic, which would also explain the fatigue.

The marks could also have been caused by the accident.

But I don't want to think about that. Because thinking about it would mean remembering it, *reliving* it, and I'm not prepared for that yet. I doubt I'll ever be. I've put that horrible day into a box and put the box up on a high shelf in the back of my mind for safekeeping.

But knowing as I do that my mental health is fragile, I decide to attend a local grief group.

The meeting is held in a room at the seniors' center. A dozen or so folding metal chairs are arranged in a circle in the middle of an expanse of ugly brown carpeting. Against one wall, a rickety wood table is dressed with a white plastic cloth and set up with coffee and tea service and a tilting stack of Styrofoam cups. Posters of smiling seniors are tacked around with reminders to get your annual flu shots. The lone window looks out over the parking lot and the rainy evening beyond.

A few people are already sitting down when I arrive. I can tell by the way they're chatting that they all know each other.

Feeling anxious, I head over to the table with the coffee and pour myself a cup. As I'm debating whether or not I'll stay or run out the door and make a quick escape, a woman walks up beside me and reaches for a Styrofoam cup.

"First time?" she asks, pouring herself a coffee.

"Yes. You?"

"Oh no. I've been coming to this group for six years now."

She turns to me, smiling. She's brunette, fortyish, and chic, wearing heels, an ivory Chanel suit, and a huge diamond ring on her finger. Her skin is flawless. Her haircut costs more than my entire outfit. She's incredibly pretty.

I feel like a clod of dirt standing next to a unicorn.

She says, "You don't have to participate if you don't want to. There's no pressure to join in. You're welcome to simply sit and listen. That's what I do. Sometimes just being around other people who understand what you're going through is enough. Jan's the group leader."

She gestures to a lanky gray-haired woman in a flowing paisley dress who's walking through the door. Jan greets the group and takes a chair, dropping her bulky purse onto the floor.

"I'm Madison," the woman beside me adds.

"Hi, Madison. I'm Kayla. Nice to meet you."

I want to ask why she's here but don't. I don't know the rules yet. And I don't want to offend someone being so nice who can probably tell I'm panicking.

As if she can read my mind, she says, "My daughter was kidnapped when she was four years old. The police never found her."

I almost drop my coffee. Instead, I cover my mouth with my hand and whisper, "Oh my God. I'm so sorry."

Madison takes a sip from her cup, then stares down into it as if searching for something.

"It was my fault. I let go of her hand while we were shopping at the mall. Just for a second, to check a text from my husband, but when I looked up, she was gone."

She lifts her head and meets my eyes. Her own are haunted.

"That's the worst thing. That it was my own fault. That and not knowing if she's still alive. The FBI said if a missing child isn't found within twenty-four hours, they most likely never will be. They gave up on the search after six months because there were no leads. It's as if Olivia disappeared into thin air. And every day since, I wonder what happened to my baby. Who took her. What they might have done to her."

Madison's eyes glaze over as if she's gazing at something far away. Her voice drops.

"Olivia would be ten years old now. I can't tell you how many hours I've spent searching child pornography sites on the dark web, looking for her. The only thing keeping me from killing myself is the hope that one day, I'll see a girl in one of those awful videos with one blue eye and one brown, and I'll get to hold her again."

I think I might throw up. My hands shake so badly, the coffee in the cup sloshes around, almost spilling over the rim.

Madison turns her haunted gaze to me. Her sophisticated veneer has dropped. She seems to have aged ten years in a few minutes, leaving her looking like exactly what she is:

A woman living in hell.

Tears welling in her eyes, she says hoarsely, "Do you think she could forgive me?"

I want to burst out sobbing. But I rest my shaking hand on her forearm and say, "There's nothing to forgive. The person who took her is evil. It wasn't your fault."

She smiles sadly. "That's what my therapist says. But I don't believe it. Neither did my husband. He left me for someone else. Someone much younger. I just heard they're having twins."

A voice calls out, "If everyone would like to sit down, we can get started."

Stunned and sick to my stomach, I glance over at the group. Jan is waving to two people just coming through the door. When I turn back to Madison, she's already pulling away.

I grip her arm and say desperately, "Has it helped you, this group?"

She looks at me for a brief moment before saying softly, "What do you think?"

Then she turns and walks away. She takes a seat at the circle and looks down at her coffee.

No one greets her. She doesn't acknowledge anyone else, either. It's as if she's in her own little bubble of pain, cut off from everything else.

I picture myself six years from now, telling a stranger at this very coffee table about what happened to my husband and having her ask me if the group has helped, and know without a shadow of a doubt that my answer would be the same as Madison's.

A big fat fucking no.

I set my cup down on the table and walk out without looking back.

Across the street from the senior center is a bar called Cole's. Its yellow neon sign glows like a beacon. Ignoring the rain and not bothering with the crosswalk, I run straight across the boulevard and plow through Cole's heavy wooden front door.

The moment I step inside, I spot Aidan Leighrite sitting in a booth in the corner.

8

~

He notices me right away. He was about to take a drink, but freezes with his glass of beer halfway to his mouth.

It's too late to pretend I didn't see him. So I send him a curt nod and walk over to the bar. I slide onto a stool and look in the opposite direction, examining the décor.

A lighted mirror behind the bar displays shelves of liquor. Red leather booths line one end of the room and the opposite wall. At the other end of the room, a pool table is brightly lit from above with a lamp bearing the Budweiser logo. The rest of the place is dark and smells like stale beer, french fries, and tobacco.

It could be any bar anywhere on the planet.

I find the ordinariness of it oddly comforting.

"What'll you have?"

The bartender, a bespectacled hipster wearing suspenders with jeans and a knitted black beanie on his head, looks all of eighteen years old. It makes me feel ancient, and I hate him for it.

"Johnnie Walker Blue," I tell him. "Three fingers. Neat."

"Nice," he says, nodding. As if I give a shit about his opinion.

Calm down, Kayla. He's just doing his job. I send him a weak smile to make up for my unkind thoughts. He gives me a look like he's worried I might be hitting on him, and quickly spins away, reaching for a bottle.

I prop my elbows on the bar, drop my head into my hands, and sigh.

From beside me, a low voice says, "You okay?"

My heart sinks. I don't bother looking over. I already know who it is. "That's the third time you've asked me that, Mr. Leighrite."

"And that's the fifth time you've called me by my father's name. I didn't like my father. Which is why I keep asking you to call me Aidan."

When I lift my head and look at him, he's leaning on the bar, gazing down at me with those dark eyes. His expression is serious, bordering on intense, but I don't think it's about the name thing.

I think he's worried about me.

That makes two of us.

"I apologize."

"Accepted," he says instantly. "What are you doing here?"

The hipster bartender sets my drink in front of me, then walks off to take care of another customer. I pick up the glass and hold it aloft. "Enjoying some exceptional Scottish whiskey."

"Without your husband?"

I freeze. Then I remember how to breathe and take a swig of scotch. "How observant you are."

He gazes at my profile with such unwavering focus, I want

to ask him if he's trying to memorize it so he can pick me out of a police lineup.

Then he slides onto the stool next to me.

Shit.

"No need to make that face. I don't bite."

"I'm not making any face. And the biting thing is debatable."

"You don't like me very much, do you?"

I exhale heavily, then take another swig of scotch. "This will sound cliché, but it's not you. It's me."

"You're right. It does sound cliché."

"If I told you the reason, you'd understand."

"So tell me the reason."

He sits facing me with his thighs spread open so one of his legs is on either side of my stool. I'm not trapped—I can turn the other way on the stool and hop off—but somehow, it feels as if I am.

I look at him from the corner of my eye. He's in a black T-shirt and black leather jacket tonight, with jeans to match. Even his boots are black. He looks more like the founder of an underground fight club than ever.

"I . . . I'm going through kind of a rough time."

"Your house," he prompts.

I get the feeling he knows my rough time has nothing to do with my house. He just wants me to keep talking. I clear my throat, lick my lips, and debate how much to tell him.

"It's more personal than that."

A couple takes the two stools to my left. They're laughing and talking about the movie they've just seen. The man slings an arm casually around the woman's shoulders, pulling her in for a kiss. Watching them, I'm shot through the heart with an arrow of anguish.

The kiss. The companionship. The simple joy of being with someone you love, sharing a laugh and a drink.

Thinking you have all the time in the world until, out of nowhere, that clock stops ticking.

My throat closes. My eyes sting. I stand abruptly and set down my drink. In a strangled voice, I say, "I have to go."

Without a word, Aidan picks up my glass, takes me gently by the arm, and steers me away toward the booth he was sitting at in the corner.

Struggling not to cry, I let him lead me over to it. I sit first. Instead of sitting across from me, he slides in beside me.

When I stiffen, he says, "You can cry if you need to. Nobody can see you from here."

He's right. His bulk blocks out the rest of the bar. It's just the two of us, facing the wall with a framed copy of *Dogs Playing Poker* hanging on it.

I slouch down, lean my head back against the booth, and press my fingertips into my eye sockets.

We sit there like that for what seems like a long time, the jukebox playing in the background and the low hum of conversation and clinking glasses in the air. Eventually, I hear the sound of a glass sliding over the tabletop toward me.

"Whiskey will help. For a while, anyway."

I peek through my fingers. The glass of Johnnie Walker Blue sits on the table in front of me. To my left, Aidan gazes down at me with hooded eyes.

I whisper, "Thank you," and lift the glass, draining it in one go.

Aidan grunts. I don't know if it's in approval or disapproval, and I don't fucking care either way.

He catches the bartender's eye, lifts two fingers, and motions for another round. Hipster boy nods, acknowledging him.

We don't speak again until our drinks have been delivered and the bartender has gone on his way.

Aidan says in a low voice, "He hurting you? Smacking you around?"

I know who he means by "he," and I almost laugh at that. Michael was the least aggressive person on the planet. He couldn't even watch a boxing match because the violence would upset him so much.

"No."

Aidan's silence seems doubtful.

I know I don't owe this guy any explanation, but he's being kind to me, and he's obviously concerned, so I reluctantly tell him a half truth.

"He . . . left me."

"You're separated?"

That's one way of putting it. "Yes."

He takes a long draw of his beer, then swallows and sets the glass down. "Never married, myself. Can't see the point to it."

"You'd see the point if you'd ever been in love."

"You say that like you think I haven't."

"Have you?"

He takes another swig of beer. Licking his lips, he gazes at me.

"No."

"Then you don't know what you're missing."

His gaze grows penetrating. "Yeah, it looks like all kinds of fun."

That stings. I break eye contact and sip from the new glass of whiskey. "It's worth it. No matter how bad it can get, no matter if it all falls apart in the end, it's worth every minute."

"Even when you wind up crying in a bar next to a stranger?"

"Yes. And I'm not crying. And technically, you're not a stranger."

He huffs out a breath through his nose that might be a laugh. "Okay. I'll take your word for it."

He throws his head back and drains the rest of his beer. I drink more of my whiskey and fiddle with my wedding band, twisting it around my ring finger with my thumb. Aidan notices.

"Can I ask you a personal question?"

"It would be great if you didn't."

Ignoring that, he says, "Do you find me attractive?"

My breath catches. My heartbeat takes off at a gallop. I set the glass down on the table and say carefully, "I'm married."

"That wasn't my question."

"Aidan—"

"Because I think you're beautiful. Sad, a little bitchy, but fucking beautiful. I want you to come home with me tonight."

Floored, I gape at him. "*What?*"

He doesn't smile. He doesn't respond. He simply stares right into my eyes and waits.

I rip my gaze away from his and fix it on the framed copy of *Dogs Playing Poker* while I struggle to get my breathing under control. "I don't sleep with strangers."

"You just said I wasn't a stranger."

"Fine. I don't sleep with recent acquaintances, either."

"Look at me."

"I'd rather not."

He takes my chin in his hand and turns my head so I'm staring into his eyes.

"Do you find me attractive?"

My body erupts into flames. I swallow nervously, then say, "No."

"Right. Let's try that again. And this time, be honest with me. Do you find me attractive?"

I pull my lower lip between my teeth and chew on it. His gaze drops to my mouth, then moves back up to my eyes.

Keeping his hand on my chin, he says gruffly, "That's what I thought. So come home with me. Let me make love to you. You need it."

I pull away and cover my eyes with a hand. "I can't believe you just said that."

"Nobody's ever told you they wanted to fuck you before?"

My face is so hot, it feels sunburned. My ears, too. "I should get going."

"Don't run away."

"That's usually what people do when they're scared."

"You're not scared of me. You're just surprised. They're two different things."

"How would you know if I'm scared or not? You don't even know me!"

"I know enough."

I choke out an astonished laugh. "Goddamn, you're really sure of yourself, aren't you?"

"Look at me, Kayla."

"I can't. I might melt into a flaming puddle of embarrassment."

"You shouldn't be embarrassed that you want to fuck me."

"Oh my God! Will you listen to yourself?"

He pulls my hand from my face and doesn't let go of it. He cups his other hand around my cheek and gently turns my head toward him.

When I'm looking at him, he says, "You said you were a good BS spotter. So tell me if you think this is BS. I want you. You want me, too. You're sad. I want to make you feel better, even if that only means for tonight. You're not afraid of me. You know I won't hurt you. You're just a little fucked up right now, you're not used to people saying exactly what they mean, and you're not sure how to handle it."

His gaze drops to my mouth again. His voice comes out husky. "And you want me to kiss you."

My heart pounding painfully hard, I say faintly, "You're insane, is that it? You're a crazy person."

"You know I'm not."

"I can honestly say I don't even know my own name right now."

"It's Kayla," he says softly, then leans in and presses his lips against mine.

It's barely a kiss. There's no tongue. There's hardly any pressure. It's only the slightest brush of his mouth over mine, then it's over.

And I'm gasping.

Shaking and gasping for air, because my lungs are being squeezed in a vise and every drop of adrenaline my body can produce has flooded my bloodstream.

That non-kiss was *electric*.

Staring deep into my eyes, he whispers, "You want another one?"

I pause to take a ragged breath as he watches me from inches away, his eyes feral. "I'm not sure. I'm feeling overwhelmed. My brain isn't working right, so I can't really give you an honest yes or no."

"Okay," he says, lightly stroking his thumb back and forth over my cheekbone. "You let me know when you decide."

Then he withdraws and motions to the bartender for another round of drinks.

I almost collapse facedown onto the table, but manage to control myself. I take a gulp of whiskey and let out a heavy, uneven breath. "I won't be able to drive home if I have any more to drink. Or is that your plan?"

"My plan is to get you naked and find out how you sound when you come."

"Holy . . ."

"I don't want you drunk, though. I want you to remember everything so you come back for more."

"You sound confident that I would."

"I am. And you will."

I shake my head in disbelief. "It must be fantastic to go through life with such self-confidence."

"It is. I want to kiss you again."

"Can you please give me a minute to regain my footing? I feel like someone just pushed me off a cliff."

"You're fine."

"How do you know?"

"Because you don't want to cry anymore."

I think about that. "You're right. I don't."

"You're welcome."

He's bizarrely self-confident, but I have to admit, he's not cocky. There's no arrogance in the way he speaks. It's as if he's simply stating facts, then letting me decide how I want to react to them.

I don't know if his straightforwardness is refreshing or weird.

He's right about one thing, though. I'm not afraid of him. He's not what you'd call normal, at least in terms of my experience with men, but he only makes me nervous, not afraid.

I think the nervousness could also be described as turned on, but I'm not ready to think about that yet.

I ask, "Would it be okay if we sat across from each other?"

"Sure. Any particular reason why?"

"I'm finding your presence a little overpowering."

He chuckles. "I'll move, but I'm just gonna give you a heads-up that I'll still be overpowering across the table."

"That's probably true."

"Plus, you'll be forced to look at me. This way, you can avoid my eyes and stare at that ugly painting all you want."

That makes me smile. "You're an interesting guy, Aidan, I'll give you that."

"Thank you. I think you're interesting, too." His voice drops. "Those eyes of yours are fucking amazing."

My cheeks and ears grow hot again. The heat burns even hotter when he adds, "I want those eyes open when you come for me."

My mouth goes dry. I have to take another sip of whiskey before I can speak again. "Not that I'm saying I'm going to sleep with you, because I'm not, but just for the sake of conversation, you should know that I'm a lights-out kind of girl."

"Not with me, you're not."

I shake my head in disbelief. "I really can't believe this."

"Why's that?"

"Because conversations like this don't happen in real life."

"Just because you haven't had them before doesn't mean they don't happen."

He keeps making all these very good points, which is highly irritating. "Are all bachelors nowadays so . . ."

"What?"

"I'm searching for a word."

"Blunt?"

"Explicit is closer to what I'm thinking."

His chuckle is low and dangerous. "You haven't heard explicit yet, Kayla."

I finally tear my gaze away from the wall in front of me and turn to look at him. His eyes are warm and so is his expression, but I shiver anyway.

I say firmly, "I'm not having sex with you."

"Okay."

"I'm serious, Aidan. I'm not in the right headspace to be hooking up with anyone right now."

"I hear you."

I narrow my eyes and examine his expression. "Why does that sound like you still think I'm going to sleep with you?"

"Because I do. But I could be wrong. It happens."

We stare at each other for a moment, until he says softly, "I hope I'm not, though. I really want to make you come."

I don't understand how he manages to be completely inappropriate and also ridiculously appealing. Whatever this sorcery is, I need to get away from it before I do something stupid.

"I'm going home now. It's been an interesting conversation, one I won't forget for a long time."

His gaze drops to my mouth. With obvious regret, he says, "I won't forget it, either."

He glances back up to meet my gaze. "But if you change your mind, I live right upstairs, over the bar. I'm home every night after six, and I'm up until after midnight. If you come later than that, you might have to knock a little louder, because I sleep like the dead."

"I'm not going to knock on your door, Aidan."

"Okay."

"Please stop saying that. You make the word sound nothing at all like what it means."

His lips curve upward. His dark eyes dance with a mischievous light. He murmurs, "Whatever you say, boss," and it sounds like he thinks he knows me better than I do.

Then he stands and gestures toward the door. "Have yourself a good evening."

I dig in my back pocket for cash, which I set on the table. Aidan looks at me like I just stomped on his big toe.

"Don't do that," he says.

"Pay for my drinks?"

"Make it transactional."

"I'm being fair."

"You're being emasculating."

"That's ridiculous."

"Yeah? You a man?"

I send him a sour look. "Not the last time I checked."

"Then you don't know what's emasculating. Keep your money."

With perfect timing, hipster boy arrives with our round of drinks. It feels like Aidan ordered them a century ago. Before he can set them down, I stand.

I tell Aidan, "If we were on a date, I'd let you pay for my drinks. But I fired you, and this isn't a date, so I'm paying. It was nice to see you again." I pause. "I'm searching for a more accurate word than nice, but nothing comes to mind."

The hipster sets the drinks on the table and says, "Baffling. Bewildering. Disorienting. Strange."

He looks back and forth between us, then turns around and leaves again.

Gazing at me with burning intensity, Aidan says, "Always liked that kid."

"Goodbye, Aidan."

"Good night, Kayla."

I know the difference in our farewells is deliberate on his part, but with nothing else to say, I turn and walk out.

9

Dear Kayla,

Thank you for writing me back. As for all the questions you asked, none of them matter. I'm sorry if that sounds rude, but it's the truth.

I'll always tell you the truth. I can't do otherwise.

Here's a verse you might appreciate:

> But already my desire and my will
> were being turned like a wheel, all at one speed,
> by the Love that moves the sun and the other stars.

What do you think?

Dante

10

I found the letter in the mailbox this time. No mystery appearances on the kitchen table, but still a big mystery about why it came in the first place.

Because I don't know this guy.

Mr. Mysterious ignored my threat to turn his letters over to the detective, so he either thinks I'm bluffing or he doesn't care.

I stand in the kitchen under the flickering light and read the letter again. The verse means nothing to me. Not that it should, because it originated from the mind of a lunatic.

I wish I could tell Michael about this. What a laugh we'd have. Right before he called the police.

I know that's what I should do, but I'm absolutely exhausted. Maybe in the morning I'll have the strength to pick up the phone and tell a nice police dispatcher that I have a crazy pen pal and could they please go over to the prison and tell him to stop writing me letters, but for now, all I want to do is sleep.

Sleep and forget about Aidan Leighrite and his sorcery.

I've still got adrenaline coursing through my veins from that chance meeting. The way he looked at me. The things he *said*.

"My plan is to get you naked and find out how you sound when you come."

To my eternal disbelief, I actually considered his offer for a moment.

It was shock. It had to be. In my normal state of mind, I'd have smacked that guy right across the face, barged out of the bar, and filed a complaint about him with the Better Business Bureau. Who talks to a customer like that?

A former customer, but still.

Actually, did I ever technically hire him? We negotiated pricing, but I didn't sign any kind of contract. It didn't get that far. I threw him out of my house first.

Oh God, who cares? This is all too much for me.

I make sure all the doors are locked and the drapes are drawn. Then I go upstairs, put the letter with the others in my underwear drawer, and go to bed.

I fall asleep within minutes, but in the middle of the night, something wakes me.

Groggy, I lie in bed listening into the dark. It's stormy again, and the wind is blowing. Rain peppers the roof. A tree branch scrapes against a windowpane somewhere downstairs.

No, that wasn't a tree branch. It was a floorboard creaking.

It sounds like someone's creeping up the stairs.

I sit bolt upright in bed, my heart hammering. I listen hard, trying to hear over the crashing of my pulse, but the sound doesn't come again.

Did I imagine it? Or is someone in the house?

I try not to panic. I try to be logical. The house is old and makes all kinds of odd noises, especially when there's a storm. Things are blowing around in the yard . . . maybe the sound was a lawn chair toppling over. Or a draft sighing through the living room curtains. Or a total figment of my imagination, seeing how I'm still adjusting to sleeping alone.

All those things make complete sense until the floorboard creaks again and I have to stifle a scream.

I leap from bed, run to the door, and lock it. Heart pounding, I grab the flashlight from under the bathroom sink. It's big, heavy, and the only thing I can think of to use as a weapon. Then I crouch down on the side of the bed opposite the door and sit there, shaking and hyperventilating, clutching the flashlight like a baseball bat.

I don't know how long I huddle like that before I decide I'm being silly.

If someone broke into the house, I'd have heard a window smash or a door being kicked in. I'd have heard more footsteps, not just a few groaning boards, because the stairs creak with every step. I'm just being paranoid.

That has to be it.

The alternative is too terrifying.

I stand, wincing when my thighs cramp. I go to the door, put my ear against it, and listen. I hear nothing more than the rain on the roof. I decide to put on some clothes and quickly change out of my nightgown into jeans and a shirt.

Then, with the flashlight in hand but not on, I carefully open the bedroom door and peer out.

The hallway is pitch-black. It's a moonless night, and the cloud cover is thick. I listen into the darkness for a moment, then tiptoe down the hall in my bare feet and look over the railing to the living room below.

It's dark down there, too. Dark and silent. Nothing moves.

Then my skin starts to crawl because I have the creepiest feeling I'm being watched.

Get out of the house!

It's not even a coherent thought. It's more like a subliminal thing, as if the ancient part of my brain screamed a warning at me.

With my heart in my throat and my hands shaking, I make my way down the stairs as quickly and silently as I can. I grab the car keys off the console table in the foyer and run out of the house in a full-blown panic, not even bothering to bring my purse.

Ten minutes later, I'm pounding on Aidan's door.

He opens up wearing nothing but a pair of faded jeans that hang low on his hips. His hair is mussed, his stomach is flat, his chest is covered in tattoos.

He's fucking magnificent.

The horrible thought that he's not alone flashes through my brain, right before I blurt, "I'm so sorry to disturb you. I'm going now."

He grabs me by the arm and pulls me inside before I can run away.

Closing the door behind me, he demands, "What's wrong? What happened?"

My teeth start to chatter. This is when I realize I'm soaking wet, because I ran out of the house into the rain without a coat on. Or shoes, for that matter.

Or underwear.

I cross my arms over my chest in an attempt to hide my breasts under the thin T-shirt I'm wearing. "I th-thought s-someone broke into my h-house."

His dark brows pull together. "So you came here?"

I'm a moron. I'm the stupidest person to ever walk the face of the earth. For the safety of the rest of humanity, I should be locked away in a government-operated facility for the rest of time.

He must see the distress on my face, because he says gently, "That wasn't a reproach."

I make a mental note that this hot roofer has a good vocabulary, but get distracted when he adds, "You're wet."

His gaze moves slowly down my body, taking in my soaked clothing and my bare feet. It travels back up again, getting snagged on my lips before finally settling on my eyes.

His voice husky, he says, "Let's get you warm. Then you can tell me what happened."

He leads me inside by the elbow, sits me down at his kitchen table, and disappears into another room. For a towel, I suppose, though he could be calling the cops to tell them to pick up the crazy lady who just showed up soaking wet on his doorstep in the middle of the night.

Shivering, I look around.

His place is small but tidy. The kitchen and living room are next to each other in an open-concept design. The space is visually separated by a set of open bookcases, with a sofa and chairs on the other side along with the TV and a coffee table. Down the hallway where he disappeared must be the bedrooms.

I'm surprised how clean and neat it is, considering a bachelor lives here. There aren't even any dirty dishes in the sink.

He returns with a fluffy white towel in his hands and commands, "Stand up."

Though I usually get grouchy when someone barks orders at

me, I obey without protesting. He wraps the towel around my back and shoulders and starts to rub my arms with it.

Without looking at my face, he says, "Don't be embarrassed."

"Easy for you to say. You're not the wet idiot standing in a stranger's kitchen at one o'clock in the morning."

"I'm not a stranger, remember? And you're not an idiot."

He seems irritated that I called myself that. Or maybe his irritation has to do with my unexpected arrival, which would make a lot more sense. The poor man has to go to work in the morning, and now he's got a soaking psychopath to deal with.

He pulls the towel up over my head and starts blotting the rain from my hair.

My face flaming, I say miserably, "I think I might be dying of humiliation."

"You're not dying of anything. Be quiet and let me do this."

I close my eyes and stand there wondering how a person would know if they lost their mind. But I force myself to stop thinking about it because the signs of insanity probably include imagining the rain is a burglar and fleeing for help to the home of the roofer you fired and turned down for sex.

In a conversational tone, Aidan says, "We're gonna have a discussion later about why you chose me to come to when you were scared, but in the meantime, walk me through what happened."

I'm too chicken to look at him while I talk, so I keep my eyes shut and tell him everything. When I'm done, he says, "You don't have a security alarm?"

"No."

"We'll fix that tomorrow."

I finally get the courage to look at him. His expression is a nice combination of amusement and concern. Those dark eyes of his are warm, but his brows are still drawn down.

Resisting the urge to reach up and pet his beard, I say, "What do you mean?"

"You know what I mean. And you're still shivering."

"I can't help it. I'm freezing."

He stops rubbing my head with the towel. "I'm gonna say something now. Don't freak out."

"You should've just said it. Now I have to freak out."

"You need to change into dry clothes."

I frown at him. "Why would that freak me out?"

"Because the dry clothes you're gonna change into are mine."

We stand a foot apart, me shivering with cold, him smoldering with heat, until I say, "I doubt you have anything that would fit me."

He smiles. "Look at you, not freaking out at all."

"Oh, I am. But I've done enough weird things for one night, so I'm keeping it on the inside."

"Come with me."

He leads me by the hand out of the kitchen and down the hallway into his bedroom. While he goes into his closet and turns on the light, I stare at his bed, which consists of one pillow and a blanket on top of a mattress laid out right on the floor. The only other things in the room are a simple wood dresser on one wall and a bookcase stuffed with books on the other.

"Yeah, I know. Super deluxe. Here."

He's back, holding out a black sweatshirt so large, I could wear it to dinner with a belt and heels and be well dressed.

I take it from him and clutch it to my chest like a security blanket. The towel is still draped around my head and shoulders. I'm still shaking with cold.

I feel utterly ridiculous.

"Aidan?"

"Yes, Kayla?"

"I'm really sorry about this. I promise I'm not a giant basket case. I'm just a little one."

Looking very serious, he strokes a strand of damp hair off my cheek. He murmurs, "You're not anything but beautiful." After a pause, he adds, "You don't have to freak out about that, either. I don't try to seduce traumatized women who run in from the rain."

"Okay. Thanks for that. Um . . . do you possibly have a pair of sweatpants I could wear with this?"

"You'd be swimming in them."

"I know, but . . ."

"But what?"

I take a deep breath and say it. "I'll be extremely self-conscious if my coochie is hanging out."

He blinks in confusion.

"I don't have any underwear on."

"Oh. *Oh.*"

"Yes. So."

"Wait. You came over here with no underwear on?"

"I promise it wasn't premeditated."

When he lifts a brow, I sigh. "I got dressed in a panic. I didn't have time for panties."

"Or a bra, either," he says, his voice lower.

I wince. "You noticed."

"Are you fucking kidding me? Of course I noticed." He

pauses. "I also noticed that your cheeks get really red when you're embarrassed."

I say drily, "Thanks for the info. Are you giving me sweats or not?"

"I don't own a pair of sweatpants."

"Oh."

"I can put your jeans in the dryer, though." When I don't say anything, he adds, "Or we can just stand here and stare at each other. I'm good with that, too."

"Why?"

After a beat, he says quietly, "I like looking at you."

There's a funny sensation inside my chest. Like a tightening, but also a loosening at the same time. I'm pretty sure it means I'm about to do something I'll regret.

I shrug my shoulders and let the towel drop to the floor. Then I pull my wet shirt over my head and stand naked from the waist up in front of Aidan.

His gaze drops to my chest. His lips part. His pupils dilate. He remains perfectly still as he gazes at my bare breasts with burning eyes.

I whisper, "I want you to do more than look."

In a gruff voice, he replies, "Whatever you say, boss," and grabs me.

11

His mouth is somehow both soft and hard. It becomes evident quickly that this man not only knows how to give an incredible, barely-there butterfly kiss, he also knows how to give a kiss that's devouring.

And so. Damn. Good.

He holds me tightly in his arms as he takes my mouth, and I shiver against him, skin on skin, my pulse flying. I'm not even sure if I'm holding myself up or he is. We kiss passionately until he moans into my mouth and pulls away, panting.

He cups my breasts in his big rough hands and bends down to kiss them.

When his hot mouth closes over a hard nipple, I gasp at the sensation. I gasp again when he sucks. When his teeth scrape over that nipple at the same time he tweaks the other one between two fingers, I moan and sag against him, digging my hands into his hair.

I don't care if this is crazy. I don't care if this is wrong. I don't care about anything right now except losing myself in this beautiful beast for a while.

My fucked-up life will be waiting for me right where I left it tomorrow.

Aidan picks me up. I wrap my legs around his waist and lower my head, hungry for his mouth. He gives it to me, thrusting his tongue between my lips and gripping my ass. We kiss as he turns and walks toward the bed and don't stop kissing as he kneels on the mattress, lowers me down, and drops on top of me.

His weight. God, his weight is amazing. Michael weighed one sixty-five after a big meal. Aidan must be well over two hundred pounds of pure muscle.

He kisses my jaw, my neck, my chest. My breasts again, too, roughly and greedily. I arch my back and close my eyes, loving how his beard feels against my skin. How hard he's breathing. How he's not treating me like I'm a fragile, breakable thing, but as if he thinks I'm strong enough to handle whatever he wants to give me.

And I want him to give me everything.

Like right fucking now.

Squirming underneath him, I say breathlessly, "Take off my jeans. Hurry."

He lifts his head and gazes at me with hot eyes. "What's the rush?"

"You just told me I'm the boss. So I'm telling you to hurry."

Holding my gaze, he lowers his head and traces his tongue round and round my aching nipple. Which I take to mean that him saying I'm the boss was only a figure of speech.

He moves to the other nipple and does the same thing. Braced on his elbows, he lies on top of me between my spread thighs and goes back and forth between my breasts, sucking and licking, until I'm whimpering and begging him not to tease me.

"I'm not teasing you, baby," he says in a throaty voice. "I'm giving you what you need."

I'd pass out, but I don't want to miss anything.

He kisses and licks his way down my stomach to the waistband of my jeans, then slides the tip of his tongue underneath it. When I shudder, groaning, he chuckles.

Then he rips open the button, pulls down the zipper, shoves his face in the opening, and inhales.

He makes a noise deep in his throat. A primal, masculine sound of desire that sends a shiver straight through me. With another fast movement, he yanks my jeans down my hips, exposing me.

He buries his face between my legs and starts licking.

Moaning helplessly, I plunge my hands into his hair and time the movement of my hips to the strokes of his tongue. I can't open my thighs wider because they're now restricted by the waistband of my jeans, but it doesn't matter. Aidan knows exactly what he's doing. He slides his hands under my ass and lifts my hips, gripping my ass cheeks and French-kissing my pussy as I writhe and moan in desperation.

Shuddering, I gasp his name.

"Come on," he whispers hotly, flicking his tongue back and forth over my throbbing clit. "Let go, baby."

I've never had a man call me that before. Michael didn't use nicknames, and the boyfriends I had before him didn't either. I don't know why I find it so insanely sexy, but I do. I don't want him to call me Kayla ever again.

He stops licking to suckle on my clit like he's drawing milk from a nipple. I orgasm in his mouth, mindlessly crying out his name.

He continues sucking until I beg him to stop because it's too sensitive. Then he stands up, pulls my jeans the rest of the way down my legs, pops open the buttons on his fly, and tears his own jeans off.

I get a split-second view of thigh tattoos and an erection surrounded by dark pubic hair before Aidan is on top of me again, kissing me passionately as he slides the head of his cock up and down between my pussy lips to get it lubricated.

He shoves it inside me with one sudden, forceful thrust.

As I cry out, he growls into my ear, "Tell me if I need to pull out, or I'm gonna come inside you."

Without waiting for an answer, he starts to fuck me deep and hard.

And I love it. God help me, but I do. He said he was going to make love to me, but this is far more animalistic than that. It's rough and rowdy, and I have to fight back the laugh of euphoria that wants to break from my chest.

When he takes my mouth again, I taste myself on him. Some dim part of my brain recognizes that all the lights are on, and I should probably be feeling at least a little self-conscious, but there's no room for that. With every powerful thrust of his hips, he's taking me out of my head and deeper into my body, making me feel everything.

My hard nipples dragging against his chest.

His fingers pulling my hair.

Our teeth clashing as we kiss deeply.

The noises we're both making and the sounds of our bodies

joining. I think I can even hear his heart pounding as madly as mine.

Then he startles me by rolling to his back and taking me with him. Panting, I stare down at him in a haze of pleasure. I flatten my hands over his broad chest.

He licks his lips and runs his hands up and down my body, pausing to squeeze my breasts, then follows the shape of my rib cage and waist down to my hips. He digs his fingers into the flesh there and flexes his pelvis upward, driving himself deeper inside me.

"Move," he orders through clenched teeth.

The man doesn't have to ask twice. I bounce up and down on his hard cock until my thighs are aching and both of us are groaning and sweating and he says, "You need to come?"

"Yes!"

He presses his thumb against my clit and keeps it there as I work my hips, madly gorging myself on his thick shaft.

He commands darkly, "*Then do it.*"

It's as if he threw a switch. My vagina starts to convulse, clenching around his dick in violent, rhythmic pulses. They're so powerful, I lose my breath. I drop my head back, close my eyes, and sink my fingernails into his chest muscles, listening to him grunt in pleasure as he fucks me and I come hard on his cock.

He reaches up and roughly squeezes my breast. "So fucking good," he hisses. "Jesus Christ. Kayla. Fuck. I'm right—"

He breaks off with a groan and comes inside me, jerking.

I look down at him.

His eyes are closed. His head is tipped back on the pillow.

His abdominal muscles are clenched and so are his jaw and biceps. His skin gleams with a light sheen of sweat. A vein is popped out and pulsing wildly in the side of his neck, and I understand with a flash of brilliant clarity that this felt as good for him as it did for me.

That feeling of euphoria returns. Without knowing I'm going to do it, I start to laugh.

Breathing hard, Aidan opens his eyes and gazes up at me. He says gruffly, "You good?"

I grin at him. "Don't worry, I'm not having a psychotic break or anything. This is just, like, *wow*."

His dark eyes flashing, he returns my grin and squeezes my hips. He looks like a pirate who just found a shitload of gold treasure.

I'm hit with the sudden awful thought that he might think this is just another average Thursday night for me. Like maybe hopping into bed with semi-strangers is par for the course, and this was nothing special.

I don't want him to think that.

So I say, "I promise I don't normally do this. Actually, I've never done this before."

"Had sex?"

I thump him on his chest. "You know what I mean, funny guy."

Still grinning, he grabs me around the waist and rolls me to my back, keeping his cock inside me. He settles his weight between my legs and leans down so our chests are pressed together. Then he kisses me deeply, holding my head in his big hands.

When we come up for air, he murmurs, "Lucky me."

I wrap my legs around his back and my arms around his shoulders and sigh in contentment.

He nuzzles my neck, inhaling deeply into my hair, then exhaling with a noise of pleasure. He whispers, "I wanted to get you dry, but I ended up getting you even wetter, didn't I?"

"Don't sound so pleased with yourself."

He chuckles. "I am, though. That was incredible."

A little shiver of satisfaction runs through my body. Then I start to worry what I'm supposed to do next. Stay? Sleep? Put my wet clothes into his dryer and pace around in simmering embarrassment until I can run away?

He raises his head and stares down at me. "You're spending the night."

I blink in surprise. "Are you a mind reader or something?"

"No. Why?"

"Um. No reason."

"Bullshit."

"Okay, fine. I was just wondering if I should go home now."

"I just told you that you're spending the night. You can leave in the morning and have the rest of your life to worry that this was a mistake, but for tonight, you're staying right here."

He flexes his hips when he says "here," letting me know he's not done sexing me up yet.

"What if I want to leave?"

"You don't."

"You seem pretty sure of that."

He kisses me softly on the lips. Smiling, he says, "I like it when I irritate you."

"That's unfortunate, because I like it when I'm not being irritated."

"Your mouth gets all puckered and your nose wrinkles up. You look like a prissy little old lady."

"Whoa, slow down with the compliments, Romeo! I'll swoon hard and hit my head on something."

"Know what I just realized?" he whispers, eyes burning.

I say tartly, "That your life is in danger?"

"That now I know what you sound like when you come."

"So what about it?"

He lowers his head and bites my earlobe, then says gruffly, "So it's my new favorite sound. I want to hear it again."

Then he thrusts his hips, driving into me.

My moan is broken. Eyelids fluttering, I say, "How are you still hard?"

"I'm not done fucking you yet, that's how."

"Oh, that reminds me. You promised you were going to make love to me, not fuck me."

"Semantics." He thrusts again.

I say breathlessly, "No, I remember. You said make love."

"I said I'd give you what you need. Which is exactly what I'm doing." He thrusts again, this time leaning down to suck hard on the side of my throat as he does it.

I moan softly, arching against him, tilting my head to give him better access to my neck as I rock my pelvis into his.

It makes him chuckle darkly. "See?"

Tugging on a lock of his hair, I whisper, "Time to shut up now, Aidan."

"Yes, ma'am."

Without another word, he snaps his hips, driving his hard cock into me. He does it again when I shudder and moan. He keeps up the pace, fucking me relentlessly and kissing me all over my neck and breasts, until I start to buck and cry out, clawing my fingernails into his shoulders.

His mouth next to my ear, he says in a guttural voice, "Is this what you need, baby? You like it rough? Or do you want me to recite some poetry and make you a cup of fucking tea?"

"This! This!"

His laugh is so dark and pleased, it makes me shiver. I orgasm listening to that laugh and wondering what the hell I've gotten myself into.

12

I wake in dim, gray morning light in Aidan's arms.

My head rests on his chest. His heart thumps a slow, steady beat beneath my ear. He's got both his big heavy arms wrapped around my body, holding me tight, even in sleep.

I take a moment to orient myself to this new version of reality where I'm waking up on a mattress on the floor with a man who lives over a bar and has more tattoos on his chest alone than everyone else I know has combined, and decide almost instantly that I like it.

Him, I mean.

I like him.

That surprises me. I'm not prone to liking people in general. I mildly distrust most people until I get to know them better, which is usually when I decide I don't ever want to see them again.

Michael and I had that in common. A vague disappointment in and aversion to the human race as a whole. It's a miracle he was so good at his job, considering he had to interact with so many people on a daily basis in his classroom.

Thinking about Michael sobers me. He'd be shocked if he could see me right now.

"What are you doing?" he'd cry, his brow creased in dismay. "The man probably doesn't even have a college degree!"

He was a snob about higher education. It was a point of contention between us that I was satisfied with my bachelor's degree in fine arts and had no desire to go for a master's.

But of the two of us, I was the more practical one. And tighter with money. I couldn't justify going further into debt for an additional degree that wouldn't help me earn more. But to Michael, education was its own reward.

I found paying the bills on time plenty rewarding enough.

His voice thick with sleep, Aidan says, "You awake?"

"Yeah."

"Good. I need to fuck you again."

As I laugh softly, he rolls me over to my back and kisses my neck. "You're not even awake yet, Fight Club."

He lifts his head and gazes down at me with heavy-lidded eyes. "Fight Club?"

"That's what I thought when I first saw you. That you looked like the founder of a fight club." Then I grimace. "Is that bad?"

"No. Because I am the founder of a fight club."

I gape at him. "Seriously?"

"No. I just wanted to see what you'd do when I said that."

"Ugh. Your terrible sense of humor is showing again."

"Can't say I didn't warn you."

He is very, very handsome in the muted morning light. I reach up and brush a lock of dark hair out of his eyes, tracing my fingertip across his forehead and over a silky eyebrow. I whisper, "I like your widow's peak. It's sexy."

"So's your gorgeous ass."

I can feel myself blushing. "Thank you."

He rubs his cheek against mine, dragging his beard against it, and says into my ear, "Almost as sexy as that desperate little moan you make when you're getting close to coming for me."

I hide my face in his neck, close my eyes, and wish I could do something about how furiously I'm blushing. My face feels as if it's on fire.

He chuckles. "Don't be shy. I love it."

Because I have no idea how to respond to that, I whisper, "Okay."

Kissing my neck, he whispers back, "How do you want me to fuck you, sweet Kayla?"

Oh God. There isn't enough time in the world to cover all of it. "Um . . . vigorously?"

He drops his forehead to my shoulder and dissolves into soft laughter.

"It wasn't that funny."

"I'm only laughing because that's exactly what I wanted you to say."

"Really?"

"Yeah." His voice drops. "Or in other words, rough."

When I just lie there and stare at him in nervy silence, he says slowly and deliberately, "I'm gonna devour you, little bunny rabbit, piece by tasty piece. I'm going to eat. You. *Up.*"

A thrill goes through me.

It's not fear. It's closer to exhilaration, an unbridled kind of joy that I'm wholly unfamiliar with. The strangest urge to leap from bed and make him chase me has me saying breathlessly, "Not if you can't catch me, you aren't."

His entire body tenses. His eyes, already so dark, turn black. His nostrils flare, and I swear to God, Aidan disappears, replaced in an instant by a predator.

A dangerous, beautiful predator, poised to shred me to bits with sharp teeth.

With a little scream of delight, I roll out from under him and scramble to my feet. I run naked out of the bedroom and down the hallway, my heart hammering, his dark laughter ringing in my ears.

But there's nowhere to escape to. His apartment is small, and I'm not about to run naked out into the street. So as he strides down the hallway, I look around wildly for somewhere to hide.

"Nowhere to go, little bunny," he growls, standing at the end of the hallway and gazing at me with hunger in his eyes. He stalks closer, never taking his feral gaze off me. Between his legs, his cock is long and stiff, bobbing with every step. "You're trapped. Surrender."

I laugh and tell him an outrageous lie. "Sorry, Mr. Lion King. This bunny isn't in the mood to be breakfast." Then I run into the kitchen, putting the table between us, and wait to see what he does.

Well, he lunges, doesn't he? Because that's what hungry lions do.

He chases me around and around the table as I scream and do my best to outmaneuver him. But he's so damn fast! When I pull out a chair to try to block him, he knocks it aside with a powerful swipe of his hand and sends it crashing against the floor. I turn and flee into the living room, but he catches me by the wrist and spins me around, yanking me against his chest.

He crushes his mouth to mine and kisses me ravenously.

I give in to it for a moment, calculating it will make him let down his guard, then break away. My plan is to run into the bathroom and lock the door behind me, but it's shot to hell when Aidan tackles me from behind. We fall onto the living room rug and start wrestling for control.

It's over in seconds. He's much too strong. I'm no match for all those damn muscles.

"Such a wily little bunny," he growls, eyes flashing. He grabs my wrists and pins them to the floor over my head, then straddles me.

Still squirming and trying to escape, I cry out in frustration.

His laugh sounds elated. "Bad bunny," he whispers. "So *bad*."

He kisses me hard, then flips me onto my belly so easily, it's ridiculous. Then he flattens his hand between my shoulder blades, pins me to the rug, and gives me a stinging swat on my bottom.

When I yelp, he does it again.

"Ow!"

"Say you're sorry for trying to run away, bunny."

"No! I'm not sorry!"

As I hoped he would, he spanks me again, then slides his hand between my legs. He makes a low sound of pleasure in his throat.

"Not sorry, but steaming hot and slick. I think my little bunny needs to get fucked right here on this rug."

When he slides a thick finger inside me, I groan.

He demands, "Tell me you want me to fuck you."

I know this is all part of the game. I'm the mouse and he's the cat, and he wants me to give him permission to rip my guts out and eat me. But mice don't give cats permission to eat them, and neither will I.

"No!"

His chuckle sounds pleased.

He withdraws his finger from inside me and spanks me again, on both ass cheeks this time, stinging swats that leave me breathless and so turned on, I start to grind my pelvis shamelessly against the rug to try to find release.

Aidan leans down and bites my ass. It stings almost as much as the spanking did, and I love it.

"My bunny likes to get spanked, doesn't she?"

"No! Let me go!" Panting, I squirm helplessly.

His voice low and dark, Aidan says, "Oh, I won't be letting you go, my sweet little bunny. You're never gonna get away from me."

It shouldn't excite me the way it does. The rational part of my brain knows that this is a dangerous game I'm playing with a man who's all but a stranger, and I should end it now, before things go too far. I should tell him calmly that I'm afraid and I want him to stop, and I should walk out of this apartment and never see him again.

The only problem is that I'm not afraid.

And I don't want him to stop.

And most of all, I do want to see him again.

I want him to take me out of my head and keep me there, because it's a dark and scary place I'd rather not spend too much time in.

But there's no way I can win this game by brute strength. He's got me beat in that department. So this little rabbit is going to have to use her brains.

I stop fighting and say innocently, "Would it be okay if I used the bathroom before we do this? Sorry, I just realized I needed to go."

After a surprised pause, Aidan says, "Sure."

The moment he removes his hand from my back and swings a leg over me, I push myself up and leap to my feet. Grinning down at his surprised face, I say, "Sucker."

Then I laugh and bolt from the living room.

He catches me before I'm even halfway down the hall.

Grabbing me by the arm, he does some kind of ninja move and throws me over his shoulder. As I squeal and squirm, he turns around and strides into the kitchen.

He drops me on my feet next to the kitchen table.

Gripping my upper arms and gazing down into my wide eyes, he whispers hotly, "Such a bad fucking bunny."

He spins me around, pushes my upper body down onto the tabletop, spreads my legs apart at the ankle, and grabs my wrists in his hands, gathering them behind my back.

He thrusts inside me so suddenly, I arch and cry out in shock.

Bending over me, he growls into my ear, "You're gonna take it hard as punishment for running away from me. Ready?"

"Yes!"

His groan of pleasure is the last soft thing he gives me.

Then he bites my shoulder and fucks me, driving into me hard, over and over, thrusting so powerfully, the table jumps and skips over the floor. His hands squeeze my wrists, his teeth scrape my skin, his grunts of dominance ring in my ears, and I can't remember the last time I felt this free.

I rest my cheek against the smooth wood of the table, close my eyes, and surrender completely.

"Get ready to take my cum, baby. Open that sweet pussy wide."

His voice is a harsh rasp near my ear. In response, I can only manage a low, broken moan. After two more hard thrusts, the motion of Aidan's hips falters. He groans. Releasing my wrists, he digs one hand into my hair and the other into my hip and yanks me back savagely against his pelvis as he grinds into me and climaxes.

With my neck arched and my hard nipples skimming the table, I orgasm around his throbbing cock.

He collapses on top of me, pinning me down, and whispers raggedly into my ear, "Take it. Take it. Take it. Take every fucking drop, my beautiful bunny, and tell me you love it."

On the verge of sobbing, I choke out, "I love it. Aidan, I love it so much."

His breathless laugh sounds triumphant. "I know you do, baby. That's my good little rabbit."

Glowing like a rising sun burning through ancient darkness, I rest my cheek against the smooth wood and smile.

13

In stark contrast to his snarling savagery as he took me, Aidan is silent and gentle as he washes my body under the warm spray in the shower.

I'm shaky and shell-shocked, uncertain what I'd say even if I could speak, so I'm grateful he's not asking me to. He turns me this way and that, soaping and rinsing my skin, then squirts a dollop of shampoo into his palm and washes my hair.

I stand with my eyes closed and wonder what happens next.

I've never had a one-night stand, so I don't know what to expect. I don't know the etiquette involved. Am I supposed to ask for his number? No, I already have that. Do I thank him? That seems weird, but then again, this whole encounter has been weird.

Amazing, but weird.

I can only imagine how awkward the goodbye will be, me standing at his door in bare feet and my wrinkled clothes that probably aren't even dry yet, trying to act nonchalant and utterly failing. What do I even say?

"It's been great, champ! Thanks for the fabulous sausage-stuffing!"

No. I might not be the world's greatest conversationalist, but even I know that's a nonstarter.

He murmurs, "Never met a woman who thinks louder than you do."

"Sorry. I'm always up in my head."

"You don't have to apologize. Just making an observation. Tilt your head back."

I obey him, closing my eyes and allowing him to rinse the shampoo from my hair. I lean against him with my arms wrapped around his waist and my breasts pressed against his chest and wonder again what Michael would think if he could see me now.

Which is when the guilt hits me, cold and solid as a brick dropped onto my head. A nasty little voice inside my mind starts hissing insults.

Your husband hasn't been dead a full month yet, and you've already had sex with another man! How could you?

Aidan says softly, "Your body gets really tense when you start to freak out."

I exhale and remain silent. There aren't any words for what I'm feeling, anyway.

He reaches behind me to turn off the faucet. Then he palms my head and presses it to his chest. His other arm wraps around me. We stand naked and dripping like that for a while, embracing in silence, until he says, "We can do anything or nothing. I don't expect you to have any answers right now."

How does he always know what I'm thinking?

Emotion threatens to swell my throat closed, but I speak around it. "What do you want to do?"

He gives me a squeeze and pronounces, "This, as much as possible."

My laugh is soft. "That can be arranged."

Stroking my wet hair, he presses a kiss to the top of my head. "You sure? I know your situation is complicated. I don't want to make it worse."

Without thinking, I say, "So far, you're the only thing that's made it better."

I cringe when I hear how it sounds. How raw and vulnerable. How needy.

But if Aidan thinks it's off-putting, he doesn't show it. He simply kisses my head again and murmurs, "Good."

I raise my head and look at him. He gazes down at me with a faint smile, his eyes warm.

My voice wavering, I say, "Can I be honest with you?"

"That's all I ever want you to be."

"Okay. Well . . ." I inhale a breath, then let it go in a gust. "This has been amazing. I mean really amazing. Like, incredible. I don't have any experience with this kind of thing because I was married for a long time and pretty much always in a long-term relationship before that."

When I don't continue, he says, "Are you asking me something in particular, or are you just thinking out loud?"

"I'm not sure. I'm having all kinds of feelings about this."

"Me, too. You think this happens to me every day?"

I pull away and look him up and down, all that perfect rugged masculinity. "Yes."

He pulls me back against him and cups my jaw in his hand. "No. It doesn't."

He stares at me with such unwavering intensity, I believe him. Nobody can lie that well this close.

I say, "Thank God," and both of us are surprised by how forcefully it comes out.

Aidan starts to laugh. I blush from my neck to my forehead. He pulls me in and holds me tightly, nuzzling my ear. "Sweet bunny," he whispers, still chuckling. "I think you like me."

Flaming with embarrassment, I say, "Nah, I just need my roof fixed, and I thought I'd shag your brains out to see if I could get a discount."

Pulling away, he pretends to be shocked. "I already gave you a discount!"

I grin up at him. "Oh, yeah. I forgot. Two thousand all in, right?"

He glowers, but he's only playing. "Wrong. Ten thousand."

"Wait, you said five!"

His glower cracks. He starts to laugh again.

I smack him lightly on the chest. "Jerk."

"Guilty. What do you want for breakfast?"

"Don't tell me you cook, too?"

"Only the best scrambled eggs you'll ever eat."

Smiling, I say, "I guess that's what I'll have, then."

He lowers his head and softly kisses me. When he pulls back, his expression has turned serious. "I need to tell you something."

My stomach plummets. "Shit. I knew it was too good to be true."

"It's not bad."

"Then why are you making that face?"

"What face?"

"That scary serious face, like you're about to tell me you have an STD."

He opens the shower door, grabs a towel from the bar on the wall, drapes it around me, and starts drying my body. "Nope. Clean as a whistle."

Enjoying the attention, I pause for a moment of sobriety. "Me, too, in case you were wondering. I suppose we should've talked about that before all the, um . . ."

"Fucking?"

"That would be the word, yes."

He bends down to dry off my legs as I rest my hands on his shoulders. "That and your chances of getting pregnant with unprotected sex, too." He straightens and gazes at me. "Also consent and safe words. I don't normally get so carried away."

"I'm on the pill . . . wait. Back up a sec. Safe words?"

"In case I get too rough with you."

I almost laugh out loud. "There's no such thing. I love how rough you are."

He falls still. Gazing at me with unblinking intensity, he says slowly, "I could hurt you, Kayla. Accidentally, I mean. I don't want that to happen."

I like that he's so concerned with my well-being. I also like that he's taking the time to communicate that. What I don't like is the sudden and unwelcome thought that maybe he's hurt someone in the past.

Accidentally or not, it seems as if there might be a story there.

I ask tentatively, "Have you hurt someone before?"

"Yes," he says instantly. Then he closes his eyes and swallows. "Not from sex, though. And it wasn't an accident."

I'm beginning to feel alarmed, but I keep my voice steady. "Then how?"

He opens his eyes. A muscle in his jaw jumps. He inhales a

slow breath. "My father used to beat my mother. Badly. He was a raging alcoholic and very violent. He put her in the hospital more than once. It went on for years. I couldn't do anything about it when I was small, but when I grew up . . ."

I realize I'm holding my breath. My heartbeat ticks up a few notches. I whisper, "What?"

He looks away. That muscle in his jaw jumps again. When he speaks, his voice comes very low. "I'm afraid if I tell you, I'll never see you again."

That rocks me back on my heels for several reasons.

One, because whatever he did, it was obviously bad. And by bad, I mean violent. And two, he's willing to tell me, but he's afraid of the consequences. He's scared that I'll freak out and run out the door.

Which means that three, he's as into this unexpected situation between us as I am.

I don't know if there's a word for this emotion I'm feeling. Maybe because it's a jumble of so many different things at once. But I do know for certain that whatever it is he did to his father, he did it to protect his mother.

Then I remember what he said to me in the bar.

"I didn't like my father."

Didn't, past tense. Which suggests his father is no longer in the land of the living.

And right then, I discover something about myself I never knew before.

"Hey."

He glances back at me, his gaze wary and his jaw clenched.

Staring straight into his eyes, I say, "The past is dead. So whatever happened, whatever you've done, just know that I'll never ask you to explain yourself to me. I'll also never judge you for something you did to keep someone else from getting hurt. No matter how bad that something was. Life is messy, and we all have our reasons for doing what we do. I don't care about anything you did before we met."

His lips part. He stares at me in disbelief and something else I can't identify.

It could be hope.

"But from now on, I *do* care what you do. If we keep seeing each other, I expect total honesty. Got it?"

Looking stunned, he nods.

"Good. Now dry yourself off, Fight Club, because I'm starving." I wind my arms around his shoulders, lift up onto my toes, and give him a soft kiss. Against his mouth, I whisper, "Your little bunny worked up an appetite from getting fucked so well by her big bad lion."

He grabs me and hugs me so hard, I lose my breath. I feel his body tremble against mine, little shivers in his muscles that are in sync with his ragged breathing.

For some strange reason, at that moment, the verse Dante sent in his last letter crosses my mind.

> *But already my desire and my will*
> *were being turned like a wheel, all at one speed,*
> *by the Love that moves the sun and the other stars.*

The words echo in my head before disappearing when Aidan kisses me.

14

We eat breakfast at his place, then he follows me back home in his truck.

When we get to the house, he insists on going inside and checking everything out before letting me in. "Better safe than sorry," he says, leaning in the open driver's-side window of my car. "Keys?"

I hand them to him. "I don't know if I locked it, though. I ran out in a pretty big hurry."

He nods, then straightens and walks up the path to the front door.

Watching him standing there trying the handle, I suffer a moment of cognitive dissonance.

Only last month, it would have been Michael standing in his place. My charming, outgoing husband with his starched white dress shirts, polished black oxfords, and slacks with the crisp leg seams. He was meticulous about his grooming, never leaving the house with a hair out of place or the faintest shadow of a beard on his jaw.

And forget about tattoos. The sight of needles made Michael

queasy. Every single year when he went to get his flu shot, he nearly passed out in the doctor's office.

Aidan is almost his exact opposite. I doubt I could've picked someone more different than Michael if I tried.

Aidan turns then and looks back at me, waiting anxiously in my car. He lifts his chin and disappears through the front door, leaving it open behind him.

Ten minutes later, he appears in the doorway and gestures for me to come in.

Apprehensive, I hurry up the path in my bare feet. At least it's not pouring down rain today, but I'm still shivering from cold.

The sky overhead is the same dull gray of Michael's coffin.

"Anything?" I ask when I reach Aidan.

"All clear. Come inside."

I walk into the foyer, hugging my arms around myself. I'm wearing Aidan's big black sweatshirt, the arms rolled halfway up so they're even with my wrists. A pair of my shoes are under the console table. I shove my feet into them, not bothering to tie the laces.

Aidan says, "Everything was locked. No signs of a break-in. I checked upstairs, too."

I'm relieved but also feel silly, seeing how I ran from the house as if I were being chased by demons. My overactive imagination is getting the best of me.

"Great. Thank you."

"No problem."

"Why are you smiling like that?"

"Oh, nothing. I just think you're really good at drawing, that's all."

I don't know what he means for a moment. When it hits me, I roll my eyes. "You were in my office."

"Had to check the windows."

"You checked a few other things, too, I guess."

He reaches out and tugs on the sleeve of his sweatshirt, pulling me toward him. Then he wraps me in his arms and grins down at me. "I think that pet rabbit the little boy has is *really* cute."

I smile. "Yeah, I bet you do."

"So you're an artist?"

"Illustrator. Children's books mostly, though I do the occasional calendar and magazine piece."

He leans down and gently presses his lips to mine. "You're crazy fucking talented, Kayla."

That compliment makes me feel as if gravity has ceased to exist, and the only reason I'm still tethered to the earth is that his arms are wrapped around my body. "Thank you."

"Aw. Look at my bashful little bunny with her red cheeks."

"Shut up before I kick you in the shin."

Chuckling, he leans down and kisses me again. "Bashful and bitchy. My two favorite things."

"Call me bitchy again and we'll see how far you can walk with a ruptured spleen."

He tries to muffle the sound of his laughter by pressing his face to the side of my neck.

I shove against his chest half-heartedly. "Jerk."

"You don't think I'm a jerk," he says softly, then kisses me again, this time more deeply.

No, I admit to myself as his tongue delves into my mouth. *No, sir, I do not.*

We kiss until both of us are breathing hard and the little pulse of heat between my legs has grown into an ache. Then the guilt swamps me again, and I pull away, pressing my fingers to my lips.

Aidan searches my face. "You okay?"

"Yeah."

When I refuse to meet his eyes, he takes my chin in his hand and tilts my head up so I'm forced to look at him.

"What is it?"

My mouth has turned dry. I moisten my lips and swallow. "I'm feeling a bit . . ." I clear my throat. "Uncomfortable."

He seems surprised. "With me?"

"With doing this in my house."

After a brief pause, he says, "Okay." Then he steps back, releasing me.

"Oh God. I'm sorry. I didn't mean to hurt your feelings."

"No, I get it."

He can't possibly get it, but I give him points for trying. "It's just that it was very recent. My separation from my husband." I clear my throat again. "And I keep expecting him to walk in the door at any minute. It's just weird for me. I'm sorry."

"You can stop apologizing," he says softly. "I said it's okay."

Cringing, I wring my hands together. "I know, but I can tell it's not, and now I feel like a dick."

"You're not a dick. I'd kiss you again, but I don't want to make it weirder for you than it already is. So here's the deal: I'm gonna call my buddy Jake, who owns a security company. He's gonna come out and set you up with an alarm. In the meantime, I've got a meeting I need to get to, but after, I'm gonna get to work on that leak."

He nods toward the kitchen and the buckets on the floor. "I won't be able to start repairs until we get a break in the weather lasting more than a few days, but I'll put up a tarp on the roof to stop more water from coming in and remove any wet insulation from the attic so you don't get a mold problem. Okay?"

"Yes. Okay. Thank you. Oh, let me go get my checkbook—"

"One more fucking word," he cuts in, "and you earn yourself a spanking."

Startled, I stare at him. There's no smile on his face, no trace of humor.

He's completely serious.

I say tentatively, "Can I ask a question?"

He nods.

"Is it the checkbook I shouldn't be talking about, or did you just want me to be quiet in general?"

He presses his lips together and folds his arms over his chest. Now I can tell he's trying to keep a straight face. He's also trying to be intimidating, and he's pretty much failing at both things.

He says sternly, "What I meant is that I'm not taking your money."

"But we agreed—"

"One more word," he interrupts again, this time quite loudly.

Mirroring his posture, I fold my arms over my chest and stare him down. "I didn't have sex with you to get free roof repairs, Aidan."

"No shit, Kayla. I'm still not taking your money."

"Is this one of those macho man ego things? Do you really think I'm being emasculating by expecting to pay you for your time and expertise?"

"Yes and yes."

I say flatly, "That's nuts."

He unfolds his arms, leans down into my face, and stares into my eyes. "Thanks for sharing your opinion on the subject. That's the last time you get to do it. Mention money to me again, and you know what you've got coming."

When I only stand there staring at him, he prompts, "Acknowledge that you know what you've got coming."

"Why?"

"It's called consent."

I say haughtily, "I don't consent to a spanking over money."

"Don't mention it again, and you won't get one."

"Remember when I told you I liked it when I wasn't being irritated?"

Ignoring that, he adds, "But if you do mention it again, I'm considering you warned and fully informed of the consequences, regardless of whether or not you claim not to want it."

I make a screwy face. "I think your logic is flawed."

"How nice for you. Doesn't change a thing." He turns on his heel and heads toward the front door.

"Where are you going? We're in the middle of a conversation!"

Over his shoulder, he says, "Not anymore, we're not."

"Get back here right now, or you're the one who'll get the damn spanking!"

Chuckling, he disappears out the front door.

An hour later, Jake the security guy shows up. He's cut from the same cloth as Aidan: big, brawny, lumberjacky. He even has forearm tattoos and a beard, too, though his is a lighter shade of brown and has a few streaks of silver in it. I let him in and show him around. We end up in my office.

"Piece of cake," he says confidently. "Where do you want the smart hub?"

"I have no idea what that is."

"It ties all your devices together and acts as the nerve center of your security system."

When I stare at him blankly, he continues.

"We're going to connect your alarm, security cameras, and doorbell camera to a wireless hub that controls everything and interfaces with your smart phone so you can do it remotely."

Hub? Cameras? Remote control? I start to get nervous. "That sounds expensive."

Jake grins knowingly. The bright pink piece of gum he's chewing sticks out from between two molars. "Aidan said that if you mentioned money, I'm supposed to tell you that you know what happens."

My face flames. I say acidly, "Did he now?"

"Hey, don't shoot the messenger. Just doin' my job here."

His tone is light and there's a distinct twinkle in his eye. I am so going to kill Aidan the next time I see him.

"How about if we just set up a basic security thingy where I, like, punch in a code to arm the alarm?"

Jake makes a face at me as if I just insulted his mother.

"Seriously, I don't need cameras and all that other stuff. I just want an alarm to sound if someone breaks in."

"But you should have cameras so if someone *does* break in, you got it on video. It won't help the police very much if they can't identify the perp."

All this talk of perps and break-ins is starting to unsettle me. I say, "Maybe we should just forget the whole thing."

Jake laughs. "Yeah, that's not going to happen."

I'm taken aback by that. "Why not?"

"Because Aidan says you're getting a security system. Which means, like it or not, you're getting a security system."

"I see."

"Yeah." He chews his gum and eyeballs me as if he wants to say something, but doesn't think he should.

"What?"

"Nothing. Not my business."

"Uh-huh. Except your face thinks it is. Spit it out, Jake."

He debates with himself for a moment, then says, "You seem like a nice girl."

"Yikes. That sounds bad."

He holds up a hand. "Hear me out. And do me a favor and don't repeat this, okay?"

I nod, anxiety blooming in my stomach.

"I've been friends with Aidan since high school—"

I cut in, "If you're about to tell me he's a flagrant womanizer, I really don't want to hear it."

"No, that's not what I was going to say."

"Good."

He cocks his head and frowns at me. "But if he was, you wouldn't want to know?"

"Like you said, it's not my business."

He makes another face, and now I'm beginning to get exasperated.

"What now?"

"Just never met a woman who wouldn't want to know if she was getting involved with a skirt chaser is all."

"Fine. Is he a skirt chaser?"

"No."

I throw my arms in the air. "You're killing me! Get to the point already."

"Okay, look. I'll be straight with you. Aidan doesn't get close to people. Doesn't trust them."

His pause seems meaningful. I say, "And . . . ?"

"He's had a rough time pretty much his whole life."

When he stops and snaps his gum, I think I know what he's getting at, and my cheeks grow hot again.

"Are you suggesting that I'm taking advantage of him? Because I specifically told him that I would pay for everything—"

"He likes you," he interrupts, his voice low. "And Aidan doesn't like anybody." He glances pointedly at my ring finger, then meets my eyes again. "I don't want to see him get hurt."

After a beat where my brain resets itself and my heart melts, I say softly, "I like him, too. And I'm not going to hurt him, Jake. I promise."

He gives his gum a few doubtful grinds with his molars.

I wonder what Aidan said to him about me, but I won't ask. Jake wouldn't tell me, anyway. He's a loyal friend, and there's the man code and all that. I'm lucky I even got this much out of him.

"Listen. I suggest a compromise. How about if you install something that isn't FBI-level surveillance, but also isn't bare bones. I won't be able to figure out anything too sophisticated, but I also don't want you to have to deal with Aidan's wrath if he doesn't approve, so let's shoot for somewhere between James Bond and Inspector Clouseau. Can we do that?"

He blows a bubble, pops it, then grins at me. "We can do that."

I stick out my hand, and we shake on it.

Which is when I happen to glance over Jake's shoulder out my office window and notice someone standing in the yard, down near the water's edge.

Partially hidden by the trunk of a tree, the figure appears to be a man. Though he's too far away to discern any facial features, and his eyes are obscured by the brim of the hat he's wearing, I have the distinct feeling that he's staring right at me.

I catch a glint of white as the man bares his teeth like an animal.

A gust of wind whistles down the chimney. Goose bumps form on my arms. A shiver of fear runs through my body, chilling me to my bones.

"I'll get my equipment from the truck and get to work," says Jake.

I glance in his direction as he walks out of the room. When I turn back to look out the window, the man by the tree is gone.

15

Feeling rattled but also brave because Jake is in the house—and it's daytime—I decide to take a walk out to the water to investigate.

Bainbridge Island is only a thirty-five-minute ferry ride from Seattle, but it feels as if it's on a different planet. Much of it is covered in thick cedar woods or dedicated to nature preserves, but there's a quaint downtown area with cozy coffee shops, boutiques, and restaurants. Miles of trails that follow the rugged coastline and hilly interior make it a hiker's paradise. At five miles wide and ten miles long, with a population of only twenty-five thousand, the island is small, but is also a perfect spot for people who work in the city but don't want to live there.

Michael and I settled here when he accepted the position as head of the Ph.D. program at the University of Washington.

That seems like a lifetime ago.

I was a different woman then. A younger, happier woman who hadn't yet tasted any of life's bitter betrayals.

How naïve we are when we're young. How easily we trust that the sun will keep rising and setting, warming our days.

And what a terrible blow it is to discover it isn't the sun that makes things bright, but the people who love us, so that when they're gone, everything is plunged into darkness.

The property covers more than two acres. It's forested with mature evergreen trees and separated from the water's edge by a long stretch of lawn and a narrow, rocky beach. Bundled in a heavy winter coat with a knit hat pulled down over my ears, I cross the back porch and take the steps down to the lawn, then follow the walking path to the water.

I avoid going anywhere near the dock or glancing in the direction of the boat tied to it.

Michael christened her *Eurydice*. I always hated that name. I told him it was bad luck to name a boat after a nymph from Greek mythology who got trapped in the underworld, but Michael said he liked it. He found it romantic that Eurydice's husband, Orpheus, loved her so much, he followed her to hell to beg Hades for her release.

When I pointed out that the story ends in tragedy, Michael just laughed at me. "It's only a story," he said, and gave me a hug.

As it turns out, I was right. Greek myth or not, doomed is doomed.

Hindsight is a real bitch sometimes.

When I arrive at the tree I saw the man standing under, I look closely at the ground. If I can find footsteps, I'll be able to tell where he ran off to. The ground is muddy around the trunk and bare of grass, so I should be able to spot something.

But there's nothing there.

No footprints. No disturbed earth. No sign of the person who stood and stared at me.

My hair whipping around in the cold breeze, I turn and look back toward the house. From here, I can see directly into my office. The house sits slightly higher than the shoreline, but my office windows are large and the room is brightly lit. My drafting table faces the door, so when I sit there, the light and the window are at my back.

Which means someone might have been standing here staring at me as I've worked for some time now, and I wouldn't have known.

I look both ways down the shore. It's empty. My only company are the seagulls wheeling overhead and the dark waves lapping restlessly at the shoreline.

Whoever he was, he's long gone.

A glint from the ground near my shoes catches my eye. I lean down and pick a coin out of the mud. I wipe it off with my thumb, and my breath catches.

It's a buffalo nickel.

Minted between 1913 and 1938, the coins can be worth anywhere from thirty-five cents to three million dollars, depending on the year and condition. This particular coin is stamped 1937. It's a D type, which shows the buffalo with only three legs instead of the usual four, and is worth exactly $2,560.00.

I know that because Michael had it valued. It had been his grandfather's. He carried it everywhere with him. He swore it brought him luck.

My heart beating faster, I curl the coin in my fist and hurry back to the house, trying to convince myself that cold tingle down my spine is only the wind.

A few hours later, Jake has finished installing the security system.

Aidan has still not returned.

Jake shows me how to use the system hub, which he mounted on the wall in my office next to the light switch inside the door. Then he installs the app on my iPhone so I can view the video feeds in real time, so in case someone rings the doorbell, I'll be able to see who's there without leaving the room. He also put a camera above the back door that captures a wide-angle view of the yard.

"How long has this been recording?" I ask, wondering if it caught the man by the tree on camera.

"About twenty minutes. It just went live. You've got enough memory in the system for a week's worth of imaging, then it will record over itself and erase the old stuff so you're not paying for extra data storage, which can get pricey."

So there's no recording of the yard at the time I saw the figure. I'm disappointed, but there's nothing to do about it. At least from now on, I'll be able to see if he pays me another visit, even when I'm not around.

Jake says, "I've mounted code entry boxes at the front and back doors, and inside the garage next to the laundry room door. If the system is accidentally tripped while the alarm is armed, you've got thirty seconds to disarm it with your code before it automatically notifies us. If you don't make it in time, tell your password to the operator who calls, and they'll cancel the alarm."

His smile is rueful. "And try not to let that happen, because we charge a hundred bucks every time you accidentally set off the alarm."

"Ouch."

"Yeah, we're mercenaries."

"I thought you owned the company?"

"I do."

"So when you say 'we,' you actually mean you."

He laughs. "You sound like my wife."

"I bet she's a highly intelligent woman."

Grinning, he shakes his head. "Now you sound even more like her."

"Great minds think alike. Out of curiosity, is there a way to get a notification on my phone if the cameras catch movement?"

"Sure, the app does that if you want me to set it up like that for you. Some folks don't like it because you'll get pinged every time a squirrel crosses the lawn or a car drives past the house. Can get annoying."

"Is there a size setting? Like so maybe it will miss a squirrel but capture a person?"

"No, but I can reduce the field to where the camera will still record everything, but it will only produce an event notice and ping your phone if someone, say, walks within five feet of the door."

This is all sounding a little more complicated than I'd hoped. I picture myself scrambling in panic for my phone every time it buzzes only to find a rodent scampering across the front porch.

"Let's skip the notifications for now. I can always turn them on later, right?"

"Sure can. All I need from you now is for you to program your passcode into the hub. Then I'll show you how to use the code box. Then we're all finished."

He walks me through the process of inputting my code and

demonstrates how the system works, which doesn't take long. Then he's packing up and shaking my hand.

Walking him to the front door, I say, "I know I'm not supposed to mention the *M* word, but you have to let me do something for you, Jake. This was really above and beyond."

"Don't worry about it. If you keep what I said about Aidan between us, I'll consider us even."

I open the door and stand back to let him by. "I will. And thank you. Really. This means so much to me."

He pauses to smile down at me. "Hope I see you again, Kayla. It'd be real nice if Aidan had a girl me and the wife could double-date with. I know he feels like a third wheel sometimes."

Surprised to hear that, I say, "Has it been a while since he's been serious with someone?"

He chuckles in a way that makes me think there's a long and involved story behind it.

"You could say that. You take care, now."

He ambles down the path to the driveway and climbs into his truck, waving as he revs the engine.

I wave back, go inside, and lock the door, hoping my new alarm system is unnecessary but not entirely believing it.

⁓

By the time Aidan returns, it's dark.

"Sorry I'm late," he says when I open the door to his knock. "Meeting was a clusterfuck. Almost missed the last ferry." He glances past me into the foyer. "Okay if I come in?"

"Of course."

I swing the door wide and step back to let him through it.

He walks into the foyer and inspects the security code box on the wall. "Jake do a good job for you?"

Smiling, I close the door. "Jake's awesome."

He cuts his gaze to me. "Yeah?"

"Yeah. I like him."

"You say that as if it's a surprise."

I shrug. "I'm not a fan of people in general. I take it on a case-by-case basis. But Jake's a good egg."

"He is," he says softly, his eyes shining. "And same here about not being a fan of most people."

"We should start a club. Introverts United, Seattle chapter. You can be the president."

"We're not introverts. We're misanthropes. Big difference."

"That reminds me. I've been meaning to tell you that I admire your vocabulary."

Gazing down into my eyes and looking as if he'd like to grab me and gobble me up, he says gruffly, "Yeah? Anything else you admire, little rabbit?"

Hearing that nickname reminds me of our sexy chase around his kitchen table. My whole body turns warm. "I'll make you a list."

We gaze at each other for a moment until he reaches out and sweeps his thumb over my burning cheek.

He murmurs, "Good. You can recite it to me next time I'm inside you."

Somebody just picked me up and dropped me into a volcano. Searing heat envelops my skin. The breath I pull into my lungs is scorching. I wouldn't be surprised if I looked down to find all my clothes burnt to ashes in a pile at my feet.

When I lick my lips, there's a moment where I'd swear he

was about to lunge at me. But he controls himself, dropping his hand from my face and turning businesslike.

"I'm gonna get that tarp up now."

"What? Now? It's dark outside!"

"So?"

"So I don't want you falling off my roof and breaking your neck!"

He stares intently at me, his gaze sharpening. "Two things."

"Oh no. Why do I get the feeling this is going to end badly for me?"

Brushing right past that, he says, "Number one. I don't fall off roofs, no matter how steep they are."

I cross my arms over my chest and resist rolling my eyes.

"Number two," he says more softly, "so what if I did break my neck?"

I blanch. "Aidan, that's not funny."

"Nobody's laughing. Answer the question."

He's very serious now, staring at me with burning intensity, an odd light behind his eyes. I don't know why, but my pulse goes haywire.

I drop my arms to my sides and say, "Please don't make me answer that."

"Why not?"

"Because I don't think I'm ready for this conversation yet."

"What conversation?"

He steps closer. His intensity burns even brighter. We stand inches apart, so close I can feel his body heat, but he doesn't touch me. He merely gazes down at me with hooded eyes, waiting.

Staring up into his dark eyes, I whisper, "The conversation about how I feel about what's happening between us."

He says instantly, "Yeah, we're gonna do that. Right now. Because I almost went fucking crazy thinking about you today, and if you're not into this, I'd rather know sooner than later."

I close my eyes and exhale a shaky breath. "Did you forget our little chat in the shower so quickly?"

"Nope. Look at me."

I open my eyes. When he's got me good and trapped in the bonfire of his gaze, he says, "I know you're not comfortable getting close in your house, and I'm respecting that. Otherwise, I'd already have you naked. Understood?"

Damn, he's intense. I swallow nervously and nod.

"Good. Now talk."

I debate with myself in silence for a while, but Aidan doesn't push. He simply stands there staring at me like I'm about to dispense some mystic secrets of the universe that have been lost to the human race since we were cave dwellers.

Finally, I say, "Okay. But I'd like to ask that after I say what I'm going to say, that you don't make a big deal about it."

"Define big deal."

I huff out a breath and shake my head. "I think you know what I mean, Fight Club."

A faint smile lifts his lips. "Yeah, I do. Just wanted to keep you talking."

"Has anyone ever told you that you're a jerk?"

"Yeah. You. Twice. You didn't mean it either time. Get back on track, and tell me what I need to hear."

I thrust my hands into my hair, close my eyes, and count to ten. The man is impossible.

"You can stand there with your hands pressed against your

head for as long as you want, but I'll still be standing right here waiting."

"I believe that." I open my eyes, drop my arms to my sides, and stare up at him. "Okay, Aidan. Here's the deal. I like you. Which I'm sure you already know, by the way, this is just your way of torturing me."

I pause for a beat, but he doesn't deny it, so I continue.

"If you fell off my roof and broke your neck, it would seriously fuck me up."

When he opens his mouth to interrupt me, I hold up a hand. "I'm not finished. You'll get your turn."

A low growl of displeasure rumbles through his chest, but I ignore it.

"I'm very attracted to you." Recalling how wantonly I rode his dick and how hard I came for him, the heat in my cheeks flares hotter. "I think we've already established that beyond any doubt. I also feel safe with you. And for some bizarre reason, I instinctively trust you, which doesn't happen for me with anyone, but especially with men. It took six months of dating before I let my future husband see the inside of my apartment, so this thing we've got going on here, despite being brand-new, is different. I don't know anything beyond that, and I hope you won't press me for more, because I tend to act like a cornered wolf when I get backed up against a wall, and believe me when I tell you that's not pretty."

I fall silent. Fierce and unblinking, Aidan stares at me.

I add sheepishly, "I also, um, have never, uh, role-played or whatever it was we were doing when you were chasing me around your apartment, and . . ."

Aidan practically shouts, *"And?"*

I blurt, "And I loved it. I want to do it again."

Then I stand there vibrating with embarrassment and wishing I could take it back.

After an interminable period wherein I suffer in silent humiliation, Aidan says, "Okay."

Disconcerted, I blink. "What do you mean, okay?"

His smile comes on slow and hot. "Just what I said." He points at the ceiling. "I'm gonna go up on the roof and take care of that tarp now."

And the bastard turns on his heel and walks out my front door.

He walks out!

I holler after him, "You know what? I was only joking! I made all that up!"

He can't hear me, but it makes me feel better anyway.

16

⌣

Dear Dante,

I debated about whether or not to write you again, seeing as how I think you might be unstable. But you could also just be lonely, and if anyone knows about loneliness, it's me.

The verse you sent was very poetic.

I'm sorry, but I can't think of anything else to say about that right now.

What I _would_ like to say is that I hope you're not dangerous and about to be granted parole, because boy, would I look stupid when the police find my dead body and our correspondence. I can already see the headline:

"World's Dumbest Woman Ignores All Logic and Writes Letters to Prisoner Who Eventually Kills Her!"

Okay, that's a lot, but you get my point. We've all heard about the prison pen pal romance gone wrong thing. _Not_ that I'm suggesting there's anything romantic here, mind you! Just that I'll look really stupid if you break out of prison and kill me.

Especially after writing that last line.

Anyway. I most likely will shred this before it has a chance *to be mailed. But on the off chance that I don't, please consider being truthful about what you did to be sentenced to prison. I suppose I could get my detective friend to tell me because people in his position probably have access to all kinds of sensitive information, but I'd rather hear it from you.*

That's it for now. I doubt you'll ever read this letter, because I'm ninety percent sure I'll tear it up, but if I don't, well . . . curiosity got the best of me.

Unsolved mysteries can drive a girl out of her mind.

Sincerely,
Kayla

17

〜

It's three o'clock in the morning when I finish the letter. I've been up since one, pacing around my office, unable to sleep. My mind spins with a dizzying merry-go-round of questions.

Who was the man on the water's edge?

What does it mean that I found Michael's buffalo nickel in the exact spot he was standing?

When did I decide it was reasonable to have a pen pal in prison?

Where can I locate my brain?

And finally, why did Aidan leave without saying goodbye?

Because that's exactly what happened. After walking out in the middle of our conversation, he climbed a ladder up to my roof, draped a blue waterproof tarp over one section of it, pulled out some wet insulation from the attic, then roared off into the darkness in his big macho truck as if the woman he fucked to within an inch of her life the night before wasn't inside waiting for him.

I really don't understand men.

Dealing with men is like dealing with a hostile alien species who crash-landed on the planet and decided our language and customs are too silly to be bothered with, and henceforth we should be treated with mild disdain and/or as objects of occasional sexual release before being ignored as inferior beings again.

I do feel better having the alarm, however, so that's one positive thing.

The little green light on the hub glows cheerfully at me from the wall by the door, reminding me that if nothing else, I can have the cops here in under ten minutes if I forget to disable the alarm.

Or if someone breaks in to try to murder me, but I'm not thinking about that.

I fold the letter to Dante into thirds and slip it in an envelope. I place it in the top drawer of my desk, thinking I'll decide if I want to mail it or not in the morning. Then I drop heavily into the desk chair and absentmindedly rub the buffalo nickel between two fingers as I stare at the closed drapes, deep in thought.

Until directly above my head in the master bedroom, a floorboard creaks.

I freeze, staring up at the ceiling. When nothing else happens after several excruciating seconds, I glance nervously at the security hub on the wall.

The green light glows reassuringly back at me.

I relax for two seconds until another floorboard creaks overhead, then another, and I break out in a cold sweat.

"It's the wind," I whisper, gripping the arms of my chair and hyperventilating. "It's only the wind."

My brain decides to wake up from its recent coma to remind

me that my ears can't hear a breath of wind stirring outside the windows.

I counter with the indisputable fact that no one could possibly be in the house as I locked all the doors and armed the security system before I went to bed.

My brain—the asshole—suggests with no regard to my emotional well-being that perhaps whomever is making that noise upstairs was already in the house before then.

Fuck.

"Keep it together, Kayla," I whisper as my hands begin to shake. "Nobody is in the house except you."

When the silence above my head continues for the next five minutes, I decide I'm not scared anymore. I'm mad.

At myself.

Because if I'd heard another creak, I have no doubt I'd have leapt from the chair and run screaming out the front door, only to make another surprise appearance at Aidan's apartment, making a complete fool of myself once again.

Armed with my new anger, I take a breath and go to the door. I'm fine when I step outside the office and look around. I'm fine as I creep up the stairs and peer into the master bedroom, which is exactly as I left it, no floorboard-creaking intruders in sight. I'm also fine as I check all the upstairs rooms, flipping lights on and feeling more and more ridiculous with every passing second when I find nothing out of place.

It isn't until I go back downstairs, step into the kitchen, and turn on the overhead lights that I go from fine to freaking the fuck out.

Every drawer is pulled all the way out. Every cupboard door stands wide open.

I clap my hands over my mouth to stifle my terrified scream.

I stand frozen, listening to my pulse roar in my ears. Adrenaline burns through my veins, urging me to run, but I'm rooted to the floor in fright. I can't move a muscle.

The eerie sense that I'm being watched slowly creeps over me.

I almost sob in terror. But I manage to hold it together and turn to see if someone is behind me.

But there's no one there. I'm alone.

Just me, my paranoia, and the drawers and cupboards, which all apparently have over-greased rails and hinges.

Because there's no other explanation for this. *Because the kitchen doesn't just decide to fling things open on its own.*

Except maybe it does, because out of nowhere, a jar of honey flies off a shelf and smashes to pieces in the middle of the kitchen floor.

My nerves are no match for it.

I jump, scream, and spin around, bolting toward my office. I plow through the door, slam it behind me, lock it, then dive behind the sofa, wedging myself between it and the wall.

I lie there curled in a terrified, shaking ball until the sun rises four hours later.

⌒

In the morning, I feel like a gigantic idiot.

Funny how daylight can chase away even the scariest of monsters.

Once the sun came up, I finally remembered to view the camera feed on my phone. I must have hit Play and Rewind a hundred times, but there was zero evidence of anyone coming anywhere near the house except when Jake drove off in the afternoon and when Aidan arrived and left later.

And according to my trusty security hub, the perimeter of the house was never breached.

Nobody climbed through a window.

Nobody kicked in a door.

I was here alone all night.

As for the open cabinets and drawers, I remind myself there's the distinct possibility I did that and don't remember. If I added up all the small lapses in my memory of late, I could make a convincing case for early-onset dementia.

Why on earth I might have felt the need to leave my own kitchen in such a state is a mystery, but there also could have been a small earthquake I missed that would account for it.

Right? That's plausible.

More plausible than the other things I'm not allowing myself to consider.

Regarding the flying jar of honey, well . . . I was overstimulated. It probably toppled off the shelf, not flew, and in my agitated state, I conflated it with my fright over the creaking and the stupid open cupboards to be more than it was.

I know full well I'm rationalizing, but that's what one does when one is faced with the possibility that their grip on reality is in question.

I consider going back to the grief group, but toss that idea as quickly as it comes. If I want to be depressed, I'm doing just fine with that on my own.

Then I consider calling Eddie the handyman to get the number of his shrink. But after careful deliberation, I decide that if Eddie is the end product of psychoanalysis, I might be better off steering clear of it.

If I'm going to spend hundreds a week unloading my various neuroses on a therapist, I'd like to come out the other side without the need to smoke what smelled like an entire crop of marijuana in order to get through my day.

I psych myself up to leave the office and face the kitchen, but when I get there, I feel curiously let down. In daylight, the open drawers and cabinets seem utterly benign. I expected to feel nervous at least, but the only thing I feel is slight irritation.

It's totally anticlimactic.

I shut the cupboards and close the drawers, then clean the sticky mess of honey and broken glass off the floor. Then I dump the plastic buckets of rainwater down the sink.

Thanks to Aidan's tarp, the ceiling has stopped leaking. The water stains look eerily like two big eyes staring down at me accusingly.

Gazing up at them, I mutter, "Don't give me that look. You would've been scared, too."

I debate whether or not I should call Aidan, but decide against it. I don't know what his strange performance was all about yesterday, but I do know that I'm not going to reward him for running off after insisting I show him all my cards.

Isn't that just typical, though? The minute you start talking about feelings, men suddenly go deaf and mute. It's like their superpower.

Thinking about it leaves me depressed.

I shower and dress, then work until it's late enough in the afternoon that I won't feel like a complete degenerate for opening a bottle of wine. After two glasses, I decide to go back to work.

I'm able to finish the boy-feeding-the-talking-rabbit piece I've been working on for far too long and move to the next one in the story. I need to complete twenty-seven illustrations for this book, and I've only got six weeks left to do it, so I need to hustle if I'm going to make the publisher's deadline.

Except my fingers decide they'd rather draw something else.

The tree takes shape first. It's a tall evergreen with a crooked tip and scraggly lower branches. Then the rocky strip of shore emerges. A dark sky filled with ominous clouds is next, followed by soaring seabirds and windswept water.

The figure appears last.

Tall and gaunt, the man peers out from behind the trunk of the tree, his eyes hidden by the brim of his hat, his teeth bared in an ugly grimace.

A hostile grimace.

A truly frightening one.

My heart beating faster, I set down the pen, sit back in the chair, and stare at the drawing.

Something about this man is familiar.

I can't decide what it is, but I feel as if I've seen him before. But where?

When the doorbell rings, I jump. I'm on my feet before I remember to look at the video in the app. When I grab my cell phone off the desk and navigate to the live feed, however, the front porch is empty.

Aggravated, I say loudly, "Cut it out, house!"

As if in response, the desk lamp flickers.

I freeze and stare at it in trepidation. My pulse and blood pressure rise along with my anxiety. The moment stretches out until I feel as if my nerves might snap from the strain.

I don't know what exactly I'm waiting for, but whatever it is, I'm already scared.

Then a text arrives with its cheery jingle, and I jerk so hard, I drop the phone.

I stand with my fingers pressed to my temples for a moment, trying to catch my breath, before I bend to retrieve the phone from the carpet. My hands shake so badly, I'm embarrassed for myself. But when I see the message, I exhale in relief.

You didn't call me. Now would be a good time to fix that.

"Oh, Aidan." I sigh, shaking my head. "You're going to be a handful, aren't you?"

I dial his number and try to pretend I don't already have it memorized.

He picks up after one ring. "Hello, beautiful bunny," he says in a throaty voice.

"Hello yourself."

My tone must have been less than enthusiastic because after a beat, he says, "You're mad at me."

"Mad is too strong a word. It's more like annoyed."

"What did I do to earn the ire of such a sweet little rabbit?"

Irked at the humor in his tone, I say tartly, "Maybe you need a time-out to think about it."

"And maybe you need a spanking to remind you who you're talking to."

"That threat would hold a lot more weight if you weren't laughing at me."

"I'm not laughing. I've been obsessing about your perfect little ass all day. How pink it got when I spanked it. How you moaned." He pauses. "I wonder how loud you'll moan when I fuck it?"

Ah, yes. Here comes that flush of heat spreading upward from my neck to settle in my cheeks as it does every time the man opens his mouth and says something to me.

I clear my throat of the frog stuck in it. "Are you asking in a professional capacity as my roofer? Because if so, I think I might need to lodge a complaint."

"With who? I own the company." His voice drops. "And there's no professional capacity here, baby. Don't get it wrong. This is all personal."

I'm sweating. Why am I sweating? Christ, I'm roasting alive.

Pulling at the collar of my shirt, I say, "If it's so personal, why did you leave without saying goodbye yesterday?"

"Come over here, and I'll tell you."

Stalling for time, I ask, "Where's here?"

He says softly, "You know where. And don't bother wearing panties. They'll only get torn to shreds."

He disconnects, leaving me even more disoriented and shaky than I was before he called.

I hesitate, undecided if I should go to his apartment.

I know it's not wise. I've had two glasses of wine, I have work that needs to get done, and he's a slippery slope I'm sliding down at lightning speed. A beautiful distraction from the wreckage of my life.

The dangerous thing about distractions, though, is how quickly they can grow addicting.

"And haven't you been through enough already?" I whisper, staring at the framed picture on the wall of Michael and me on our wedding day.

It was a glorious afternoon in May. The sky was cloudless for once, and the scent of honeysuckle perfumed the air. Standing beside me in a tux on the steps of the church, Michael gazes down at me. He's smiling widely, handsome even in profile, one arm wrapped around my waist.

Wearing a frothy sleeveless gown of silk and lace and holding a bouquet of pure white calla lilies, I stand next to him, looking directly into the camera.

Unlike Michael, I'm not smiling.

I recall how nervous I was that day. How my stomach was twisted into knots. How hard Michael squeezed my hands as we recited our vows. Later, he said I was so pale and trembling, he thought I might pass out right there at the altar.

I never told him that I threw up before I walked down the aisle. That's not something you want your spouse to remember. It's not something you want to remember yourself, either. There's no place for such things on what's supposed to be the best day of your life.

And so I locked it away, so effectively that particular memory hasn't surfaced since.

Until now.

I notice something in the photo I've never noticed before. A few inches below my right shoulder, there's a smudge on my biceps. Moving closer to the picture, I squint to make it out. Lifting my hand, I trace a finger over the glass where the smudge is.

But it doesn't rub off because it's not a smudge.

It's a bruise.

A small, dark bruise in the shape of a thumb.

I fall still. Something dark gathers into a storm inside me. A noise like a thousand wingbeats echoes in my ears. Beneath it, there's a faint muffled sound that could be screaming, but it sounds as if it's coming from very far away.

Or underwater.

All the tiny hairs on the back of my neck stand on end.

I feel as if an important understanding hovers just out of my reach, a key to a lock on a door I didn't know until this moment even existed.

What is it? What am I missing?

Then the desk lamp flickers again, breaking the spell. Shaking my head to clear it, I send Aidan a text with trembling hands.

Be right over.

18

Before I can even knock, Aidan yanks open the door.

He pulls me inside, kicks the door shut, takes me into his arms, and kisses me passionately.

I kiss him back, desperate for him to make me forget everything except the way it feels when his mouth is on mine.

Without a word, he pulls my T-shirt up and over my head. He flings it to the floor and kisses me again.

He's not wearing a shirt, so my breasts are pressed against his bare chest. His skin is smooth and hot, and he feels wonderful.

"I thought you were supposed to be telling me why you left without saying goodbye yesterday," I tease.

Instead of answering, he picks me up and carries me into his bedroom. I marvel that he can do that with such ease because I'm nowhere near what could be described as petite. But then he's lowering us to the mattress and pressing the long, hard length of his body against mine, and I forget about his strength because I'm too busy luxuriating in how good he feels on top of me.

"I love how much you weigh," I say breathlessly, squirming

underneath him. "You're so solid." I almost add *It makes me feel safe* but bite my tongue.

Now isn't the time to have a chat about my recent meltdown after what happened in the kitchen.

Kissing my neck, he says, "Is that number one on that list you were gonna make about all the things you like about me?"

"It's not even in the top ten. Please keep doing that. I love how your beard feels on my skin."

Into my ear, he says gruffly, "That's twice you've said the word love, little rabbit." When I don't respond, he raises his head and gazes at me with one brow arched.

Shivering, I whisper, "Um. Okay."

He chuckles.

"Hey, if you can get away with using that word to cover entire conversations, so can I."

"Oh, you think the same rules apply to bunnies as to big bad wolves?"

His tone is dark and hot, and there's a thrilling glint of danger in his eyes. Knowing exactly what I'm doing, I blink up at him innocently.

"I thought bunnies made the rules that the wolves had to follow."

"No, you didn't. Liar."

He flips me over, yanks my jeans down my hips, and spanks me.

When it's over and I'm lying there panting and trembling with need, he says softly, "Was that too hard?"

"No."

"Think about it for more than half a second before you answer."

Craning my neck, I look at him over my shoulder and meet his burning gaze. "I know you're worried you'll hurt me. Thank you for that, but I like it rough."

Gazing down at me with those dark eyes alight, he says, "We need to have a safe word just in case."

"What exactly is a safe word?"

"It's a word that makes everything stop when you say it."

"Hmm. How about cheesy?"

He arches his brows, waiting for an explanation.

"Because it *is* cheesy."

"No, it's necessary. We need to communicate clearly about these things."

I frown at him. "Since when are you Mr. Conversation? Half the time, I barely get a grunt out of you."

Kneeling over me and stroking his palm over one of my burning ass cheeks, he smiles. "That's funny."

"In what way, exactly?"

"I talk to you more in one day than I talk to anyone else in a week."

I make a face at him. "Really? How are you still in business? Do you know sign language or something?"

He bends down and bites my ass. When I yelp in surprise, he bites the other cheek, laughing against my skin.

"Such a mouthy little rabbit," he whispers, rubbing his beard over my stinging behind. Then he slides a hand between my legs, and his voice gains an edge. "And so ready for me."

I close my eyes and curl my fingers in the sheets, lying still as he glides his fingers through my wetness. He takes his time, lazily stroking my clit until I'm panting.

"Aidan?"

"Yes, baby?"

"I need more."

"And you'll get it. When I'm ready to give it to you."

I turn my face to the sheets and wriggle my bottom, attempting to hurry him along.

"Bad bunny," he whispers hotly.

"Please?"

His groan is soft. He tugs on my clit, gently pinching it between two fingers to elicit a gasp from me, along with more begging and bottom wiggling.

"Please, Aidan. Pretty please."

In a dark, sensual voice, he says, "Shake that ass one more time, and I'll assume you want me to fuck it."

I fall still. Breathing hard, my whole body trembling, I say, "D-do you want to?"

"You know I do. Know what else I want?"

I can smell him on the sheets. The earthy, warm musk of his body, that indelible, intoxicating scent of a male in his prime.

I want to roll around in these sheets like a dog in mud, getting his scent all over me, smothering my skin in that delicious smell so I can never wash it off my body.

I whisper, "What?"

He leans down near my ear, so close I feel the heat coming off him in waves.

"Everything. I want every fucking thing you have to give me, Kayla. And I want you to give it to me without hesitation. Without question. And without regret."

The sheer dominance and desire in his voice makes me shiver. My nipples are hard and my pussy is throbbing, and I'd sign over the deed to my house and everything else I own right now if only he'd hurry up and fuck me.

I blurt, "Okay."

To my great disappointment, he says, "No. We're not there yet."

"I am!"

His exhalation is ragged, sending a wash of warm air over my shoulder. "Sweet girl. I love that you said that. But you're not."

He sinks his teeth into my shoulder, making me shudder in desperation.

"How do we get there?"

"Time."

He slides a finger inside me, pressing deep. I moan, loving how it feels but still needing more.

"And practice."

He adds another finger, working it inside me as I clench the sheets.

"A *lot* of practice."

He thrusts his fingers in and out, biting me harder as he finger fucks me. I tilt my hips and spread my thighs wider, my heart racing and my body responding to him as if he's playing it like an instrument.

"Oh God. Aidan. Aidan."

Into my ear, he softly commands, "Beg me to let you come."

"Yes! Please, yes, that's exactly what I was going to say, will you please, please let me come?"

I don't care that I'm babbling. I don't care how I must look, writhing around mindlessly underneath him. I don't even care that all it took for me to hand him the reins to my mind and body was a few words, spoken in that soft, commanding tone that somehow drives me crazy.

All I care about is the fire between my legs that I need him to quench immediately.

"Look at you fucking yourself on my fingers," he growls. "Look at those greedy hips move. Does my bunny not know she's supposed to take what I want to give her?"

It's a question that doesn't require an answer. Which is good, because I'm not capable of speech at the moment, anyway.

In the most dominant voice he's used yet, Aidan says, "Here in this bed, this is what happens: I give. You take. You'll take and you'll take until you break, then you'll beg me to break you all over again."

On the verge of orgasm, I sob.

"Don't you dare let go without my permission," he growls, thrusting those long, hard fingers inside me over and over again.

I make a garbled sound of pleasure and frantically grind against his hand. My eyes roll back into my head.

Just as I'm about to tip over the edge, Aidan pulls his fingers out of me.

Ignoring my whine of protest, he pulls my jeans down my legs and tosses them away. Then he hikes me up to my knees and gives me a series of fast, stinging slaps on my ass.

It's not enough. I want it harder, I want it faster, I want him to ruin me.

I want him to make me forget my own name.

He stops spanking me the instant I moan.

Panting, he says, "Talk to me."

The only thing I can manage is a breathy and broken "More." He smooths his hand over my burning bottom, then bends down to kiss it. Then I hear the sound of a zipper being ripped open. A moment later, the head of his hard cock nudges my entrance.

Through gritted teeth he says, "Repeat the safe word so I know you remember it if you need to use it."

"Cheesy."

"Good girl."

Gripping my hips, he shoves inside me with a guttural grunt.

This time, my moan is one of gratitude.

Then he fucks me. Hard and fast, his fingers digging into my flesh. I feel the cold bite of metal on the back of my thighs and realize he didn't pull his jeans all the way down before taking me.

He couldn't wait any longer, either.

He bends over, reaching beneath me to squeeze my breast. Panting and pulling on my hard nipple, he drives into me relentlessly until my moans are so loud, they echo off the walls. My pussy clenches around his cock.

"Don't you dare," he hisses.

The warning only makes me hotter. I flex my hips in time to his thrusts, straining to get him as deep as he can go inside me, until suddenly he falls still.

Breathing hard, he moves his hand from my breast down between my legs. He slides his fingers all around, then strums his fingertips back and forth over my swollen clit.

As he undoubtedly knew it would, that instantly makes me orgasm.

Crying out, I jerk violently. My pussy convulses, clenching over and over again in hard, rhythmic waves.

"Come, baby! Ah, fuck yes, come for me!"

He sounds triumphant.

I understand then that forbidding me to climax was part of this game, that he knew every minute I'd hold back would add to my pleasure when I finally let go, and I'm stupidly grateful that he knows what he's doing, because this is exactly what I needed.

He's exactly what I needed.

A handsome stranger with secrets in his eyes and a way of looking at me as if he already knows everything there is to know about me. As if I'm a book he's read a thousand times and highlighted all his favorite passages.

As if he already knows how this is going to end.

He falls on top of me, pushing me flat onto my belly on the mattress and trapping me with his weight. With both hands clenched in my hair, he thrusts hard a few more times, then moans my name.

Shuddering, he empties himself inside my body.

I close my eyes and brace myself against the huge wave of emotion cresting to a peak above me, then surrender to its churning darkness as it crashes down and carries me, tumbling, far away.

19

Afterward, we don't speak.

I don't know if he's feeling as emotionally raw as I am or if he simply has nothing to say, but he rolls off me and goes into the bathroom, closing the door behind him.

The faucet runs. The toilet flushes. He reappears carrying a wet washcloth and a hand towel. He silently pushes me onto my back and wipes the washcloth gently between my legs as I lie there feeling as if all my bones have turned to liquid.

He dries me off with the hand towel, then rises and flips off the light switch. Then he crawls onto the mattress beside me, rolls me to my side, pulls me against his chest, and buries his face in my hair, inhaling deeply.

When he exhales, it sounds as if a hundred years of pent-up frustrations leave his body in the same breath.

Eventually, his breathing slows to a deep, even cadence that tells me he's asleep.

I lie there in the dark enveloped in his warmth and think about Michael.

Was I a good wife?

I don't know. I tried to be. More than anything, I wanted

to make him happy. He wanted me to be happy, too, and I thought we were perfect for each other. All our jagged little pieces matched. We *fit*.

But our relationship was nothing like this.

I know it's unfair to make comparisons. I also know it's unfair that I lied to Aidan about being separated from my husband instead of simply telling him the truth.

But he caught me off guard. I had no idea anything even remotely like this would happen. I wasn't prepared for the extent of our attraction, for the force of it, for the way I'm drawn to him with an intensity I feel strangely powerless to resist.

And so I simply let him believe Michael was still alive. Part of me wants to believe it as well. Part of me wants to believe this isn't the truth:

My husband is dead.

He fell off our boat and drowned.

I watched it happen.

Maybe I haven't told Aidan about it because I don't want to relive that last part. The splashing and the screaming. Michael's desperate cries for help growing weaker as the boat drifted farther and farther away.

The smell of smoke over the dark water and the awful, brittle laughter that seemed to come from everywhere all around.

I didn't tell the detective who interviewed me after the accident about the laughter. It's not exactly something I can explain.

I must fall asleep at some point, because the next thing I know, the room is light and Aidan's big hand is gently stroking my bottom. He's still behind me in the same position he was when he fell asleep.

He murmurs, "Morning, sweet bunny. Sleep well?"

Turning my head toward him, I inhale and stretch my legs, curling my toes. "I think so. You?"

He presses a kiss to my nape. His hand drifts over my hip and down between my legs. "Like the dead."

"Hmm. That big hard thing poking into my tailbone doesn't feel very dead."

He chuckles. "You can't blame him. He's got a beautiful naked woman in his bed."

When he slips his fingers inside my pussy and strokes them over my clit, I sigh in pleasure.

"I'm obsessed with that sound," he says, his voice darker. "With all the sounds you make. I can't get enough of you, Kayla."

He bites me on the shoulder. It's not hard, but it is dominant. Like something an animal would do before it mounts its mate.

"You're shivering."

"It's not from cold."

"I know, baby. Time to sit on my face."

My eyes fly open. "Pardon?"

"You heard me. And from now on, I expect you to obey an order the first time I give it."

My heartbeat surges. I lie still with my mind going a million miles an hour until I venture hesitantly, "I want to ask you something, but I don't want you to think I'm being, um, disobedient. I'm just trying to figure out the rules."

He kisses my shoulder, then my neck. Actually, kissing isn't really what he's doing. It's more like licking and sucking. As if he's tasting my skin and finds it delicious.

Nipping my earlobe, he whispers, "Ask your master for permission to speak."

Oh God. Oh dear holy God in heaven, this is actually happening. He! Just! Said! That!

Calmly lavishing my shoulders and neck with his lips and tongue, Aidan lazily strokes his fingers back and forth over my clit, which is now achingly sensitive. My nipples are, too. So is my entire nervous system, which feels as if it's about to explode.

Hyperventilating, I whisper, "May I please have permission to speak . . . master?"

His voice low and hypnotic, he says, "Yes, my perfect, pretty bunny rabbit. You may."

Then he presses his teeth to the side of my throat and slides a finger inside me.

My cry of pleasure is soft and broken. It takes me a moment to remember what the hell I was going to say. "I . . . I don't know exactly what you mean by sit on your face."

"It's not rocket science."

"Yes, but I mean, logistically, how does it work? Do I, like, brace my hands against the wall for balance?"

He sounds surprised. "You've never done it before?"

"No. And I don't want to smother you."

His laughter is muffled against my skin. Then he groans. "Fucking hell, you're sweet. You're so goddamn sweet, I just want to sink my teeth into every inch of you."

"You're doing a pretty good job of that so far."

He rolls me to my back and cups my face in his hand. Gazing intently down at me, he says, "What else haven't you done?"

"Everything that doesn't include missionary or doggie style with the lights out. Oh, and oral. But nothing . . ."

"What?"

My cheeks are heating up, damn them. "Kinky."

"Define kinky."

"I think you know what I mean, mister."

He's trying not to laugh at me. Pressing his lips together, his eyes alight, he shakes his head. "It's master or sir. No misters. I'll give you one free pass, but next time, disrespect will earn you a spanking."

I smile up at him. "You say that like you don't already know I love it when you give me a spanking."

He stares at me in silence for a moment, his laughter fading. Then his voice comes out rough.

"I wish you knew how perfect you are. How different and perfect. I've never met anyone like you. Whenever we're together, I feel like a new man. A better man. Like everything bad that's ever happened to me doesn't matter anymore because your sweet smile takes it all away."

Warmth washes over me. It seems as if the sky just opened up, and I'm being bathed in a brilliant ray of sunshine from head to toe. Feeling shy, I whisper, "What a nice thing to say. Thank you."

He stares at me, his gaze moving slowly over my features, then he kisses me deeply, his hand still cupped around my face.

Against my mouth, he murmurs, "I'm gonna lie on my back, and you're gonna straddle my face, baby. Don't worry about smothering me. I'll hold you up. Ready?"

Shimmering with need and embarrassment, I whisper, "Yes, sir."

When he exhales with the faintest of moans, I know I've pleased him.

It frightens me how much I suddenly want to please him again.

He rolls onto his back and pulls me on top of him, clasping his hands around my waist. He urges me up toward the wall, so I climb forward on my hands and knees as he scoots lower down the mattress. When my knees are on either side of his head, he pulls me down by my hips until my pussy hovers right above his mouth and I'm looking down between my spread legs at him.

He warns, "Don't come until I give you permission," and latches onto my clit with his mouth.

I gasp. My thighs quiver. My lids flutter shut. He stabilizes me by gripping my hips, then reaches up around my hips with both hands and squeezes my breasts. He fondles my breasts and pinches my nipples as he licks my pussy, and I doubt my head will ever be set on straight again.

When I moan softly, he takes one hand away from my breast and slaps me on the ass. It's hard and stings, and I love it.

I flatten my hands against the mattress and lock my elbows. I flex my hips against Aidan's mouth. He makes a soft sound of approval, so I flex my hips again.

He pulls on my hard nipple and slaps my ass, making me groan loudly in pleasure.

"Fuck my mouth," he orders. "Ride my face, baby. Don't make me tell you again."

Okey dokey, sir.

I grind my pussy against his face, laughing breathlessly when he shoves his tongue deep inside me. The laughter dies quickly because his mouth feels so damn good. I stop worrying that I might smother him and really get into it, concentrating on the feel of his hot, wet mouth between my legs and his calloused fingers pinching my nipple and digging into my hips.

A sharp contraction of my uterus makes me moan.

Still playing with my nipple, Aidan slides a finger inside me and sucks my clit with more force.

I whisper raggedly, "Oh. Aidan. Oh God, that feels *amazing*."

"You need to come?"

"Yes, please."

"Not yet."

He eats me until I'm moaning brokenly, my thighs are shaking hard, and I'm certain I'll fall over before I can climax. Then he drags his fingernails down my back, shoulder blades to ass cheeks, and laughs into my flesh when I shudder.

"You need to come, baby?"

"Yes! Please!"

"Then you better earn it."

Before I can decipher what that might mean, he pulls me down by the hips, forcing me to crawl backward a foot or so. Then he flips around beneath me, positioning himself on his back so his hard cock juts up toward my mouth and my knees are on either side of his head again.

He orders, "Suck my cock, bunny," and buries his face in my pussy.

I grasp his erection in one hand and lower my head to lick the crown. Aidan hums in pleasure, a sound that vibrates deliciously through my pelvis. Then he flattens a hand on the small of my back and forces me to lie on his stomach, skin to skin, as he lavishes my pussy with his tongue and I suck on his dick.

He thrusts up into my mouth. I flex my hips against his tongue. We're both moaning and frantic, our skin slick with sweat, and if he doesn't give me permission to come soon, I will anyway.

When I make a high, whining noise in the back of my throat, he knows I can't hold out any longer.

"Swallow my cum, then you have my permission to orgasm," he says, panting. "But not before. You ready?"

I make a desperate sound of assent around his hard cock and keep sucking and sliding my hand up and down his shaft.

"Good girl."

Swirling his tongue around and around my engorged clit, he thrusts up into my mouth, stretching my lips open until my eyes are watering and I'm fighting the urge to gag. Then he climaxes with a grunt, spilling hot semen onto my tongue in thick pulses.

I suck and swallow over and over again, breathing through my nose, my entire body trembling. Aidan spanks my ass three times, hard, then shoves a finger deep inside my pussy.

Choking on his cock, I convulse around his finger.

"That's my perfect good girl," he growls, thrusting with his hips, driving his cock deeper down my throat. "Swallow every fucking drop as you come for me."

Blind with pleasure, helplessly jerking, I sob around his erection and do as I'm told.

He praises me with words I hear but don't understand. I'm somewhere far off, hurtling through space, my mind ablaze with fireworks, my body utterly beyond my control.

I'm a stranger to myself at this moment. Someone with no limits and no worries, a woman at once perfectly at peace, yet completely astonished by her actions.

He's pulled a string I didn't know I had hidden inside and unraveled me from the inside out.

Then he flips me onto my back, tosses my ankles up over his shoulders, shoves his still-hard cock inside me, and unravels me all over again.

20

Later, I lie beside him, my head resting on his chest, my leg thrown over his, my body boneless. I'm a bowl of jiggly Jell-O, quaking and spent.

I've never felt so alive.

Gazing up at the ceiling, Aidan murmurs, "Need to ask you a question. And I need you to be honest when you answer."

I wait silently. He didn't give me permission to speak, and I'm still not really clear how and when all these rules of his apply, so I stay on the safe side and say nothing.

His chest rises and falls with a deep breath. "What are the chances of you getting back together with your husband?"

A sudden sharp jab of pain stabs me beneath my sternum. I squeeze my eyes shut against it. "Zero."

"Yeah?"

"Yes."

"Then why are you still wearing your wedding ring?"

I think about it for a moment. "I don't really know. Habit, I suppose. Does it bother you?"

"Yes and no."

He doesn't explain himself further. I get the sense he's waiting for me to say something, but I can't be sure. "May I please ask a question?"

He murmurs, "Sweet bunny. You can always ask me anything."

"Really?"

"Why do you sound surprised?"

"Because I'm not sure when we're doing the permission thing and when we aren't, and I don't want to get into trouble." I add more softly, "Or displease you."

His groan is low. Pulling me closer, he kisses the top of my head.

"Kayla," he whispers. "Everything about you pleases me."

Snuggling closer to him, I smile. "You can see my problem, though, right? I mean, I don't have any experience with this kind of thing."

He rolls me onto my back and lifts up to an elbow, staring down at me with blazing intent.

"Me neither."

I laugh right into his face. "That's a total lie!"

"I wasn't talking about sex."

My laughter dies. Confused, I gaze up at him with knitted brows. "Then what are you talking about?"

He flattens his hand over my chest, right above my heart.

"This. Us. You and me. How it's so easy. How it's so simple. How it just feels right. But you're still wearing your wedding ring, and you don't feel comfortable kissing me in your house, and that tells me everything I need to know about where your head's at. And I get it, I really do. Your whole life has been turned upside down. It's understandable that you're not ready for this.

"But I gotta be honest. I won't be a rebound. I won't be the guy you distract yourself with for a while to make yourself feel better, then walk away from when you do. So I think I should cut my losses now before I get my heart shredded, because I can already tell you're gonna wreck me if this goes on much longer and you leave."

That knocks the breath out of me. I lie there staring up at him with wide eyes and a pounding heart, shocked by his honesty.

When I pull myself together, I discover to my surprise that I'm really freaking mad.

I say firmly, "No."

Dark eyes burning, he stares at me. His silence makes me even angrier.

"You don't get to decide how this is going to go before it's even gone anywhere, Aidan. I understand not wanting to be a rebound, but you could just say, 'Hey, we'll take it slow,' or 'Let's talk about your expectations here,' but instead, you unilaterally decide you're breaking up with me? Before we're even officially an item? Fuck that. That's not how this works. You can boss me around in bed all you want, but when it comes to making decisions about our relationship, we're doing that shit together. I refuse to be a one-night stand."

After a moment of blistering silence, he says gruffly, "It's already more than a one-night stand."

"Fine. A three-night stand. Whatever." I glare at him until something in his eyes melts.

"Relationship? That's what you're calling this?"

"I said what I said. Deal with it."

"Oh, bunny," he breathes, a thrill in his voice, "you're *this close* to getting the spanking of your life."

I want to drum my heels against the mattress in frustration. And maybe scream a little, too. But I lie still with my lips pressed together and my nostrils flared, internally shouting curses at him.

Then I remember that I don't have a single goddamn leg to stand on. My anger is misplaced.

He's not the one holding back an important detail about their personal life here. That's all me.

But *then* I remind myself that I have absolutely no idea what the man is or isn't holding back. Other than that he owns a roofing company, has a friend named Jake he's known since high school, and that he may or may not have unalived his own father, I know zilch.

Which makes this entire conversation all the more bizarre for both of us.

I close my eyes and exhale a hard breath.

Aidan commands, "Eyes on me, Kayla."

I open my eyes and glare at him. "Oh, are we back to master and slave again? Pardon me while I go online to find a chiropractor to treat my whiplash."

He drops his head and puts his mouth next to my ear. "Do you have any idea how hard I want to spank you right now?"

I can't help myself. I smile. "The feeling is mutual."

He rolls on top of me, smashing me into the mattress with his body weight.

"Oof!" I flail weakly at his back, slapping him. "You're crushing me!"

"You love it," he murmurs, holding my head between both hands and gazing down at me with hot eyes. "Now stop bleating and listen to me."

I fall still, flinging my arms down to the mattress a little too dramatically, as evidenced by the quirk of his lips.

"Drama queen."

"Tyrant."

"You bet your sweet ass I am. And you like that about me."

He waits for confirmation while I glower at his chin.

"Kayla."

I know what that warning tone in his voice means. I exhale, rolling my eyes. "Okay, yes, I like it." I can't resist adding, "Usually."

Chuckling, he kisses the tip of my nose. "Brat. As I was saying . . ." His voice drops to a whisper. "Thank you."

Damn, he sure has a way of taking me by surprise. "For what?"

He shakes his head, which I take to mean I won't get an explanation.

I say brightly, "Hey, I have an idea!"

"What's that?"

"Why don't you teach me sign language so that when you suddenly decide you don't want to use your words anymore, we can still keep talking."

My stare is pointed. His glower is dark. Then I smile at him because he obviously got my point, and I'm not really in the mood for more arguing.

I wrap my arms around his back. Knowing full well what the answer is already, I ask innocently, "So are you ending it with me or what?"

I can't decide if his expression is admiration or aggravation. Maybe a combo of both.

He says bluntly, "You want me to?"

Crap. He turned it back around on me. "No."

Searching my eyes for any sign of ambivalence, he says more softly, "You sure? It's not too late to walk away from this."

I'm unsure if it's my imagination or not, but it seems as if there's a vague threat buried in there somewhere. As if he thinks there's an invisible line in the sand we haven't quite crossed yet, but once we do, there's no turning back for either of us.

I slide my hands over his shoulders and into his hair. Staring into his eyes, I nod.

"Say it out loud," he orders.

"I'm sure."

After a long period of silence, he pronounces, "Okay."

I dissolve into disbelieving laughter. "God, you're nuts."

His dark eyes glittering, he says softly, "You have no idea."

Right back at you, stud.

⌒

After a shower and a serving of Aidan's awesome scrambled eggs, I tell him I should probably get going.

Sitting across from me at his kitchen table, he shovels a forkful of eggs into his mouth. He doesn't respond until long after he's finished chewing and swallowed. I'm not sure if he's deliberately taking a moment to think about his response or if he's just really into those eggs.

Looking at his plate, he asks, "You got things to do today?"

"I'm behind on work."

He nods thoughtfully.

"What are you up to?"

"I work on the house on Sundays."

"What house?"

"My house."

Surprised, I say, "You have a house?"

He glances up at me and nods. "Building one on the other side of the island."

"You're *building a house*? From scratch?"

"No, from origami swans."

I smile at him. "There's that devastating sense of humor again. Seriously, you're really building a house from the ground up?"

He gives me a look like I should already know he's fully capable of that and any other project he might set his mind to. Like, say, constructing a spacecraft from recycled aluminum cans.

"Wow, Aidan. That's impressive."

He nods, turning his attention back to his eggs.

"Can I see it?"

He freezes. His eyes flash up to mine. He says gruffly, "You want to?"

"Of course I do. Why are you shocked?"

He shakes his head and looks down at his plate. I impatiently let him ruminate on his answer, knowing he might never provide one but holding out hope.

Then he says quietly, "Still not sure what the parameters are."

It's not a lot, but it's enough. "Me neither. How about if we figure it out as we go along?"

He glances up to meet my gaze. "Or we could decide right now."

"Is that what you want?"

His nod is curt.

I smile at him and tease, "So we're negotiating."

He says sourly, "Funny."

"It's just that I remember how it's your favorite thing."

Without missing a beat, he says, "Being inside you is my favorite thing. Making you come is my favorite thing. Knowing you don't do one-night stands but you made an exception for me is my favorite thing. Everything else is now a distant second."

I chew on the inside of my cheek as my ears grow hot.

He says more softly, "Tell me to stop talking like that and I will. I don't want to scare you."

I consider him. In a simple white T-shirt and jeans, he's tense and unsmiling, and so handsome, it seems impossible.

Holding his gaze, I say, "You know you don't scare me."

"I meant scare you away."

"I know what you meant. My answer's the same."

We stare at each other across the table until he pushes his plate away and sits back in his chair. His voice low and his gaze burning, he says, "Come here."

He's got that predatory look in his eyes again, as if he's the hunter and I'm his prey. Every nerve ending in my body responds to it, standing on end at full attention. My pulse, respiration, and body temperature jump.

Moistening my lips, I stand and slowly walk around the table.

As soon as I'm within reach, he grabs my wrist and pulls me down onto his lap. He sinks his hands into my hair and brings my face close to his as I flatten my hands over his pecs.

Gazing deep into my eyes, he says gruffly, "Tell me what you want."

I don't even have to think about it. "To keep doing this. To get to know you better. To spend time with you and see where it goes."

He licks his lips. His gaze drops to my mouth. "What else?"

I swallow nervously, then whisper, "To please you."

"You don't have to say that."

"I know."

His breathing turns ragged. His erection digs into my bottom. Beneath my palms, his heart drums a fast staccato beat.

"Give your lion a kiss, bunny. Make it sweet."

The roughness of his tone and the need in his eyes make me tremble. I take his face in my hands and press a soft kiss to his mouth. Then I rub my cheek against his, closing my eyes and sighing in pleasure as his beard tickles my skin.

He murmurs my name.

"Yes, sir?"

A delicate little shudder runs through his chest when I call him that. He mutters, "Christ. You're gonna be the death of me, aren't you?"

"Oh, come on, Fight Club. You're tough. You can handle it."

He kisses me, devouring my mouth, softly groaning into it as he holds my head steady and takes what he needs. When he breaks the kiss, we're both breathing hard.

He gazes into my eyes with an expression of agony. Surprised, I trace a fingertip over his bottom lip and whisper, "Aidan. What is it?"

He clenches his teeth so hard, a muscle in his jaw flexes. The shake of his head is short and final.

He's not going to tell me what's wrong.

I sigh again, foreseeing a lot of this silent nonsense in our future.

"May I please have permission to tell you that you're a pain in the ass?"

A hint of humor surfaces in the dark depths of his eyes. "Careful, sweet rabbit."

I blink innocently. "Oh, did I not do that right?"

He lowers his lids and gazes at me as a dangerous growl rumbles through his chest.

"Okay, fine. I'll be good." Smiling, I give him a peck on the lips. "Can we go see your house now? I can't wait to find out what kind of place a lion king builds for himself. I hope you remembered to leave space on the walls to hang all the bunny rabbit pelts you must've collected."

Releasing his fists from my hair, he cups my face and kisses me softly.

"The walls are bare," he murmurs. "I never wanted to catch a bunny before now."

Inside my belly, a million tiny butterflies take flight all at once.

They drop to the ground, killed by a sudden arctic freeze, when Aidan adds firmly, "But it's time for you to go home."

I grumble, "Wow, talk about a buzzkill. I see all that time you spent in charm school was a total waste of money."

"You said you need to work. I won't get in the way of that. And use that smart tone with me again, and you'll earn yourself—"

"I know. A spanking."

"No. You like it too much. It's a reward. Next time you sass me, you'll be punished."

I assess his serious face with narrowed eyes. "Punished how?"

"Try me and find out."

He smiles at my poisonous expression. Then he sets me on my feet, stands, and walks me to the front door.

Opening it, he says, "I'll talk to you soon. In the meantime"—he gives my ass a swat—"stay out of trouble."

He leans down, gives me a firm, quick kiss, pushes me over the threshold, then shuts the door in my face.

Miffed, I shout, "Goodbye, Aidan!"

From the other side of the door comes a low laugh. "See you later, Kayla."

I head down the stairs to the parking lot, wondering why he never says the word goodbye and why he avoided my questions about it both times I asked him.

More mysteries to add to his growing collection.

I'm lost in thought as I get in the car and start it, but freeze when I see what's sitting on the dashboard above the steering wheel.

A 1937 D-type buffalo nickel.

21

∽

I stare at the coin with my heart palpitating and my mind recoiling as if it spotted a rattlesnake.

After a while when I get up my nerve, I reach for it with a trembling hand. It feels abnormally cold in my fingers, as if it's been stored in a freezer.

But it hasn't been in a freezer. It's been where I left it, in a drawer in my office desk.

And now it's here.

In my car.

The car parked outside the bar that Aidan lives above.

I glance around, but there's no one in sight. The parking lot and sidewalks are deserted. There are a few cars parked along the street, but they're down a block or so, near a bakery.

Truly frightened, I stare at the coin again.

One of only two things happened here. Either I took it from my office drawer and don't remember doing that—or leaving it on the dash—or someone else took it from the drawer and left it here for me to find.

Which makes no sense. Who would do that? And why?

Starting to shake, I drop the coin into the cupholder between the front seats and reach behind the passenger seat for my purse. I only brought the key inside to Aidan's with me last night, but now I can't be certain if I locked the car doors or not. Did I unlock them a moment ago?

I don't know. I don't remember.

How can I not remember?

As I dig into my purse for my cell phone, my panic builds. I navigate to the security app and load it. I curse when I realize I'll have to rewind about twelve hours of video feed to see if anyone was in the house while I was gone.

"But that can't be possible," I whisper. "The alarm would've been triggered."

Which means I would have received a call from Jake's security company, but there isn't one. The notifications are blank.

So the only remaining possibility is that I left the coin here and forgot.

I lean my forehead against the steering wheel, close my eyes, and take deep breaths, trying not to hyperventilate.

This memory problem has to be caused by more than stress, but I'm extremely wary of doctors. Both my parents' deaths were caused by medical misdiagnosis. My mother's when her doctor misdiagnosed her lung cancer symptoms as asthma, and my father's when his doctor told him those chest pains he'd been having for the past twelve hours were nothing more than heartburn. The doctor prescribed antacids, when in fact the culprit was a heart attack. By the time Dad was admitted to the emergency room, it was too late.

And didn't I read somewhere that most deadly infections people get are picked up inside hospitals?

"You need help," I tell myself. "Stop rationalizing."

PEN PAL • 171

But what would I even tell a doctor? "Hi, I'm Kayla! I've been hearing strange noises in my house, jars fly out of my kitchen cupboards on their own, my memory has more holes in it than a spaghetti strainer, I've got a new pen pal in prison, and I started an intense sexual affair three weeks after my husband died with a man who calls me his bunny rabbit!"

And let's not forget the mysteriously reappearing buffalo nickel and the weird guy in the hat who spied on me from behind a tree and didn't leave any footprints behind. *In mud.*

Psych ward, here I come.

Just breathe, Kayla. Just calm down and breathe.

Back at the house, I'm worried I might not have armed the alarm before I left, but it's working as it should. I enter in my code to reset it, then stand in the foyer, listening.

For what, I don't know.

The house is silent. When I enter the kitchen, I half expect to see more open drawers and cupboards, but nothing is amiss. I go from room to room, checking things out, until I'm satisfied there are no bogeymen hiding in closets or behind doors.

Only I'm not really satisfied. I'm paranoid, and I don't know what to do about it.

So I do what any rational person would and pour myself a glass of wine.

Then I lock myself in my office and force myself to work, ignoring the disturbing fact that I'm drinking wine before noon and trying to pretend it's normal behavior, when in reality, everybody knows denial about your drinking habits is a total red flag for alcohol use disorder.

"Oh, who cares?" I mutter, glaring at my drawing board. "I've got bigger things to worry about."

After an hour, I give up. I drop my pen and rub my eyes, then go into the kitchen and refill my wineglass. Leaning against the counter, I hit the Rewind button on the security app on my phone and settle in for some high-speed, backward video viewing.

I have a bad feeling that daily reviewing of the damn camera feed is about to become my new hobby.

It takes a while to get through it all from the time I left last night to when I returned this morning, but I find nothing unusual. Around dawn, two squirrels chased each other across the driveway. Just after midnight, a fat raccoon trundled out from the woodpile on the back porch and wandered away into the darkness. Other than that, everything was still.

It isn't until I return to my office with another glass of wine that I see something interesting.

A little blond boy about five or six years old plays by himself on the back lawn. Dressed in a red jacket, matching pants, and yellow rain boots, he runs around grinning, chasing leaves and throwing them into the air. He falls at one point, screaming with laughter as he tumbles face-first into the grass, then rolls over and waves at the sky.

Staring at him through the window, I wonder if a new family moved into the neighborhood. Or maybe someone's grandchild is visiting? I can't think of anyone nearby who has little kids.

But why would his mother think it was a good idea to take this kid to play on my back lawn? The house sits in the middle of two wooded acres. You have to make an effort to get here. Unless they walked down the beach? And where is his mother, anyway? There's no adult in sight. Just this jolly little preschooler tearing up my grass.

Sighing, I set the wineglass on my desk and leave the room. I pass through the kitchen on the way to the laundry room, then go through the garage and out the side door to the backyard.

When I look around, however, the kid has disappeared.

I holler, "Hello? Anybody out here?"

My only answer is the lonely cry of a seagull circling far overhead.

Chilled because I forgot to put on a jacket, I walk all the way around the back of the house and look down toward the street. I see no one. The driveway is empty. I look back toward the beach, and it's empty, too. So are the woods on either side of the house.

Irritated, I mutter, "Where'd you go?"

The last thing I need is some kid breaking his leg on a rock he tripped over on my property. I can see the lawsuit coming a mile away.

I spend another fifteen minutes hunting for him, then give up and go back inside for more wine. Then I get the idea to review the camera feed from the last half hour to see where little blondie went.

But when I open the app, all I get is static. The screen shows nothing but pixelated snow.

Great. The security system works as well as the electrical system. Maybe I should just sell the place and move.

Feeling defeated, I go back to my desk and work for the rest of the day.

⁓

The next morning, I wake to the sound of the alarm screaming.

Disoriented, I jolt upright in bed and look around in panic. Gray daylight sifts through the cracks in the curtains. My robe is where I left it, draped over the arm of a chair. Nothing in the room appears to be out of order, except for the ear-piercing shriek of the security alarm.

In my panic, I fall out of bed. I hit the floor with a thud, but scramble to my feet, adrenaline burning through my veins.

Someone broke into the house.

Fuck fuck fuck oh holy fuck, someone broke into the house!

The noise cuts off as abruptly as it began, leaving my ears ringing with the silence.

Hyperventilating, I move quietly to the door, open it a crack, and listen. Within moments, I hear a female voice grouse, "Blasted thing. What a bloody racket. I'll go deaf, and that's a fact."

I nearly faint with relief. It's Fiona.

Throwing open the door, I walk down the hall and lean over the balcony that overlooks the first floor. "Fiona! It's you!"

She screams and jumps, whirling around. Gazing up at me from the foyer, she presses a hand over her heart.

Looking cross, she says, "It's ten o'clock Monday morning, dear. Of course it's me."

"Ten o'clock?" I repeat, astonished. I can't believe I slept this late, but get distracted from that thought when another occurs to me. "How did you know how to turn off the alarm?"

A strange pause follows. It seems fraught. "I entered the code."

"How did you know what code to enter?"

Another strange pause follows. She asks hesitantly, "How do you think I know it?"

Oh shit. I told her the code, that's how she knows it. I told her and forgot.

I pass a hand over my face and exhale. "Because I gave it to you. Of course I did. Sorry."

When I look at her again, she appears relieved.

"No need to apologize."

A clap of thunder rumbles through the sky. The gray morning is about to erupt into rain again. And whatever this creeping memory loss is of mine, it seems to be accelerating.

"Are you quite well, dear?" asks Fiona, tilting her head and peering at me with an expression of concern.

After a moment, I say, "No. I don't think I am. I don't think I'm well at all."

She nods, as if she already knows my condition is poor but didn't want to say anything and risk offending me. She sets her bags on the floor next to the console table, shrugs out of her woolen jacket, unwinds the scarf around her neck, lays both on the console, then looks back up at me.

In a kind tone, she says, "Why don't we sit in the kitchen and have a cup of tea and a chat?"

Without waiting for an answer, she turns and walks away.

Feeling queasy, I go downstairs. I find her in the kitchen, setting a teapot on the stove. She lights the burner, then sits down at the table and folds her hands together on top. Chewing on a thumbnail, I take the chair across from her.

I think she's going to ask me about my health or suggest I take a nice vacation in the nearest mental institution, but she surprises me by saying gently, "I've always liked you, Kayla. You're a bright, gifted young woman."

Flattered but also taken aback, I say, "Well, thank you. I've always liked you, too."

She smiles and nods in a grandmotherly way.

I look askance at her. "Why do I feel like there's more coming?"

"Because there is. And I want you to remember that this comes from a place of concern for you and your well-being."

I prop my elbows on the table and drop my head into my hands. "I know. I'm a mess. Believe me, I'm aware."

"I don't think you're a mess. I think . . ."

When she pauses too long, I glance up at her, nervous. On her face is a curious expression. It's part concern, but mostly anticipation. At least I think that's what it is. She's staring at me with a weird light in her eyes, the way a person with a gambling addiction looks at a slot machine.

"What?"

She says ominously, "I think something is troubling you."

I blink. "I don't mean to be rude, but that seems obvious."

She shakes her head. "I'm not speaking about the loss of your husband, dear."

"O . . . kay. Then what are you talking about?"

"Well, I don't exactly know. But if there's anything you'd like to get off your chest, I'm here for you. I'm a very good listener."

I stare into her piercing blue eyes and wonder what the fuck she's talking about. "Um . . ."

Leaning forward, she prompts, "Has anything unusual happened lately? In the house, I mean."

All the hairs on my arms prickle. A tiny shiver of fear runs over my skin.

"Yes, I can see that it has," she says softly. "Why don't we talk about that?"

My heart decides now would be a good time to do some acrobatics. My stomach follows suit and twists into a tight knot. My mouth goes dry, my hands tremble, and a high-pitched buzzing noise rings in my ears.

I whisper, "How did you know?"

Her smile is gentle. "I grew up with this kind of thing. Ghosts are quite common in the old country. Scotland is one of the most haunted places in the world."

I blink again, sure I've misheard. Outside, another clap of thunder rolls through the sky, rattling the windows. An odd pressure builds in the room, a friction, as if the air itself has become charged.

"Excuse me, but did you just say *ghosts*?"

"Quite so, my dear."

I sit back in my chair, laughing a little. "I don't believe in ghosts."

She gazes at me steadily. "What you believe is immaterial, Kayla. Because ghosts most definitely believe in you."

Rain begins to fall, pattering softly against the kitchen windowpanes. Drops slide down the glass like tears.

When I don't say anything, Fiona fills the silence.

"Let me give you a few examples, then you can tell me if I'm off my rocker, as your expression suggests. Have you recently been hearing strange noises? Like creaking floorboards, for instance? Have you felt unusual cold drafts? Had the eerie sense you were being watched, but no one was there?"

I swallow. It's becoming difficult to draw a breath. The high-pitched ringing in my ears grows louder.

"What about strange problems with electricity? Flickering lights, exploding bulbs, the telly turning itself on or off?"

"It's an old house. It has lots of problems."

Blowing right past that, she continues her assault on my sanity.

"Perhaps you've been having strange dreams. Maybe objects are being moved, appearing in places other than where you put them."

She must catch something in my expression, because she leans closer. "Books falling off shelves? Furniture rearranging itself in the middle of the night?"

My voice faint, I say, "A jar of honey flew out of the cupboard on its own. A coin I put in one place showed up in another. And all the kitchen drawers and cupboards were standing wide open in the morning one day when I came down."

She nods solemnly. "What about strange scents? Perfumes or strong odors? Any of that?"

I think of the odd burning smell when I run the dryer, the smell Eddie couldn't find a source to—or any of the other electrical problems in the house—and feel as if I might jump right out of my skin.

When the kettle on the stove whistles, I do jump. Suddenly, I'm scared witless.

Fiona rises from her chair, gets two mugs from a cabinet, and pours hot water into both. The tea bags go in next, then she sets one of the mugs in front of me and sits back down across from me.

As if she hasn't just given me an aneurysm, she says, "It would be proper with a drop of milk, but I've gone lactose intolerant in my old age. Would you like some?"

I barely manage a shake of my head.

"Now, now, dear, please don't be frightened. I know being haunted is a bit much for our twenty-first-century minds to deal with, but we'll get through it together."

Maybe I'm still asleep. Maybe this is just a bad dream. Maybe all that wine I had yesterday went to my head and killed more than the usual amount of brain cells.

Ever the practical one, Fiona turns businesslike. "What we need is a séance."

I say flatly, "That's ridiculous."

"No, the federal tax rate is ridiculous. This is simply a situation that needs to be remedied." She sips her tea and makes a yummy noise. "As soon as possible, I might add. The longer a spirit is trapped in this dimension, the greater the odds it will never be able to move on."

"Fiona, I don't have a ghost in the house!"

She clucks her tongue in disapproval at my tone. "I know it's alarming, dear, but please try to control yourself. Scots have a genetically built-in aversion to overt shows of emotion, and I'd hate to think less of you over something so minor as being haunted. Now, what about visual disturbances? Have you seen anything strange around the place?"

Into my mind flashes an image of the strange, hostile man in the hat hiding behind the tree who left no footprints behind. Another image comes, this one of the little blond boy playing in the yard . . .

The boy my security camera didn't catch, presenting me instead with a recording of static.

Horror creeps over me, starting at my feet and slowly moving up my body until I'm gripped in a cold, tight skeleton hand of fright.

As if her case is closed, Fiona says sagely, "Ah."

Chilled to the bone, I say, "It's impossible. Ghosts don't exist."

Fiona smiles. A bass rumble of thunder rolls through the

sky. The rain increases, peppering the windows and drumming against the roof.

Then the overhead lights turn themselves off and on three times, like a smug supernatural fuck-you.

22

"Now listen carefully," says Fiona, turning businesslike again. "I need to tell you something important."

"What is it?"

"No matter what happens, *don't* tell the ghost it's dead. They have no idea they're no longer living."

I'm convinced we're both in a padded cell somewhere having this conversation. That's really the only reasonable explanation.

When I sit there staring at her in disbelief, she continues.

"Ghosts are simply souls with a story to tell. When a person dies tragically or violently, their spirit often can't move on. They have unfinished business that keeps them tied to this realm. Until they get closure, they will remain here, haunting the people and places that meant the most to them while they were alive."

"Are you even listening to the words coming out of your mouth?"

She arches a brow. "I'm aware this is difficult for you, dear, but there's no need to be snippy."

Chastened, I sigh. "Sorry."

"As I was saying . . . What was I saying?"

"Ghosts need closure."

"Yes, that's right. And until they get it, they're stuck here, wandering the earth in misery."

She stares at me expectantly.

"You're saying we need to help this ghost who doesn't exist and definitely is not haunting me get closure."

Fiona beams. "Well done."

Stupendous. She wants me to give up art and become a guide for lost spirits. "I hope you won't be offended by this, but that is the dumbest thing I've ever heard."

I can tell by her expression that she's definitely offended.

She sniffs, lifting her nose. "All right. If you don't want my help, I can't force you to take it." She stands, takes her mug to the sink, and dumps the rest of her tea down the drain. Rinsing out the mug, she says over her shoulder, "Do you need your office cleaned today?"

"Really? We're just going to act like this conversation never happened?"

She turns to level me with a cool stare. "I was under the impression that wallowing in denial is where you're most comfortable."

"Ouch. That was harsh."

"I'm not one to sugarcoat things."

I say drily, "Gee, I couldn't tell."

We gaze at each other across the room, until I finally give in.

"Okay, even if I did go along with this insanity—which I'm not, I'm just saying *if*—what then?"

Her expression softens. She sets the mug in the drain rack next to the sink and returns to her chair. "Then we attempt to contact the spirit to see what it wants."

"You're back to the séance thing again."

"Correct."

We gaze at each other across the table as I attempt to retrieve my brain from outer space where it went for a nice rest from this ridiculous conversation.

"Or maybe I should just go see a therapist. That seems as if it might be money better spent."

"Oh, there won't be a charge, my dear. She could do it as a personal favor."

"Who's she?"

"My sister. She's a medium."

By this point, that new tidbit of information doesn't even faze me. "Of course she is. And how does one get into that line of work?"

"Well, you're born into it, aren't you? It's a gift."

I repeat doubtfully, "A gift."

"Something that comes naturally, like your artistic ability."

"Only with dead people."

"Exactly."

"And she can guarantee this non-spirit who isn't haunting me will leave after that?"

"Oh no. That's entirely up to the spirit. And there's always the chance that . . ." She chews on the inside of her cheek.

"Don't leave me hanging. I'm strung out enough as it is."

"Well, not all spirits are friendly ones. Some of them are vengeful and full of rage."

I chuckle. "So they used to work at the DMV."

Her blue eyes glitter. Her voice drops. "This isn't a joke, my dear. One must exercise extreme caution when dealing with beings from another realm. They're very unpredictable. If provoked to anger, they're quite capable of violence."

The shiver of fear I felt earlier returns, skimming over my flesh and leaving goose bumps in its wake. "How can a ghost be capable of violence if it doesn't have a body?"

"The same way it can rearrange furniture or knock something off a shelf."

"I don't understand."

She gathers her thoughts for a moment. "A spirit is energy manifesting itself, akin to an electrical storm gathering force until it discharges a bolt of lightning. When a spirit is upset, that emotion—that energy—is transformed into a physical outcome. Hence your open cupboards and drawers."

She glances upward. "Or your flickering lights."

I stare at the ceiling in trepidation, half expecting to see a grinning green goblin floating over my head. "So . . . theoretically speaking, not that I believe any of this . . . the spirit who lives in my house is mad?"

She replies softly, "I'd say the spirit who lives in this house is bloody furious."

When I look at her, startled, she adds in an offhand tone, "Or spirits, plural. This house is very old. There's really no telling how many restless souls are lurking about. Could be dozens."

"*Dozens?* You're saying I'm living in hell?"

"Hell is a state of mind, my dear. Reality is simply what we believe it to be. Each of us makes our own truths, even ghosts."

That statement is the most unsettling thing she's said so far. "Okay, but I still don't believe in ghosts. Wouldn't that put a damper on a séance?"

Fiona lifts her brows. "Do you suppose God is affected one way or another if people don't believe in him?"

"I mean . . . maybe his feelings get hurt?"

She sighs. "I can't make cookies without sugar, my dear."

"Great. Now you're speaking in code. Also, you totally *can* make cookies without sugar. They're called sugarless cookies. Diabetics eat them all the time."

She regards me balefully. "My, what a wonderful chat we're having. I'm so glad for this chance to get to know you better."

"Ha-ha. Back to the cookie thing. What did that comment mean?"

"It means your skepticism won't interfere with a medium's ability to connect with a spirit, but I'm afraid it *would* cause you to interpret anything you might experience as a byproduct of indigestion or some such. You'd rationalize it away."

I think about that for a moment. "That does sound like me."

"Just as I thought. So perhaps you should take a while to mull it over." She smiles. "See if any more pranks from your ghost might open up your mind."

"Pranks? I don't like the sound of that."

"Well, from what you've told me, so far it seems your spirit has been acting relatively well-mannered . . ."

She trails off and stares at me, unblinking.

I say, "That pause has got to be the creepiest thing I've ever heard."

"I'm simply suggesting that ghosts, like people, have moods. I'd be willing to bet you haven't seen the worst of it yet."

I press my cold fingertips to my closed eyelids and heave a sigh. "Fine. Let's assume for argument's sake that there is a ghost or ghosts living in this house. What other things should I be on the lookout for?"

Fiona cheerfully ticks off a list. "Orbs of light. Whispering voices. Strange dreams. Shadowy forms glimpsed in your peripheral vision or unnatural shadows where there shouldn't be any. Misplaced items. The radio or television changing stations on their own. Feeling a touch—"

"A touch?" I interrupt, horrified. "A ghost could *touch* me? Gross!"

She purses her lips, gazing at me as if I've gravely disappointed her.

"I said *feeling* a touch. It's a sensation. If you recall, dear, ghosts don't have bodies. So naturally, it would follow that they don't have hands. Please pay attention."

I swear, I'm going to give this woman such a smack.

But I get distracted from that thought when she says, "Another thing that could happen is that you begin to be physically influenced by the presence of the spirit. So you might begin to experience headaches or lapses in memory, things like that."

Headaches? Lapses in memory?

I stare at Fiona with my mouth hanging open.

Perplexed by my expression, she says, "What?"

When I find my voice again, I say weakly, "I think I just had a revelation."

Eyes bright, she leans eagerly over the table. "*And?*"

"There's no and. Just . . . there was this little boy."

She blinks in confusion. "Boy? What boy?"

"I saw him through my office window playing out on the back lawn, but when I went outside to find him, he was gone. And the security feed was all static when I reviewed it, as if it had been erased. Or hadn't recorded at all." My throat arid as a desert, I swallow. "Because he wasn't really there."

Fiona is wearing such an odd expression, it makes me nervous.

She asks, "What did this little boy look like?"

"Blond. Maybe five years old. He was wearing a red rain slicker and little yellow boots. And he seemed happy, running around and laughing." I shake my head in disbelief. "I thought he got lost and wandered into my backyard."

Fiona looks down at the table. She spreads her hands flat over the top. She appears to be calculating something.

"What's wrong?"

After a beat, she puts on a bright smile. "It's only that I've never heard of a happy ghost. Typically, spirits who linger on this plane are here because of a tragedy they haven't gotten over. They're usually sad or angry."

"Oh." My laugh borders on hysterical. "Well, the other guy definitely fits the angry slot."

"What other guy?"

"I saw this man spying on me from behind a tree in the backyard. He looked really pissed off. He bared his teeth at me and everything. But he didn't leave any footprints in the mud, and now I'm thinking the only people who don't leave footprints in mud are people who don't have bodies."

I cannot fucking believe I just said that.

Blinking like an owl, Fiona repeats slowly, "Bared his teeth."

"Yeah. He freaked me out. Though I couldn't really see much of his face, just that weird grimace. He was tall and gaunt and had a trench coat and a hat on, pulled low over his eyes."

I gasp, sitting up straighter in my chair. "Oh God! Do you think he might have hurt the little boy? Like maybe that's why they're here, because they're linked somehow?"

A strange expression crosses Fiona's face. After a moment, she nods. "Perhaps. Maybe they lived in this house long ago. Maybe they were father and son. Or maybe they're from two completely different time periods and something tragic happened to each one of them. The possibilities are endless. Sometimes ghosts are drawn to one another and wind up haunting the same area, even though they didn't know each other in life."

We stare at each other. Finally, I say, "Not that I believe in ghosts."

"Of course not."

"Right. So when can your sister come and do the séance?"

"I'll ask her and find out."

"Great."

We stare at each other again. Then she says urgently, "The most important thing, Kayla, is for you to remember what I said about not telling a ghost it's dead. If you see these spirits again before we can arrange a séance and hopefully assist them to the Other Side, just allow them to do whatever they're doing undisturbed. Don't try to interact. And especially don't do anything to anger them."

Feeling chilled all over again, I ask, "Why is that so important?"

"Because a spirit lives in a world of its own making. It only sees what it wants to see. It's blind to reality. Wandering spirits must be ready to accept that they no longer inhabit the world of the living. They must be gently coaxed to that understanding and accept it through their own free will, or they might retreat further into their fantasy world, dooming themselves to be locked in the darkness for eternity, beyond all hope of reaching the Other Side and thus achieving peace."

She pauses, then adds quietly, "In effect, they'll be damned."

I don't want to be the cause of any random spirit being damned, so even though I don't believe any of this and am probably dreaming this entire conversation, I say solemnly, "I promise I won't tell them they're dead."

"Good."

She gives me a reassuring smile and rises from the table, leaving me alone in the kitchen with my figurative and literal ghosts.

Then I walk into my office, take the letter I wrote to Dante out of the drawer, and grab an umbrella from the stand next to the front door. I go outside in the rain, headed to the mailbox.

If I'm being haunted by the spirits of a happy little boy and a hostile dude in a trench coat, I might as well commit to having a pen pal in prison.

At least he's alive.

It's not until I'm raising the red metal flag on the mailbox that something Fiona said comes back to me like a slap across the face.

"When a person dies tragically or violently, their spirit often can't move on."

My heart pounding, I whisper, "Michael."

As if in response, a crackling burst of lightning rips jagged claws of brilliant white through the dark and stormy sky.

23

Dear Kayla,

I had this cat when I was a kid. Orange tabby, skinny thing, hated everybody. Except me. That cat loved me. I loved him, too, though I didn't know it until he got hit by a car. Before that, I thought OJ was a menace. (That was his name, OJ. After orange juice. Not very creative, I know, but I was eight.)

Once the cat died and he wasn't around anymore, I realized how much I loved him. That stupid cat had been my best friend, but I only realized it in hindsight.

Funny thing, isn't it, hindsight? It's memory, but with new understanding tacked on, so that the past means something different than it did before.

And the only way to find that meaning is to look for it.

Look to the past.

Dig up those graves.

Examine the bones you find there.

I've been doing my fair share of that lately. I've got so much time on my hands in this place, thinking about the past has become the main way I spend my days.

You asked what I did to land myself here. The simple answer is that I loved someone too much.

You see, I learned a lesson from OJ's death. I learned that love means nothing unless it's acted upon. Love isn't real without intent. It's a verb. It isn't passive.

But most of all, love means sacrifice.

Whatever love asks of you must be given, no matter the price.

And I'd gladly give what love asked of me a thousand times over. Even if I had to do it every day until the end of eternity, I'd slice open my own veins with a razor blade and happily bleed myself dry.

Dante

24

It's Saturday. The rain has fallen steadily day and night this week, tapering to drizzle only to gather strength and pound the saturated ground once again.

I sit in my office with Dante's letter in my hands as I gaze out the window into the dreary afternoon. The sound is a murky iron gray, its waters uneasy, whipped to white peaks by gusty winds. The house exhales an occasional wistful sigh, but otherwise is silent.

It's been that way since my talk with Fiona last Monday. Eerily silent, as if it's holding its breath.

It's not the only one.

I've barely slept all week. I walk around on eggshells, my nerves screaming at every gust of wind or tree branch scraping a windowpane. But nothing out of the ordinary has happened. There have been no more sightings of the little boy or the man in the trench coat, no unexplained smells or flickering lights.

Out at the end of the dock, the *Eurydice* bobs restlessly in the choppy water. Drawn by some irresistible force, my gaze returns to it again and again.

I know it's only my frazzled nerves that make it seem like the boat watches me back.

I work through the remainder of the day with Dante's letter simmering on the back burner of my mind until a text comes through on my phone.

You win. Call me.

It's Aidan. We haven't spoken in six days. I'm not feeling particularly cooperative, so I send him a text back instead of calling.

What did I win?

I can almost feel his irritation that I disobeyed his order to call him in the three bouncing dots as he types his reply.

You were supposed to contact me first.

Frowning, I type back.

I didn't realize it was a competition.

The phone rings. As soon as I pick up and say, "Hello?" Aidan's displeased voice is in my ear.

"I was giving you space. Didn't think it would turn into distance."

"There's no distance. It's just been a weird week."

After a pause, he asks, "You okay?"

"There's honestly no accurate way to answer that. By the way, I miss you."

His voice softens. "Yeah?"

"You know I do."

"I hoped. Kept thinking I'd hear a knock on my door and open up to find a soaking wet, barefoot stunner in a see-through shirt on my doorstep."

That makes me smile. "Isn't that what every man wants?"

"Maybe, but I'm the one who got it." His voice lowers an

octave. "Get your sweet ass over here, bunny. I need you naked in my bed. You've made me wait long enough."

"You made yourself wait, Fight Club. You could've picked up the phone days ago."

"Told you I was giving you space."

"Not that I wanted it."

"I'm interested in giving you what you need, Kayla, which might not coincide with what you want."

And I'm interested in my body's reaction to those words, which is a confusing mix of desire and annoyance. I'd like to tear off all my clothes and kneel at his feet, but at the same time, I'd like to hang up on him.

I know I'd only call him right back, though, so I'll skip it.

"And exactly what is it you think I need, Aidan?"

"To forget everything so you can remember who you are again."

That takes my breath away. Not only because of the darkly sensual way it was spoken, but also because he's right. My heart beating faster, I moisten my lips and whisper, "Yes."

"I know. Now get over here. You have ten minutes. Any later than that, and you'll be punished." He hangs up.

I sit with the phone clenched in my hand and my stomach turning somersaults, wondering if I should wait thirty minutes before I leave just so I can see what my punishment would be.

I decide I'm not quite that brave yet. I'm out the door in under a minute. And once again, Aidan opens the door to his apartment before I even have a chance to knock.

Wearing only a pair of faded blue jeans, he's barefoot, bare chested, and beautiful. I laugh as he drags me into his arms and kicks the door shut behind us.

"Do you stand there and listen for my footsteps on the stairs?"

"Yep. It's all I can do not to run out to the parking lot like a fucking lunatic the minute your car pulls up."

When I grin at him, he warns, "Don't gloat."

"I would never. My God, you're even more handsome than I remember."

He plants a big kiss on my mouth and says gruffly, "Sweet little rabbit. How do you want to get fucked?"

Thrilled, I whisper, "Any way you want."

With one arm wrapped tightly around my back, he takes my jaw in his hand and holds my face firmly like that as he growls, "Any way I want . . . *what*?"

I melt. I melt like a Popsicle dropped onto hot asphalt on a blistering summer day. All other thoughts but of him fly out of my head.

As if it's the most natural thing in the world, a hidden default mode I was unaware I was born to operate on, without a single second of resistance, I simply surrender.

I say breathlessly, "Any way you want, master."

He kisses me as if he's been starving for my mouth his entire life.

I cling to him, feeling his heart beating wildly against my breasts, feeling as if I've been sucking helium and might at any moment rise up to the ceiling and bob there, laughing and buoyant. He always makes me feel so alive, untethered to anything solid and utterly careless.

He makes me feel free. And holy hell is it amazing.

Breaking the kiss, he yanks my T-shirt off over my head and

tosses it aside. My jeans get torn off next. He growls in disapproval when he sees me wearing panties and pulls them down my legs impatiently. When I'm standing in front of him fully nude, he rips open the fly of his jeans and orders gruffly, "On your knees."

I sink to my knees on the hardwood floor like a grateful supplicant and take his jutting erection in my hands.

"Suck, bunny."

The moment my lips slide over the engorged head of his cock, he moans and tilts his head back, closing his eyes. He sinks his fingers into my hair and raggedly whispers my name.

"So fucking sweet. Everything about you. Love your sweet mouth, my good girl."

His gruff praise is candy to my ears. It's heroin injected into my veins. It's hot euphoria running along every nerve ending, setting me on fire. I suck so eagerly on his dick, he has to warn me to slow down.

"Pace yourself, baby. You'll get my cum, but not yet."

He opens his eyes and gazes down at me, running his thumb over my top lip as I bob my head, taking him deep in my mouth, then going shallower again.

"Look at you," he says hotly. "On your knees for me. My hard cock in your mouth. Your eyes begging for me to fuck you. Do you have any idea how beautiful you are? How perfect?"

Feeling crazed, I close my eyes and swallow him as deep as I can, gagging a little as I shove his girth down my throat.

"So fucking perfect," he whispers. "Kayla. My beautiful, obedient girl."

I moan around his cock, sucking frantically as I stroke his

shaft with both hands. My pussy throbs. My nipples ache. I need him to fuck me so badly, I moan again, trembling with need.

He knows. Of course he knows. His laugh is soft and dark.

"You need to spread your legs for me and take that cock deep, don't you, baby? You need your master to fuck you."

The vein on the underside of his penis throbs against my tongue. His fingers tighten in my hair. Right now, he could order me to throw myself out the window, and I probably would.

"Yes, you do. Greedy girl. Let me watch you finger fuck that gorgeous pussy while you take my cock down your throat. But don't you dare come without my permission."

I shove one hand between my legs and frantically start rubbing my clit. I'm soaked already, desperate, breathing hard through my nose and shaking all over.

He cradles my face in both hands and flexes his hips, guiding his cock in and out of my mouth, controlling the speed and depth, controlling every part of me.

He whispers, "Oh, fuck yes, baby. Fuck *yes*."

I gaze up at him. Our eyes lock. His lips are parted, and his eyes burn. They burn straight through me, flaying me open until I'm totally exposed, raw and vulnerable. Mewling around his cock, I shove a finger inside the aching space between my legs.

"Don't come," he orders in a soft, stroking voice as he imprisons me in his mesmerizing gaze. "Be a good girl and hold out for me."

I'm going out of my mind. I beg him silently with my eyes. He licks his lips, watching me.

A contraction deep in my core makes me suck in a sharp breath through my nose. Aidan fists a hand in my hair and pulls my head back. His dick pops out of my mouth.

Breathing hard, he bends down until he's staring into my wide eyes from only a few inches away. He says in a guttural voice, "Did you disobey your master?"

I'm panting so hard, I can barely answer. "No. No. I promise."

He doesn't believe me. With a growl, he pushes me onto my back on the bare wood floor and kneels over me, flattening one hand over my sternum and pressing down so I'm pinned. The other hand he slides between my legs. He hisses when he finds me soaking wet and ready for him.

He thrusts a finger inside me, shushing me when I groan.

"Arms over your head. Spread your legs. One more sound, and you'll be punished."

Quaking, I lift my arms over my head and rest my clasped hands against the floor. Then I spread my thighs and bite my bottom lip, praying I'll be strong enough to remain silent as I've been instructed.

He's still for a moment, watching my face with avid eyes, that finger sunk deep inside me waiting for the rhythmic clench of orgasm. I'm almost there—*almost*—and if he moves his finger at all, I'll tip over the edge and start fucking his hand desperately as my climax rips through me.

"Sweet little bunny," he whispers, elated. "You're trying so hard to be good, aren't you?"

I nod frantically.

He slides the hand pressed against my sternum over to one breast and fondles it for a moment before he pinches the hard nipple. Pleasure ripples through my body in waves that head straight down between my legs. Though I'm unable to control the way my thighs quiver and my back arches from the floor, I remain silent, breathing shallowly through my nose.

Between his legs, his erection juts out from the open fly of his jeans. It's big and glistens with my saliva, the crown flushed red. The shaft is thick, taut, and mapped with veins.

I want it. I need it. I need him to impale me on it and fuck me senseless as he growls filthy things into my ear and perfumes my skin with his scent as he grinds against my body.

"Eyes on me, Kayla."

I meet his dark gaze and whisper, "Yes, sir."

Though I was supposed to be quiet, I can tell that he's pleased with me.

For my reward, he rolls me onto my belly and spanks my ass smartly, going back and forth between each cheek until I'm almost crying with need.

He stops just short of spanking me into an orgasm.

When I whimper, my cheek pressed against the floor and my eyes squeezed shut, he says through gritted teeth, "You're the most beautiful thing I've ever seen in my entire life. You better run away now, little rabbit, or I'll rip you to fucking pieces."

Knowing relief isn't too far away now, I sob as I scramble to my hands and knees, then leap to my feet.

Snarling like an animal, he slaps my ass. I yelp and jump, then tear out of the kitchen with my heart in my throat. I barely get his bedroom door slammed and the lock on the handle turned before he's pounding on it, demanding I let him in.

When I refuse, he kicks the door open.

It smashes against the wall. A few books fall off the bookshelf and tumble to the floor. A chunk of plaster drops from the ceiling. Aidan stands in the open doorway, breathing hard, nostrils flared, eyes as fierce as a hungry predator's as he gazes at me, backed up against the far wall.

He growls, "On your hands and knees on the mattress."

I shout defiantly, "No! If you want me, you have to catch me!"

His grin is wide and lethal.

I feint left. He lunges. I dart the other direction, too fast for him to spin around and grab me. With a laugh of victory, I run from the bedroom and down the hall.

He catches me in the living room, pulling me back against his body and wrapping an iron arm around my ribs. As I struggle to get free, he laughs, nuzzling his nose into my hair and inhaling deeply.

"You think you're strong enough to get away from me, bunny?"

"Yes!" I twist and squirm helplessly.

"I don't think so." He bites my shoulder, reaching around to touch me between my legs. His voice drops. "What I think is that you're about to get fucked very, very hard."

I might faint. My pulse is wild, I'm panting in desperation, and I feel strangely weightless, as if I'm disembodied, floating outside of myself.

Aidan drops to the sofa, bringing me down with him, then flips us over and pins me under his weight.

Hot and stiff, his erection pokes against my stinging ass.

He takes a moment to enjoy my helpless struggles and cries and merely lies on top of me, his bare chest burning my back as he sniffs my hair, shoulders, and neck and grunts in pleasure.

"Let me go!"

He chuckles. "Say the safe word, and I will."

The smug bastard. He knows I won't say the fucking safe word.

I scream in frustration. It makes him laugh.

"Bad bunny," he whispers, his tone jubilant.

"No!"

"Oh, yes, you are. And you know what bad bunnies get, don't you."

It's not a question, but it still requires an answer.

"Set free!"

He puts his mouth next to my ear and says hotly, "No, baby. They get fucked in the ass by their masters until they promise to be good."

I almost orgasm then. My pussy clenches with need. I groan in desperation, wriggling my butt against him.

Gripping my wrists with one hand, Aidan slides the other between my legs. He rubs my pussy lips, spreading the wetness up between my ass cheeks. When his fingertips glide over my anus, I squeal.

He slides his finger in up to the knuckle. I cry out, stiffening.

"This is mine," he says darkly. "I'm gonna claim it. If you don't want that, say the safe word right fucking now."

Trapped beneath him, I'm helpless, but not completely. I know all it would take is one word to turn this whole thing around. If I said the safe word, I know he'd stop instantly and release me. I know it without a doubt, and that's what keeps me on the right side of the fine line between pleasure and fear.

I turn my face to the cushion and sob his name.

He exhales a moan filled with desire and dark satisfaction. "Yes, baby. Say my name when I fuck you. Scream it when you come for me."

He spits on his fingers, rubs his saliva all over the sensitive knot between my ass cheeks, then holds me down as he guides the head of his hard cock inside me.

I cry out, shuddering.

"Take your master's dick," he commands, and shoves it all the way in.

It burns and leaves me breathless, my eyes watering and my ass muscles clenched. Aidan doesn't move his hips again, he simply lies on top of me, breathing heavily against my hair, both hands now wrapped around my wrists.

His total dominance over my body—a dominance that I not only allow, but crave—makes something fragile inside my chest snap like a twig.

A tear slides over the bridge of my nose. Trembling, full of him and chaotic emotion, I whisper brokenly, "Master."

He groans. In a faint, breathless voice, he says, "Sweet girl. My good girl. Beg for me."

I close my eyes and obey. "Please, master. Please fuck me. Fuck me hard."

He withdraws and pumps back into my ass with a sharp snap of his hips.

My sob is broken and grateful.

He does it again, thrusting harder, then again with a grunt when I moan.

It stings like a son of a bitch, but my clit is throbbing and my hard nipples rub with delicious friction against the coarse fabric of the sofa with every thrust, so I beg him to keep going, canting my hips up and back like the greedy little thing he's made me.

Releasing my wrists, he grabs my hip in one hand and pushes

against the sofa with the other. He rears back to his knees, keeping his cock inside my ass and bringing me with him. He steadies me and braces one foot against the floor, then grips my hips in both hands as he kneels behind me.

Then he fucks me hard and deep, driving into my tender ass with relentless force as I cry out deliriously and his heavy balls slap against my pussy.

"Master! Master! Please may I come?"

He pants, "Yes, baby. Give it to me."

He reaches around between my legs and firmly tugs on my swollen clit.

It sets off an instantaneous chain reaction.

I gasp and buck. My pussy clenches rhythmically. My mind blinks offline as my body takes over, responding to his touch on a level beyond conscious control.

"Aidan! Oh God, Aidan, I'm coming! I'm coming!"

The sound that breaks from his throat is guttural, animalistic, and thoroughly pleased.

Then he shoves his thick finger inside my throbbing pussy, and his sounds are drowned out by my high, wavering scream of pleasure.

He shudders, lets out a primal roar, and comes inside me.

I break down into tears, sobbing helplessly in sweet surrender as this beautiful beast of a man drags me down with him into the dark.

25

Afterward, I'm an emotional mess.

I lie facedown on the sofa with my ass in the air, sobbing into the cushions, trembling all over, sweaty and spent. Aidan is bent over me, breathing raggedly. His hot forehead rests between my shoulder blades.

I can't say exactly why, but something about the way we play together is so cathartic. Every time, it's as if I've been baptized and reborn into a lighter version of my own body. Even though we're pretending he's in control, I always know, deep down, that I am. And even though we can get rough, there's an underlying sense of care and safety that makes me feel adored like I've never been before.

"Oh, baby," he whispers. "Don't cry. It's okay, sweetheart. It's okay."

He presses the gentlest of kisses to my spine and slowly withdraws from my body. Then he drags the afghan off the back of the sofa and wraps me in it. He sits, pulls me onto his lap, and surrounds me with his strong arms.

"So fucking beautiful," he murmurs, kissing my forehead

and wet cheeks. "You're my good, beautiful girl. Are you hurting? Did I hurt you?"

"No. It was perfect. You're perfect. I loved every minute." I bury my face in the crook of his neck and cry harder.

He tightens his arms around me and gently rocks me, cooing soft words. He strokes my hair and caresses me, calming me and cradling me like a baby.

We sit like that until my tears have stopped and I'm sniffling, trying to stifle the occasional hiccup.

He inhales deeply, exhales, and glides his fingertips lightly along the side of my face. Resting his cheek on the top of my head, he says softly, "Tell me what you need from me."

I've never had a man ask me that before.

Well, technically, it was an order, not a question, but I'm not splitting hairs. Dazed, sore, and thoroughly satisfied, I sit and think seriously about it for a while before deciding I need more specifics.

"Do you mean now or in general?"

"Both. I want to know what makes you happy. What will make you feel all the time like I do right now."

I peek up at him. "How do you feel right now?"

He gazes down at me, his eyes endless and dark. Tracing my lower lip with his fingertip, he says, "Reborn. Forgiven. Or maybe . . . I don't know." He struggles silently for a moment. "Freed."

I ask shyly, "I make you feel free?"

"Like I've been living in a dark cave my whole fucking life, and I just stumbled out into the sunlight."

Tears stuck in my throat, I close my eyes and snuggle closer to him. With a hitch in my voice, I whisper, "I've never met anyone like you."

His chuckle is soft and dark. "I'll take that as a compliment."

"It is. I always feel safe around you. You bring out a side of me I didn't even know existed before. I feel like I could tell you anything, my darkest secret, the worst thing I've done that I'm most ashamed of, and it would be okay." I hesitate. "Except . . ."

He stills. "What?"

"When you walk away in the middle of a conversation, I get really frustrated."

After a moment, he nods. "Okay. I won't do that again."

Encouraged, I keep talking. "And when you shut down and don't tell me what you're thinking, I get confused. You're very intense in some ways, very communicative and open and right in my face, but other times, you seem like you're hiding from me."

I pause to think again. Then I venture, "Like maybe you're worried how I'll react if I get to know the real you?"

He kisses me, brushing his lips against mine with a tenderness that makes my chest ache.

Then he murmurs, "What I'm worried about is giving my heart away to a woman who's still wearing a wedding ring."

The sadness in his voice makes my heart flip-flop. I whisper, "Oh, Aidan. I'm sorry."

"You don't have to apologize. Or explain yourself. I don't ever want you to feel obligated to explain yourself to me. I know you're just taking this one day at a time."

By "this" he means "us." This thing we're doing together, whatever it is. And he's right, in a way. I am taking it one day at a time. There's no other way to take it. He crashed into my life like a meteor falling to earth, right when I was the most broken I'd ever been.

Only I don't feel broken when I'm with him.

Too overwhelmed to continue with the conversation in my emotionally raw state, I say, "Okay. You want to know what I need to be happy right now?"

"Yes."

I smile up at him and tug on his beard. "A glass of wine and a hot bath."

His lids lower. He smolders at me in silence for a moment. "I can do that for you."

"Thank you."

He raises his brows. "Aren't you forgetting something?"

I spread my hand over his jaw and smile wider. "Thank you, sir."

He stares deep into my eyes for a long moment. Then he says quietly, "Kayla, be careful with me."

Surprised by that, I ask, "What do you mean?"

"I know you think I'm strong. But the problem with strong things is that they're brittle. They can't bend under stress. They just break."

Before I can respond, he picks me up and carries me into the bathroom.

❧

I soak in bliss for an hour, up to my neck in bubbles, sipping a glass of Cabernet. Aidan comes in and out of the bathroom, bringing me little bites of cheese and slices of apple, feeding them to me from his fingers and watching me chew as if it's the most fascinating thing he's ever seen.

The way he looks at me is addictive.

Because I like it so much, it's also a little scary.

I don't think I'm ready for this. It seems as if he isn't, either. We're magnets who don't want to be magnets, pulled together by invisible elements beyond our control.

I don't have the words or the will to tell him it would be wiser if we slowed down this runaway train before it veers off the tracks and kills all the passengers. Besides, aren't we past that point, anyway?

The obvious answer is yes. We are. We skipped the dinner dates and polite conversation and jumped straight to kinky fuckery.

Not that I'm complaining. It's simpler this way, and simple things are beautiful. And with my recent state of mind, small talk would be a stretch.

Wearing only his jeans, Aidan sits on the toilet with his elbows propped on his knees. "Going out to the house tomorrow."

"Is that an invitation, or are you just informing me of your future whereabouts?"

A faint smile curves his lips. "It's an invitation, smartass. Which you already knew. What's the answer?"

"The answer is yes. Which *you* already knew."

"Don't want to assume anything." He glances at my ring finger, then looks away. "Don't know your schedule."

Tell him. Just tell him about Michael. Tell him what happened. He deserves to know.

Does he? There's no commitment here. And I'm not the only one holding things back. I barely know anything about him. Hell, I don't even know how old he is!

I go back and forth mentally for a few seconds, arguing with myself, until he startles me by asking, "How old are you?"

I laugh uneasily. "God, that's strange."

"What is?"

"I was just thinking I don't know how old you are when you asked me that."

"I'm thirty-five."

"I'm thirty."

We gaze at each other. He murmurs, "What else were you just thinking?"

Buying myself time, I slowly set the wineglass on the edge of the tub. I sit up and look down at the bubbles, shimmering in iridescent clumps, clinging to my knees and breasts.

"I was thinking about my husband."

Aidan remains silent. I can't even hear him breathing. I feel him waiting, though, feel the new tension in his body as clearly as if his muscles were my own.

"Actually, that's not exactly it. I was thinking I wanted to tell you something about him."

I swallow. My pulse starts to race. I don't know why this should be so difficult. I told Eddie the handyman my husband was dead, and *he'd* never railed me up the ass and called me his bunny.

When I draw a shaky breath and squeeze my eyes closed for a moment to gather my courage, Aidan orders softly, "Eyes on me."

I look at him. He stares back at me with unwavering intensity, his eyes fierce.

"Is he hurting you? That's all I want to know."

There's something wild in his gaze, a dangerous glint that

makes me shiver. I draw my knees closer to my chest, wrapping my arms around my shins. "If I said yes, what would you do?"

His answer is hard and instant. "Kill him."

My pulse flying and my eyes wide, I whisper, "Aidan."

He stares at me, waiting.

Finally, I say, "Is that what you did to your father?"

He replies without flinching or looking away. "Yes."

I exhale, close my eyes, and drop my head to my knees.

His voice lower, he says, "You don't have to be afraid of me."

"I'm not."

Sounding unconvinced, he adds, "I'm not a danger to you. I'd never hurt you."

"I know."

"But you're hiding."

"I'm . . . fuck, I guess I am. I'm just processing. Give me a minute, please."

We sit in silence broken only by the occasional sound of water dripping from the faucet. Then he kneels next to the tub and takes my face in his hands.

He says urgently, "I'm older now. Smarter. Had a lot of time to think about what I did. And if it comes to it again, I'll be better prepared."

My heart hammers against my sternum. "I'm going to pretend you didn't just tell me you know how to get away with murder."

"Pretend whatever you want. The reality is that if I find out a man put his hands on you in anger, he won't ever be able to do it again."

He kisses me gently, pressing his mouth to mine in an unspoken promise. I wrap my hands around his wrists and kiss him back, opening my lips for his tongue when he slides it inside. He probes deeper, angling my head to take what he needs as I shiver in the cooling water.

Then he breaks the kiss and presses his forehead to mine.

"Kayla. You answer me now. And tell me the truth. Is he hurting you?"

Tears welling in my eyes, I say, "No."

He pulls away and gazes at me, frowning. "Then why are you gonna cry?"

"Because I just realized I'm crazy. I'm literally, certifiably insane."

"Why would you say that?"

A lone tear crests my lower eyelid and meanders down my cheek. My chest aching, I whisper, "If I were sane, I wouldn't think you threatening to kill someone for me was so beautiful."

He stares at me for a long moment, his eyes burning. Then he stands, pulls me to my feet, and lifts me out of the water. He carries me, dripping wet, into the bedroom and lays me on the mattress.

Without a word, he kneels between my legs, spreads my thighs open, and leans down to put his mouth on my exposed sex.

When I moan and arch, he reaches up with both hands and encircles my wet breasts, squeezing them gently before thumbing over my nipples.

I guess this is his way of telling me we can be crazy together.

I sink my hands into his hair and sigh. His beard scratches my thighs. His delicious hot tongue delves deep inside me. The rough pads of his fingers glide back and forth over my rigid nipples, and soon I'm panting and moaning loudly, rocking my hips in time with the motion of his tongue.

When he pinches my nipples, hard, I come in his mouth, shuddering and crying out his name.

He sucks my clit until I'm limp, then rises and pulls his jeans off. Then he lowers himself on top of my body and enters me.

With his hands in my hair and his face turned to my neck, he says gruffly, "If you decide this isn't what you want, promise me you'll end it before I fall in love with you."

"I promise," I whisper, fighting tears all over again.

"Good." His voice drops. "But so you know, you don't have much time."

"Aidan—"

"Hush now."

He makes love to me with a careful tenderness he hasn't shown before, handling me as if I'm made of porcelain. When he climaxes, it's with a soft groan of desperation, as if he knows this thing we're doing is big and dangerous, capable of annihilating us both.

I understand exactly how he feels.

26

Sunday morning dawns brilliant blue. The rain clouds have been chased away by the sun, and for the first time in weeks, it's gorgeous out.

Aidan makes us breakfast—scrambled eggs, of course, but also toast and bacon—then we shower together. He hums as he washes my body, grins as he towels me dry afterward, whistles as we dress.

Aidan in a good mood is intoxicating. With his face lit up, he's even more handsome than usual.

Because the weather's nice, he suggests we make the trip to the house on his bike. When I agree and tell him I used to ride motocross when I was a kid, he stares at me in disbelief, looking me up and down.

"You?"

"Don't judge a book by its cover, lover boy. I know I look like the girl next door, but inside, I'm more like *The Girl with the Dragon Tattoo*." I pause to think. "Except without the tattoos, the genius IQ, the computer skills, or the eidetic memory." Then I brighten. "I am antisocial, though."

Aidan chuckles. "What you are is adorable."

"Right?" I agree, pretending that didn't just make me light up like the sun.

"Yes. Let's see if I have a jacket you can wear, bunny."

"I won't fit into one of your ginormous jackets."

He rummages around in his closet, emerging with a black leather bomber so large, I might as well use it as a tent and go camping in it.

Smiling at my expression, he orders, "Put it on."

I climb into it. Then I stand there looking like somebody's idea of a hilarious joke. "If I wear this, the wind will catch me, and I'll sail behind you like a balloon."

"Don't worry, my giant helmet will weigh you down."

He isn't kidding. He hands me a helmet fit for the super-villain Megamind. When I laugh, he says, "Can't help it. My brain is huge." He grins. "Among other things."

I say sweetly, "You're thinking of your ego."

He swaggers past, swatting me on the ass as he goes. "C'mon, little rabbit. If you're good, I'll feed you a carrot later on." He turns and winks.

I'd like to make a smart remark, but damn, I also really want that carrot. So I bite my tongue and follow him out the door.

There's a small garage behind the bar where he keeps his Harley, a shiny macho thing custom-made to scare old ladies and little dogs and deafen everyone else. It starts with a rumble and idles at an eardrum-piercing volume, vibrating the earth under my feet.

Aidan jerks his chin, indicating I should climb on behind him. When I do and I've got that lovely vibration going between my thighs, I decide I should look into purchasing one for myself.

I might never leave the house.

Wrapping my arms around his waist, I hold on tight as we take off with a roar.

It's only a ten-minute ride to the other side of the island, but it's so beautiful, I'm wishing it were longer. The air smells crisp and fresh, the hills are awash in golden light, and everywhere I look, I see a million shades of green, from pale apple to dark emerald. The whole world seems steeped in it.

We round a turn and pass a roadside farm stand, then a winery. Then we're descending a hill into Port Madison, a historical waterfront neighborhood full of parks and walking trails. A few more turns and we're on a long dirt driveway lined on either side by tall trees. The driveway ends on a flat parcel of shaggy grass directly overlooking the calm crystal waters of Hidden Cove.

Aidan parks under a giant cedar and cuts the engine. I hop off first, pulling the helmet from my head and looking around in awe.

"Wow. This view is incredible."

He swings his leg over the bike and pulls on the chin strap of his helmet. When he's got it off, he sets it on the seat of the bike and smiles at me.

"Lots of space for a bunny to play in, huh?"

My cheeks heating, I twist my lips and look at him.

He laughs at the expression on my face. "C'mon. The house is up here."

I thought we were on the main parcel, but he's pointing toward an incline beyond a break in the trees. He holds out his hand. I take it and follow behind him up the gentle slope on a path that looks well-worn.

When we reach the top, I stop short and gasp.

The frame of a house sits in the middle of a semicircle of giant Western white pines that stand at least one hundred feet tall. Facing the water, the house has two stories, a foundation, a roof, and not much else. There are no interior walls or windows yet. No landscaping or driveway, either. It's more of a sketch, the outline of an idea, but the idea is taking shape beautifully.

"There's gonna be a wraparound porch in the front," says Aidan softly, gazing proudly at the bare bones of his home. "And a path over there that leads down to the dock."

He looks at me, eyes shining. "I'm gonna get a boat. Nothing big. Little flat-bottomed lake boat I can putt around in for cocktail hour."

An image of the *Eurydice* pops into my head, bobbing silently at the end of the dock under a cloudy, ominous sky, but I push it aside to focus on Aidan. "How long have you been working on this?"

"Couple years now."

Wide-eyed, I look around. "And you're doing this all yourself?"

He chuckles. "I wish. Plumbing and electrical go in next, and that's when things start to get expensive." He looks back at the house, draws a deep breath, and smiles. "A lot of it I can do in trade. Which is good, because I don't have the cash to finance this project. The cost of lumber alone nearly had me going broke."

I move nearer to him. Still gazing at the house, he winds his arm around my shoulder and pulls me close.

"At the risk of being punished, I need to tell you that I'm definitely going to pay you now for the work you're doing on my roof."

His laugh is soft. He tilts his head back and closes his eyes, enjoying the sun on his face. "You're lucky I'm in a good mood, bunny, or your butt would be burning."

I wind my arms around his waist and rest my cheek on his chest. "Promises, promises."

He kisses the top of my head. Then we stand there in comfortable silence, our arms around each other, listening to the breeze playing through the trees. The sound of faraway children's laughter drifts to us over the water.

Aidan asks softly, "You ever want kids?"

My pulse goes wild. My hands start to tremble. I close my eyes, bury my face in his chest, and whisper, "Yes."

There's a slight change in his energy. A new tension creeps into his arms. "Was that the wrong thing to say?"

I shake my head. "No, it's just . . . I tried once. We tried."

He rests his cheek against the top of my head and tightens his arms around me. "You don't have to tell me."

"It's okay. It's not a secret or anything." I blow out a breath. "I had a miscarriage. I was pretty far along."

A memory hits me like a punch to the gut: pain, screaming, blood coursing down my bare thighs. Crawling over the office floor and sobbing, trying desperately to get to the telephone on the wall. It's a jumble of impressions that come all at once, like a clip from a movie played too fast with the sound turned all the way up.

But whose voice is that? The screaming doesn't sound like mine. It's a stranger's voice, full of rage, bearing down on me like a hurricane.

The memory disappears as quickly as it came, cut off as if a plug was pulled on a projector.

It leaves behind the distinct and chilling impression that big chunks are missing. That something important has been left out.

Or erased altogether.

I search for anything more, but nothing comes. I've hit a brick wall.

"You're shaking," says Aidan, sounding worried as he hugs me tighter. "What is it, Kayla? What's wrong?"

"Nothing. Just hold me, please."

He envelops me in his arms, holding me tight. I cling to him, swallowing down the acid taste of bile.

After a few minutes, when I've calmed down a bit, Aidan says softly, "I don't mind if you're not ready to talk about certain things. You can just say that, and I'll accept it. I won't push. But don't lie to me again, okay?"

I whisper, "I'm sorry."

His voice turns firm. "Say you won't lie to me again, Kayla."

"I won't. I promise."

Nuzzling my cheek, he murmurs, "Good. Because you don't have to. You never have to hide from me."

My voice cracks when I say, "I don't understand how you're so amazing."

He kisses my neck, my ear, my cheek, soft butterfly kisses filled with tenderness.

"I'm only amazing when I'm with you. The rest of the time, I'm nobody."

I burrow closer to him, needing his solidity, loving how safe I feel in his warm embrace. He makes a sound of pleasure low in his throat and inhales into my hair. Then he's kissing my neck again, only this time, his mouth is more demanding.

"I love the way you taste, bunny," he says gruffly. "Love the way your skin tastes. Love your smell, too. And how you lose control when I make you come. And how you look at me. The way you look at me makes me feel like a goddamn king."

He sinks a hand into my hair and gently pulls my head back, exposing my throat. Holding me against his body, he licks and kisses a path from my earlobe to my collarbone, pressing his teeth into my skin every few inches as if he wants to take a bite of me and gobble me up.

When I exhale a small moan, he squeezes my ass and flexes his pelvis against mine, pressing his erection against my hipbone.

My response is instant.

My nipples harden. My heart pounds. My skin heats, and my pussy tingles. I've never met a man I had a physical reaction to like this, so effortlessly and instantly. Not even my husband.

With my eyes closed and my face turned to the sky as he kisses my throat, I say, "Such a hungry lion. I hope you can run on an empty stomach."

Smiling, I push him away and gaze at him coyly, fluttering my lashes.

Then I turn and bolt toward the pine trees.

Laughing, he calls out behind me, "You have ten seconds before I come for you, little rabbit!" Then he starts counting aloud.

A thrill in my blood, I tear across the grass and past the house, pumping my arms and legs as fast as they'll take me. Once I've hit the stand of pines, I hide behind a massive trunk and risk a quick peek around it.

Aidan advances toward me in an easy lope, grinning darkly.

I scream and start running again.

Beyond the stand of tall pines is a small meadow surrounded

by a thickly wooded area. Realizing the property must be several acres in size, I run toward the woods with my heart in my throat, not daring to look behind me. Breathing hard, my thighs burning, I break through the tree line at a flat-out sprint.

Underfoot, the ground is soft and uneven, covered in a moist blanket of grass and leaves. Before I've gone twenty feet in, I catch my toe on a half-buried tree root and go flying.

I land on my stomach. My breath is knocked from my lungs. I lie stunned and panting for a moment, then try to scramble to my feet.

I'm too late. My lion has already pounced.

Growling, he grabs me around the waist. We tumble to the damp earth. I put up a fight, struggling to get free as he laughs breathlessly and wrestles me. Then I'm on my back and he's on top of me, biting my neck as he pins my wrists to the ground.

He laughs in exultation as I squirm beneath him.

"Bad bunny."

"Let me go!"

"You have leaves in your hair, bunny. Where else might you have leaves, I wonder?"

He flips me onto my stomach and yanks his leather jacket off me, throwing it aside.

"Hmm. Not here. Maybe under your shirt."

As I struggle and holler in protest, he strips my shirt from my body and sends it flying. Then he's growling into my skin as he rubs his beard on my shoulders.

"My naughty little rabbit needs to get fucked in the woods, doesn't she?"

"No!" *Yes.* "Get off me!"

He slides a hand under my torso and roughly squeezes my

breast. Into my ear, he says hotly, "I'm gonna fuck you so hard, bunny. You're gonna take your master's cock on your hands and knees, totally naked, in the middle of the woods."

I nearly faint with desire and give in right then. But as this game is all about the chase, it wouldn't be much fun if I let him win so easily.

"I won't!"

Struggling wildly, I somehow manage to knock him off. I'm up and running in a heartbeat, my hair flying out behind me, my bared breasts bouncing. Cool air mists my heated skin.

He catches me as I'm skidding around the gnarled trunk of a pin oak. Yanking me into his arms, he kisses me ravenously. Off-balance, but still in the game, I stagger, my heart racing as I try to push him away.

He's so strong, though. He's just so damn *strong*. His strength surrounds me.

He yanks down the zipper of my jeans, turns me around, and pulls them down my hips. I try to get away, but he has such a tight hold on me, I'm helpless. When he slaps my bare ass, I yelp, jumping.

Then he pushes me against the trunk of the tree and holds me there as he continues to spank me.

Whimpering, I claw at the trunk. Rough bark scrapes my breasts and stomach. My ass jiggles with every strike of his hand, flooding my pussy with shockwaves of pleasure.

The spanking stops abruptly when Aidan thrusts his hand between my legs.

His mouth pressed to my ear, he says, "Ooh, soaking wet. You need me to fuck this pretty wet cunt nice and hard, don't you, bunny?"

I sob.

"Yes, you do. I know you do. And you know how much I want to."

He shoves two fingers inside me and finger fucks me from behind as I squeal and struggle.

"Ah, God, baby, you're fucking perfection. My dick is so hard for you. I need to come deep inside this perfect pussy while you scream my name."

He pulls his fingers out of me and slides them all around, spreading my wetness. He tweaks my engorged clit, making me yelp, then spins me around and pushes me back against the tree trunk.

He thrusts his slick fingers into my mouth.

"Taste yourself, bunny. Lick all that sweet honey off."

He bends down to suck on my rigid nipple as I obey his command, my eyes rolling back in my head.

He pulls my jeans roughly down my thighs. Without taking them all the way off, he throws me over his shoulder and starts walking, his arm wound around my waist, one hand spread over the back of my thigh, his fingers digging possessively into my flesh.

I kick and struggle, but my jeans restrict the movement of my legs. He's hobbled me.

When I shout in frustration, Aidan laughs and slaps me on the ass.

"Here," he says, stopping. "This looks like a good place for my bunny to take her master's dick."

He drops me on my feet onto a soft patch of earth, then pushes me down until I'm on my back. Straddling my hips, he grabs my forearms. I swing wildly at him, struggling for release.

"*No*, bunny," he breathes, eyes wild with need. "Stop fighting me now. Time to get fucked."

"Argh!"

I refuse to stop. Obviously enjoying himself, Aidan allows me to wrestle him for a few moments before he yanks off my shoes and pulls my jeans from my ankles. When I'm completely naked, he flips me onto my stomach and drags me up to my knees.

The ripe, damp smell of the earth fills my nostrils. A cool breeze washes over me, forming goose bumps all over my bare skin. Far overhead, birds sing and leaves whisper in the boughs of the trees.

Seeing me nude and helpless with bits of forest floor clinging to my breasts, belly, back, and bottom excites Aidan so much, he's panting.

"Look at you all covered in dirt. My sweet, filthy girl."

He spanks me several times, forcing me to balance on my elbows so I don't topple over sideways. Then he fondles my exposed pussy, pinching and stroking it as my stinging ass throbs with heat.

He groans. "You're so wet, baby. God, you're so fucking wet, it's all over your thighs. My pretty little bunny is so ready for me."

His voice is gruff and exultant, filled with lust and triumph. He sounds as if he's hanging on the last thread of restraint, and as soon as he lets go of it, an animal he normally keeps tightly bound will be unleashed.

I'm about to be devoured, and we both know it.

Head hanging down and eyes closed, I moan.

Through gritted teeth, Aidan orders, "Beg me to fuck you now, Kayla."

I whisper, "Please, master. Please fuck me."

I hear the sound of a zipper being torn open, then the crown of Aidan's hard cock nudges my entrance. He grabs me by my waist and shoves his erection deep inside me. When I cry out in pleasure, he starts to thrust his hips, driving into me over and over again.

"Aidan! Aidan!"

"Tell me you're mine."

"Yes! I'm yours!"

"Tell me you love my cock."

"I love it!"

My cries echo off the trees. He reaches under me and palms one of my swinging breasts, squeezing it roughly, then pulling on the nipple. It feels so good, I moan again.

"Dirty little bunny," he growls hotly. "You can't get enough of your master's hard cock. You want my cum, too, don't you, dirty girl? You need your master to fill you up until you're dripping with it."

My arms give out. I fall forward. My cheek scrapes the damp ground as Aidan fucks me from behind, fully clothed and in control of every part of me.

His laugh is dark and pleased. "Yes, good girl, you take it like a sweet little cum slut should. Look at that plump pink pussy, stuffed with her master's fat cock. I'm stretching your pussy wide open, aren't I, bunny?"

When I moan again, shuddering and sweating and very close to orgasm, Aidan chuckles.

"Maybe my dirty bunny needs her other hot little holes filled, too."

He shoves his thumb into my ass.

When I cry out, he leans over and thrusts his other thumb into my open mouth.

Then he continues to fuck me, bent over and riding me hard from behind as I suck desperately on his thumb and jerk my hips back to meet every one of his thrusts.

"Time to take your master's cum," he pants, his tone urgent. "But I want those eyes on me."

He withdraws and throws me onto my back.

Panting, my heart racing, I stare up at him as he looms over me, his engorged cock jutting from his jeans, his chest heaving, his dark eyes burning like fire. Spreading my thighs, he falls on top of me. He fists his dick in his hand and finds my wet center, then forces it inside me with a grunt.

When I moan and grab on to his jacket, he grasps my wrists and pins my arms to the ground.

He starts to fuck me again, hovering over me as he holds me to the earth and stares into my eyes.

I beg brokenly, "Please. Please, master. Please may I come?"

His eyelids flutter. He whispers my name.

But he doesn't give me permission to let go.

My pussy and clit throb with every thrust of his hips. My back arches from the ground. My nipples ache so badly, it's painful. My lids slide shut, and I whimper.

Aidan releases my wrists and grips my head in his hands. "Look at me," he orders.

I stare up into his burning eyes as a white-hot coil of pleasure winds tighter and tighter in my core and my thighs start to shake uncontrollably.

"You ready, baby?" he whispers, the motion of his hips growing frantic.

Unable to speak, I merely nod.

"Eyes on me when you come. Don't look away. I want you to give it to me looking right into my eyes." After another few thrusts, he snarls, "Now."

I suck in a breath and grind wildly against him. My climax hits hard, and I moan but don't look away. I stare wide-eyed up at him as my pussy contracts over and over around the huge, invading length of his cock, buried deep inside me.

"Oh, fuck, Kayla," he breathes. "Jesus fucking Christ, here I come."

His entire body jerks. Deep inside, I feel his dick throb. Then he's moaning and thrusting shallowly as he spills himself into me, staring straight into my eyes.

The intimacy is so intense and overpowering, I lose my breath. My chest feels as if it's being crushed by an invisible force.

He feels it, too. I can tell because his eyes fill with anguish.

He says my name on a strangled breath, then gives me a desperate, devouring kiss.

All the way through it, we both keep our eyes open.

27

We lie entangled on the forest floor, breathing hard, but otherwise silent. Then he groans and drops his face to my neck, hiding his eyes.

Staring up at the endless blue sky, I wrap my arms around his shoulders, knowing instinctively that this time, he's the one falling apart.

"It's okay," I whisper hoarsely, dazed. "Aidan, it's okay."

He makes a muffled sound of pain.

"Shh."

I softly kiss the side of his face and thread my fingers into his hair. He's heavy and hot on top of me, trembling all over, and all at once, I'm flooded with a deep sense of peace.

Or awe, maybe. Or something else altogether. I'm not sure there's a word for it.

Whatever it is, it's beautiful.

My lips close to his ear, I whisper, "I loved it. I loved every second. Everything you did and said. Do you hear me? This is what I needed."

He exhales a ragged moan.

"My beautiful lion. You're so wonderful. You're exactly what I need."

He lifts his head and kisses me passionately, moaning into my mouth. "Kayla," he says, panting. "God. Fuck. Did I hurt you? Are you okay?"

I chuckle. "Aside from some scrapes and bruises, I'm *excellent*."

His gaze darts all over my face, searching for any sign that I'm lying. When he seems satisfied I'm not, he swallows and moistens his lips.

He says haltingly, "I got a little carried away."

"Did you ever," I reply with a grin. "Holy cannoli, what a smutty vocabulary you have. It's even better than your normal one."

After a beat, he starts to laugh. Softly, shaking his head, he laughs in relief, then kisses me again.

"I can't help it. You bring out the beast in me."

"Apparently! But now I would very much appreciate it if we could stand up. There's a rock digging into my lower back, and it's unholy painful."

"Shit. Sorry."

He withdraws, stands, tucks himself back into his jeans, and zips them up. Then he helps me stand, handling me carefully as he brushes earth and leaves from my skin.

"You're all scraped up," he says in a hushed voice, wincing as he dusts me off with feather-soft strokes of his fingers. "Your knee is bleeding."

I sigh deeply in satisfaction. "That's what happens when bunnies get fucked in the woods. I'm sure I'll be sore as hell tomorrow. Where are my clothes? I'm getting cold."

He leaves me briefly to gather my shoes, shirt, jeans, and his jacket from where he tossed them to the ground earlier. Then he helps me dress in silent concentration, handling me gingerly as if he's convinced I might crack.

His tenderness and concern are touching. He's being so sweet and gentle, the opposite of my dominant, snarling beast from only minutes ago.

It's incredible how many different people one body can hold. We all walk around with a thousand strangers inside us, slumbering quietly until someone else wakes them up. Like the jolt of electricity that reanimated Frankenstein's monster, all it takes for our sleeping giants to jump to life is a single spark.

When I'm dressed, Aidan takes my hand and silently leads me out of the woods. When we emerge into sunlight, we look at the sky, then at each other.

Something passes between us, unspoken and profound.

He looks away first, squeezing my hand and smiling.

That smile could break my heart.

⁓

We spend the rest of the day at his apartment. I have to take another shower to get all the remnants of leaves and dirt off my skin. Afterward, Aidan puts Neosporin on my cuts and scrapes and bandages my knee.

He looks unhappy as he does it, his brows drawn down, his lips pressed to a thin line.

Though my injuries are minor and gained in the most wonderful way, he hates to see me hurt.

I spend the night again. He wakes me up at dawn and makes love to me with a wordless urgency that leaves me breathless.

Then he withdraws into that quiet place inside his head where he goes when he needs to hide.

But I don't ask him what's wrong. I don't push. I let him be.

He's not the only one keeping secrets.

⤚⤙

By the time I get home, Fiona is already there. I find her in Michael's office, which sends a spike of irritation through me.

"What are you doing in here?"

Holding a feather duster, she whirls around from his desk and starts when she sees me.

"Kayla!"

"Yes, it's me. I live here, remember?"

Her smile is apologetic. "I'm sorry, dear. I didn't hear you come in. You walk like a cat."

Uncomfortable, I hesitate at the threshold. I haven't been in this room since the accident. The door has been shut, and the air is stale. Something about it makes me feel claustrophobic.

"I didn't want this room cleaned. I thought I told you that."

"Did you?"

"Didn't I?"

She laughs. "Well, if you did, I don't recall."

"Oh. Sorry. To be honest . . . neither do I."

Remembering what she said last week about the possible cause of my memory lapses, I grow even more uncomfortable. My cheeks heating, I shift my weight from foot to foot and clear my throat. "But I'd like to leave this room alone for the time being. It's just . . ." I gesture helplessly. "I haven't gone through any of his things yet."

She says gently, "Oh, dear. I completely understand. I'll start on the kitchen."

"Thanks. Um . . . about that séance thing we talked about."

Fiona brightens. "Yes, I spoke with my sister! She says we should hold it on the next full moon, which is in three weeks. Oh, and she also said you shouldn't wear any perfume or jewelry. No other accessories, either, especially cell phones. Apparently, they annoy the spirits." She chuckles. "Like the rest of us."

My laugh is small and embarrassed. "Actually, I think we should just forget about the whole thing."

Fiona gazes at me for a moment, thoughtfully pulling at the feathers on the duster with her fingers. "Oh?"

Her tone is mild, but it seems to require an explanation. I sheepishly provide one.

"I've decided I'm going to see a therapist."

She raises her brows. "How can a therapist help with your ghost problems?"

I exhale, shaking my head. "Just the fact that I even considered the possibility that I'm being haunted strongly suggests the need for therapy."

She looks as if she's about to protest, but must change her mind because she only nods.

"All right. If that's what you prefer."

"It is. Thanks, Fiona."

She walks past me, avoiding my eyes. As her footsteps recede in the direction of the kitchen, I worry that I've insulted her. I turn to go after her, but something I glimpse on Michael's desk catches my eye, and I turn back.

A folded newspaper sits on the blotter next to where Fiona was dusting. From where I'm standing, I can't read the headline, but I can clearly see the photograph that accompanies the article.

It's a picture of Michael.

My pulse surges. My mouth goes dry. I feel a bit unsteady, as if the floor has tilted. For some strange reason, I'm suddenly afraid.

I walk slowly across the room and stand beside the desk. I want to pick up the newspaper, but don't. I simply stand there and read the headline.

Local Man Drowns.

The paper has been folded over, so only the headline and Michael's picture are visible on the left side, along with part of the byline.

I'm sure I haven't seen this article before. I'm sure I didn't put this newspaper on Michael's desk. What I'm not sure of is how it got here.

Did Fiona bring it in?

My mind starts to race. I try to think of rational explanations as to why she might place this newspaper in Michael's office, but can't come up with any. She'd know it would upset me to see this. I'd chalk it up to my memory lapses, but I know I haven't been in this office since the accident.

I *know* it.

A little voice in my head whispers *Maybe it wasn't Fiona.*

Covering my face with my hands, I recite silently *There are no such things as ghosts. There are no such things as ghosts. There are no such things as ghosts.*

Something hits the office window with a sharp *bang.*

I jump, letting out a little yelp, then stand with my heart palpitating and my shaking hands clutching my throat.

Nothing moves. The air is still. Outside the windows, the sky is a glowering, leaden gray.

Gathering my courage, I go to the windows and look out, scanning the horizon. I see nothing unusual. The yard is empty. The rocky beach is clear. It isn't until I'm about to turn away that I discover the source of the sound.

On the ground below the window lies the lifeless body of a blue jay. Its neck is bent at an unnatural angle. Its legs extend stiffly out from the trunk, talons curved like claws. Its black eyes stare sightlessly up at me.

There's a ghostly outline of the bird's body on the window-pane where it hit, wings outstretched in flight.

Fighting the urge to scream, I turn and bolt from the room.

I lock myself in the master bedroom. Then I pace, wringing my hands and chastising myself for being silly.

Bird strikes are nothing new. I know they perceive the reflection of the sky on glass as being more sky, and that's why they fly right into windows and break their little necks. It doesn't *mean* anything.

Only it feels as if it does.

It feels sinister. Like a bad omen.

Or maybe . . . a message from beyond.

I stop pacing and stand still in the middle of the room. With my heart beating like mad, I gaze up at the ceiling and whisper, "Michael?"

Nothing happens. The moment stretches out until my nerves are frayed with tension. When a door slams shut somewhere downstairs, I nearly faint in terror.

I tell myself it's only Fiona, but don't quite believe it. That eerie feeling of being watched creeps over me again, but I'm alone in the room.

Or am I?

Suddenly, everything in the room looks sinister.

The shadow behind the nightstand. The porcelain clown figurine on the bookshelf. The stuffed teddy bear in my reading chair who has, though I've never realized it before now, teeth that look weirdly human.

Then there's the indentation in the duvet cover on the bed.

That might be most creepy of all.

As I do almost every morning, I made the bed when I rose, smoothing the covers and neatly arranging the army of small decorative pillows Michael scoffed at but I adored. I like the bed to look tidy, as an unmade bed makes everything else look messy, so I'm somewhat anal about the habit. Sheets tucked in, pillows placed, covers perfectly smoothed.

But now there's a distinct indent on one side of the bed. It's the side closest to the door, the one I never sleep on.

Michael's side.

The indent is approximately the size and shape of a body.

I exhale a ragged breath and give myself a pep talk. "Calm down, Kayla. You're losing it. There are *no ghosts* in this house."

The doorbell rings. When I get my handbag from the dresser, dig my cell phone out of it, and look at the camera feed, no one is there. The front porch is empty.

That's it. I've fucking had it. I'm not about to let a stupid electrical problem drive me insane!

I quickly scroll through my call log to find Eddie the handyman's number, then stand there hyperventilating until he picks up.

"Hello?"

"Hi, Eddie. It's Kayla. Remember me? With the leaky roof and the electrical problems?"

"Sure, I remember! Hey, Kayla! How are you, man?"

"I'm good, thanks. How are you?"

His laugh is low and breathless. "Grooovy."

He sounds stoned. What a surprise. "That's . . . nice. So the reason I'm calling is because I wanted to get the number of your therapist."

"Oh, for sure! I just, uh . . ." He's silent for a moment, then says, "I don't actually remember it."

"Won't it be in your cell phone?"

He sounds confused. "Cell phone?"

Yep, totally stoned. Either that, or I was right about him living in a commune with no modern conveniences. This number must be a land line. I sigh. "How about if you just give me his name?"

"Oh, yeah, yeah, no problemo. His name's Letterman. Dr. David Letterman."

I frown. "Like the talk show host?"

Another confused pause. "Who?"

So he doesn't own a television, either. At any rate, this conversation is going around in circles. Time to say goodbye. "David Letterman. Got it. I'll give him a call. Is he in Seattle?"

"Nah, he's right down on Winslow and Olympic, across from the museum of art. That little red brick building with the green awning."

I know the building well, so I thank Eddie and promise him again that I'll give his number to anyone who might need a handyman. Though I think he's probably far more skilled at dealing pot.

When we hang up, I go downstairs to my office and google the doctor on my laptop.

There's no listing. Eddie was probably so high, he gave me the wrong name.

I consider calling him back, but decide it's a lost cause. Next, he'd likely give me the name of his dentist.

Feeling defeated, I stare at the computer screen for a while. I know therapists in Seattle will be more expensive than ones on the island, and I don't love the idea of taking the ferry back and forth to the city once or twice a week. I could try to find someone in Bainbridge, but I know the pickings will be slim.

Then I consider the possibility that maybe Dr. Letterman is the *only* shrink on the island. Or maybe he's not a shrink at all, but a voodoo doctor who'll want to sacrifice a chicken and read its entrails to see what's wrong with me. That seems a little more up Eddie's alley.

Except David Letterman doesn't sound like a voodoo name.

I'm starting to get exhausted from my little mental guessing game, so I decide I'll take a drive downtown later this afternoon after Fiona's gone and pop into Letterman's office.

You can tell a lot by someone's office. If he's got a nice secretary and the place doesn't look like it's recently hosted any black magic ceremonies, I'll make an appointment. I've got dry cleaning to pick up, anyway, and the cleaners is only a block over.

Hopefully, my clothes are still there. I dropped them off before the accident.

When a sharp pain stabs me behind my left eyeball, I mutter an oath.

Just what I need, a headache.

I lie down on the sofa and close my eyes. I must drift off to sleep, because when I open my eyes again, the light has changed. Shadows slink up the walls in long gray fingers. When I look at the clock, I'm surprised to discover I've been asleep for more than four hours.

When I emerge from my office, the house is quiet. Fiona's gone. I go upstairs and change into a fresh shirt, then drive downtown and park on the tree-lined street outside the building Eddie said Letterman's office is in.

As I'm getting out of the car, I happen to glance at the restaurant across the street.

The Harbor House is a seafood place with a patio overlooking the water and live jazz on Friday nights. It's a popular spot for tourists and locals alike. Sometimes during the summer, there's even a line to get in.

But it's not summer now, and there's no line. I've got a clear view of the restaurant's entry.

Walking through the front door with his arm slung around a curvy brunette's shoulder is a man I'd recognize anywhere, even from the back.

Aidan.

28

I freeze. My heart stops. Feeling as if I've been kicked in the gut, I lean against the car door to steady myself. Then I stand there in cold shock, trying to decide what to do.

But there's nothing *to* do. Aidan and I aren't in a committed relationship. Hell, we haven't even talked about whether or not he's dating other people. I don't know a thing about his personal life.

"Oh God," I say aloud, horrified. "Kayla, you idiot!"

He could have twenty other women on a rotating fuck schedule for all I know, with nary a condom in sight.

This is exactly how lifelong regrets are made.

I quickly get back in the car and slam shut the door. Groaning, I lean forward and rest my forehead on the steering wheel. With my eyes closed, I curse myself silently, alternating every few moments with a nice juicy curse for Aidan, too.

Not that he deserves it. No promises have been broken here. That awful pain in my chest is just my ego smarting. Or maybe it's my heart, I can't tell. Whatever it is, it's painful.

Boy, I'd *really* like to swing a hammer at a few of his most tender body parts.

When the sharp knock on the window comes, I jerk upright.

Aidan is bent over outside the driver's-side window, peering at me quizzically.

Shit.

When I don't make a move, he says, "Thought that was you. What are you doing?"

Heat rising in my cheeks, I say quickly, "Nothing. Sitting here."

After a beat, he asks, "This a bad time?"

I know what he means, and he isn't talking about my impending mental breakdown. "I'm alone."

"Okay. Back to the other question, which you answered but not really. What are you doing?"

"I was just . . . out running errands."

He furrows his brow. His gaze grows piercing. I sigh and wish for the power of invisibility, which inconveniently doesn't materialize.

"Get out of the car, Kayla."

I make a face at him. "Do I have to?"

"Yes."

He steps back and folds his arms across his chest, waiting.

I consider starting the engine and burning rubber, but decide against it. He'd probably run after me and catch me at the next stoplight. So I brace myself for an uncomfortable conversation and exit the car.

He takes my arm and leads me safely over to the sidewalk, then stands across from me with his arms folded over his chest again. He doesn't say anything. He just stands there, silently looking me over.

I say, "Okay, fine. I'll start. Hi, Aidan. How are you?"

His eyes narrow. Other than that, he makes no response to my question.

From experience, I know we could stand here all night before he tells me what's on his mind. If ever. So I point at the car and say, "I'm gonna go."

"Why are you acting so strange?"

"Me? *I'm* acting strange?"

He gets this look on his face, this annoyed look, like he's seriously considering taking me over his knee right here on the sidewalk and spanking my ass raw. A warning in his voice, he demands, "What's wrong, bunny?"

Hearing him call me that makes my blood boil.

I sternly remind myself that this man doesn't belong to me, that we have no commitments, that all the hot, incredible sexual chemistry in the world does not a relationship make, but can't quite get myself to believe it.

I'm hurt, I'm angry, and I'm embarrassed that he caught me slumped over my steering wheel because I was so hurt and angry.

But I'll be damned if I'm going to admit it. I might not have much, but I still have my pride.

I lift my chin and say calmly, "Nothing's wrong. I was out running errands. It's nice to see you."

His eyes flare with anger. His voice low and controlled, he says, "Three fucking lies in one breath. Try again, and this time be honest."

Heat pulses in my cheeks. I stare at him, aware that my hands are shaking. With every ounce of self-control at my disposal, I ask, "How's your date going, Aidan?"

He blinks. He huffs out a short laugh. He glances over his

shoulder toward the restaurant, then turns back and pins me in a look of such burning intensity, I take a step backward.

Eyes shining, he says softly, "Oh, bunny. You're gonna pay for that later."

Then he takes my arm and leads me across the street. Ignoring my protests, he opens the restaurant door and guides me past the hostess stand and through the main dining room to a table near the back.

A table where the brunette he walked in with is sitting.

Right next to his friend Jake, the security guy.

I understand instantly that my tendency to assume the worst of human nature has just come around to bite me in the ass.

Stopping tableside, Aidan gestures to the brunette. "Deb, this is Kayla. Kayla, say hi to Deb." He gives me a pointed stare. "She's Jake's wife."

Face flaming, I say, "Of course she is. Hello, Deb. Nice to meet you."

My face flames hotter when Deb bounces in her chair and claps in excitement.

"Kayla! We've heard all about you! It's so great to meet you! Come join us, please!"

"Oh, no. I don't want to interrupt your dinner."

"Don't be silly. You're not interrupting at all. I can't wait to get to know you better."

As I stand there with Aidan's big hand curled around my upper arm and my mortification painting my entire face red, Jake smiles at me. "Hi, Kayla."

"Jake."

"How's the security system doing?"

"Great, thanks."

"Good to hear." He glances at Aidan. "You gonna sit, or is your man here gonna throw you over his shoulder and stalk off into the woods?"

"There's really no telling."

Aidan puts me into a chair. He takes the one next to me. Then he props his elbows on the tabletop and stares at my profile with the intensity of an FBI interrogator.

"Aidan?" says Deb, looking confused. "Everything okay?"

He doesn't answer, but the tension in his body is enough to communicate volumes.

Looking at Deb, I say sheepishly, "He's mad at me."

Obviously surprised, she looks back and forth between us. "Why? He was literally just telling us how amazing you are before he stepped outside to take a call!"

This just keeps getting better. I want to slide under the table in shame, but manage to smile tightly and answer her. "I did something he didn't appreciate."

She and Jake glance at each other in surprise, then look back at me with lifted brows.

I feel like a world-class asshole.

After a rough throat clearing, I admit, "I saw him coming in here with his arm around your shoulders and assumed you were together."

She laughs. "*Us?* Oh, honey, I've known this guy since high school. He's like a brother to me."

Jake slings his arm around the back of her chair and sends her a lazy smile. "You've known me since high school, too. You feel like I'm your brother?"

Smiling, she smacks him lightly on the thigh. "Oh, be quiet. You know what I'm saying."

They share an affectionate kiss as Aidan continues to burn holes into the side of my face. Then he leans over and murmurs in my ear, "You were jealous."

I turn my head. There's no mistaking the glint of heat in his eyes. It's right there next to the disappointment. When I chew on the inside of my cheek, he chuckles and withdraws.

The chuckle gives me hope that my punishment for breaking my promise never to lie to him won't be too severe.

The waitress appears with a tray of waters for the table, then asks if we'd like drinks or appetizers before dinner.

Deb says, "God, yes. Give me a scotch and water, please. Easy on the water."

I can already tell I'm going to get along well with this woman.

I ask for a glass of wine, and Jake and Aidan both order beers. When the waitress leaves to get our drinks, Deb leans over the table, smiling at me eagerly.

"So, Kayla. I understand you're an artist."

"An illustrator, actually."

She crinkles her forehead. "They're not the same thing?"

"I suppose I'm a commercial artist. As opposed to a fine artist."

"Meaning you make money," says Jake with a chuckle.

"Not much," I answer ruefully. "But it pays the bills."

Deb says, "I'm so jealous. I don't have a creative bone in my body."

Jake snorts. "Don't know about that. You come up with some pretty creative stories every month when the credit card bill comes and you have to explain why you spent so much on Amazon."

She waves a hand dismissively in his direction. "I keep telling you, honey, everything I buy is absolutely essential."

"Explain to me how six pairs of identical black leggings are essential."

She turns to him in outrage. "Would you prefer I go to Pilates class naked?"

He smiles at her. "I'd prefer you do everything naked."

She turns back to me with pursed lips. "Ten years of marriage, and he's still the Energizer Bunny."

I try not to choke on the sip of water I'm taking. Under the table, Aidan squeezes my thigh. I know he's smirking without turning to look.

The waitress returns with our drinks and takes everyone's food orders. When she's gone, Jake, Deb, and I chat about nothing in particular while Aidan watches us silently. His hand still rests on my thigh, a warm reminder that I've got some groveling to get to later. And after that, when I'm alone, some serious self-reflection.

I told Aidan that what I wanted was to get to know him better. To spend time with him and see where it goes. That was the truth, but was it the whole truth?

Do I really want something more?

If I'm honest with myself . . . yes.

The thought of it scares me. I don't understand how I could possibly be ready to jump headfirst into a commitment so soon after Michael's death. What does that say about the kind of person I am?

What does it say about my marriage?

These are questions I don't really want to know the answers to. But in fairness to both Aidan and myself, they need to be asked.

"Don't you think, Kayla?"

I suddenly realize everyone is waiting for me to answer a question Deb has asked. But I've been so lost in my own thoughts, I don't know what it is. I glance around the table, my cheeks growing hot.

"Sorry, what was that?"

Deb hesitates. When she glances down at my left hand, resting on the tablecloth, I realize I'm obsessively twisting my wedding ring around my finger with my thumb. I pull my hand under the table and swallow nervously, hoping Aidan didn't catch it, but knowing he probably did.

And why the fuck am I still wearing the damn thing? What am I holding on to?

More questions that require answers.

Deb says gently, "I was just saying we girls need to stick together."

It's obvious that's not what she was saying. She's being kind, letting me know that she can tell I'm a big mess, but that she's pulling for me.

Jake, on the other hand, is giving me a steely stare. He's not cutting me any slack. He turns to Aidan and asks him how the house build is going, an obvious ploy to move the conversation in a different direction.

They talk about the project while I sit and listen in uncomfortable silence, every once in a while offering a tight smile in response to a worried glance from Deb.

This is a disaster. *I'm* a disaster. I can't even pull off a ten-minute conversation with other people without making a fool of myself. I've probably embarrassed poor Aidan in every way the man could be embarrassed, first assuming his best friend's wife is a fuck buddy, then toying with my wedding band and spacing out about my husband.

I shouldn't be here.

The moment that thought crosses my mind, Aidan drapes his arm over my shoulders and gives me a squeeze.

Flooded with emotion, I swallow and look down, blinking rapidly to clear the water from my eyes.

Deb says, "I've got to go to the little girls' room. Kayla, want to join me?"

The woman is a saint.

I nod gratefully, then stand and follow her away from the table, feeling Aidan's gaze on my back as I go.

As soon as we're inside the ladies' room and the door closes behind us, I lean against the sink, cover my face with my hands, and exhale hard.

Deb rests a hand on my shoulder. "Don't beat yourself up about it. He understands."

I drop my hands and look at her helplessly. "Understands what? That I'm a moron?"

Deb's brown eyes are as kind as the rest of her. She smiles gently at me and says, "Oh, honey. Aidan's been through hell, too. He knows the only way to get through it is to keep going until you reach the other side. You'll get there. You just have to trust the process."

She turns and locks herself into a stall. I stand staring at the closed door until the toilet flushes and she reemerges. As she stands at the sink to wash her hands, I say, "He really has told you all about me."

She pulls a paper towel from the dispenser on the sink. Drying her hands, she nods. "It isn't often Aidan likes someone, so you'll have to forgive me for getting excited. We haven't been on a double date with him in years."

She tosses the crinkled paper in the trash, then steps past me and pulls open the bathroom door. "Come on, girlfriend. If we stay in here much longer, they'll start to worry and come looking for us. And trust me when I tell you that's not something we want to happen."

"The worrying part or the looking for us part?"

She laughs. "Both."

I smile, thinking I actually quite like it when Aidan comes looking for me. Hide-and-seek is my new favorite game because of him.

When we approach the table, Aidan and Jake abruptly stop talking. Judging by their body language and the tension in the air, we interrupted an argument. Deb and I take our seats, then there's a long, awkward silence where nobody says anything or looks at each other.

When Jake scowls at my left hand, I have a feeling I know what the argument was about.

He says aggressively, "Can I ask you a question, Kayla?"

Aidan sends Jake a blistering glare and warns, "Leave it alone."

"No, it's okay," I say. "Go ahead."

He rests his forearms on the table and points at Aidan. "This man doesn't deserve any bullshit."

Aidan says through gritted teeth, "*Jake.*"

I say, "I agree, he doesn't. What's your question?"

"What are you doing?"

"What do you mean?"

"I mean what are you doing with *him*"—he pauses to send a pointed stare to my ring finger—"when you're obviously otherwise committed?"

Infuriated, Aidan turns to me. "Don't answer that." He turns back to Jake. "You're out of fucking line."

"He's just watching out for you," I say softly.

"I don't need watching out for."

As Aidan and Jake glare at each other, Deb rests her hand on Jake's forearm. She says gently, "Honey. Let it go."

Jake snaps, "The hell I will! He's my best friend. I've watched him get shit on and beat up and kicked around by life for way too long. And he's finally in a good place, after years of the worst this world has to offer." He turns away from Deb and pins me in a cold stare. "Then you came along."

He drops his gaze to my finger and stares accusingly at my wedding ring.

Aidan hisses, "For fuck's sake!"

Mimicking Deb's gesture, I rest my hand on Aidan's tense forearm. My heart pounding, I look into Jake's angry eyes and say quietly, "You asked what I'm doing. Here's the answer. The best I can, like everyone else. I recently went through a huge transition. I'm not over it. I don't know how long it will take to get over it. But in the meantime, I'm living my life and figuring it out. I'm taking things one day at a time, just trying to sort through all the confusion. But I'm not otherwise committed. There's no one else."

I turn to Aidan and gather my courage. "And today proved something to me. Seeing you with your arm around Deb, thinking you were with her . . ." I swallow around the lump in my throat. "I don't want there to be anyone else. For either of us. I'm in way deeper than I thought, and to be totally honest, it scares the shit out of me."

The emotion reflected in Aidan's eyes is overwhelming.

Deb and Jake disappear. The restaurant disappears. Everything around us fades to black. There's only me and Aidan sitting beside each other, looking at each other's bared souls.

He says gruffly, "Me too. All of it. Me too."

"I know," I whisper, tears filling my eyes.

He takes my face in his hands. "But you don't have to be scared. I'll catch you when you fall. I'll always catch you."

He tears me apart and glues me back together again, all with a kiss.

Jake groans. "Well, fuck me. I guess now *I'm* the asshole."

Deb says, "You'll make up for it by paying for everyone's dinner. Ah, and here's the waitress with the appetizers now! Perfect timing. Let's eat, guys."

When Aidan pulls away from me, I catch a glimpse of a familiar figure in the large rectangular mirror mounted on the wall behind our table. A tall, gaunt man in a gray trench coat with a hat pulled low over his eyes stands near the front door of the restaurant. Though I can't see his eyes, I feel him staring in my direction.

By the time I turn around to look at him, he's gone.

29

"Kayla? You okay?"

Aidan glances over his shoulder, following my gaze. I turn back quickly to the table and force a smile. "I just thought I saw someone I knew."

It isn't a lie. And it's not as if I'm going to sit here and admit the someone I thought I knew may or may not be a ghost, so I'll just keep this stupid smile on my face until my heartbeat returns to normal and I can stop the screaming inside my head.

There are no such things as ghosts. There are no such things as ghosts. There are no such things as ghosts.

Dear God, please let there be no such things as ghosts.

We start on our appetizers. We share small talk. We order entrées and eat. I don't remember much of the rest of the dinner, because my brain is preoccupied with trying to solve the puzzle of who the man in the trench coat is if he's not an apparition from another dimension who's stalking me all over town.

I really need to go see that shrink.

When we're finished eating and we say our goodbyes to Deb and Jake, Aidan guides me out of the restaurant with his hand around my upper arm. When he steers me toward his truck parked in the lot outside, I say, "I take it I'm not going home tonight."

"You'll be lucky if I ever let you go home at all."

Oh, boy. It sounds like I'm in big trouble. I guess that kiss at the table isn't going to make up for what happened earlier. I say nervously, "I left my handbag in my car."

He shoots me an intense look, his energy crackling. "Forget the handbag. You've got more important things to worry about."

I'm sure my gulp is audible.

The drive to his apartment is tense and silent. I keep opening my mouth to say something but closing it again, at a loss for words. It's dark by the time we arrive at his place, and it's starting to rain.

He parks, kills the engine, and turns to me, eyes glittering.

He says nothing, so I go first. "I'm sorry I wasn't honest when you asked me what was wrong."

He waits for more, his silence burning.

"I should have told you the truth, but . . . I was hurt. And angry. And felt like a fool."

"You promised me you wouldn't lie to me."

I whisper, "I know. I'm sorry."

"I believe that. But what happens next time? What happens if I ask a question you don't want to answer? You gonna lie to me again?"

Not trusting myself to speak because I'm getting emotional, I shake my head.

"No, really think about it before you answer. Do you feel you can't trust me?"

I look out the windshield into the drizzle and swallow back tears. "It's myself I don't trust. My head is all fucked up. I don't know what's wrong with me. All I know is that I want you. I want you more than anything, and I don't understand how that could have happened so fast."

He reaches across the seat and takes my hand. Giving it a firm squeeze, he murmurs, "Same. And I'm as scared as you are, bunny, but I'm not gonna let it get in the way of enjoying every fucking second. You're the best thing that's ever happened to me."

Oh God. He's killing me. I'm going to expire right here in the front seat of this truck.

I cover my face with my hands. He drags me across the seat into his arms. Then we sit there in silence broken only by the patter of the rain on the roof.

After a long time, he says in a husky voice, "You ready to take your punishment?"

A shudder runs through me. I whisper, "Yes, sir."

He kisses my temple, then whispers next to my ear, "Good girl."

What happens inside my body when I hear those words can't be normal. There's tingling, shivering, butterflies, the works. But all that stops abruptly when Aidan releases me and starts the car again.

Confused, I ask, "What are you doing?"

His only response is to pull out of the parking lot and onto the street.

"Aidan?"

"I'm taking you back to your car."

"What? Why?"

"You're going home."

"I don't understand. Why am I going home?"

When he just keeps driving silently through the rain, I say miserably, "Because that's my punishment."

Gazing out the windshield, he says, "I told you I'd give you what you need, which might not be what you want. Right now, what you need is space."

My heart in my throat, I whisper, "What I need is you."

Wincing like he's in pain, he shakes his head. "I never want you to look back at this time and think we rushed things. I never want you to have regrets. Not about us. So we're gonna slow it down to a crawl and take baby steps."

"I think it's too late for baby steps."

He glances at me. Even in the dimness of the car, his gaze is so intense, it burns like fire. When he turns back to look at the road and takes all that heat away, it leaves me freezing cold. By the time we get back to the restaurant and he parks on the street behind my car, my teeth are chattering.

Leaving the engine running, he reaches over and strokes a hand over my hair, then squeezes the back of my neck.

"Go on," he says softly.

"Why do I feel like I'm never going to see you again?"

"Because you're a drama queen. Now get your sweet ass out of my truck, bunny. Call me when you've got clarity."

"Clarity?" Emotion makes my voice high and tight. "What does that even mean?"

He leans over, takes my face in his hands, and stares right into my eyes.

"When you're ready to take off that wedding ring, you'll

have clarity. Until then, I'm not doing anything for you but muddying up the waters."

He presses a firm, closed-mouth kiss to my lips. When he withdraws, he takes my heart with him.

"Now go," he commands gruffly, staring out the windshield into the rain. "When you're ready, you know where to find me."

Fighting tears, my face hot and my heart throbbing, I say, "I don't want to leave it like this."

"I know."

"I think we can work this out another way."

"I don't."

"Aidan, please!"

"Get out of the car, Kayla."

My lower lip trembles like a baby's. A cry of anguish is stuck in my chest, making it impossible to breathe. I stare at Aidan's profile, but he refuses to look at me. He just gazes out into the rain with one hand white-knuckling the steering wheel and a muscle jumping in his jaw.

It takes all my willpower to get my hand onto the door handle. What I really want to do is fling myself at him and hang on tight, but I know it won't get me anywhere.

Once Aidan makes up his mind, there's no changing it.

I open the door, climb out, and stand on the curb in the rain, staring at him.

He hangs his head and exhales hard. Not looking at me, he whispers hoarsely, "Goddammit, bunny. Just fucking do it."

I swing the door shut. It closes with a hollow clang. The truck pulls away from the curb and drives off, picking up speed until it races around a corner and disappears from sight.

I turn my face to the sky, close my eyes, and let the rain slide over my cheeks to mingle with my tears.

⌒

I don't sleep at all that night. I lie awake in bed, staring at the shadows playing on the ceiling and listening to the rain on the windowpanes, my head full of Aidan and my heart aching with the loss of him.

I could call him, but he wouldn't answer. I could go to his apartment and pound on the door, but he wouldn't open up. I could write him a letter and beg and plead, but I know all I'd get in response would be silence.

He's doing it for me—for us—but damn, does it hurt.

The strongest medicine always tastes the most bitter.

I drag myself from bed in the morning and force myself to work. The hours pass so slowly, they feel like years. By three o'clock, I'm in such a state, I quit work for the day and head over to the building where Dr. Letterman's practice is, determined to get an appointment.

Halfway there, I spot a sign for a psychic. On impulse, I pull to the side of the road and stop.

"Readings by Destiny!" the neon pink sign declares. It beams out from a front window of a charming yellow cottage with white trim. Taped under the sign is a rough drawing of a crystal ball floating between two hands. Stenciled beneath are the words, "Today Only, $10 Special!"

Though I suspect the poster is in the window every day, I decide ten bucks is a small price to pay to have my fortune told by a woman named Destiny.

If nothing else, it will be a fun story to tell.

Walking up the stone pathway to the front door, I hear wind-chimes and smell the sweet scent of burning incense. Feeling slightly foolish, I ring the bell. After a moment, the door opens to reveal a short old woman with a deeply creased face wearing a purple jogging suit with purple leather Air Jordans.

"Hi," I say, smiling nervously. "I was just passing by and thought I'd get a reading."

After looking left, then right, the woman shuts the door in my face.

Taking that as a sign from the universe that I should abandon my ridiculous mission, I turn and start to walk away. But the door opens again and a woman's voice calls out, "Hello there! Helloooo!"

I turn to find a younger version of the first woman standing in the doorway. She's also short, but the hair piled atop her head in a complicated braided mound is black instead of white, and instead of a purple track suit, she's in a flowery teal-and-gold muumuu.

Strings of colorful plastic Mardi Gras beads are draped around her neck. Gold bangles decorate both arms from wrists to elbows. Her lipstick is bright red, and the polish on her long acrylic nails is sparkly silver. Dotted throughout her coiffure are clusters of rhinestones that look like Christmas tree ornaments.

It takes a significant amount of self-control to keep a straight face.

She wiggles her fingers at me and smiles. In a syrupy Southern drawl I suspect isn't authentic, she says, "C'mon in, sugar."

"Are you open? The other lady didn't seem very welcoming."

"Don't worry about Mama." She waves her hand so her

chunky rings catch the light. "Her eyesight and hearing isn't the best. I try to get to the door before she does, but the woman's as spry as a billy goat. Come in, come in!"

I decide her enthusiasm makes up for getting the door slammed in my face and accept the invitation.

Slightly out of breath, she closes the door behind me, then hustles me into a parlor off the hallway, excitement oozing from her every pore.

I get the feeling she doesn't get many customers on a Tuesday afternoon.

Or maybe ever.

"Sit, honey," she instructs, pointing to a small round table draped in black velvet flanked by a pair of tufted gold-and-maroon velvet chairs. On top of the table is a deck of cards and a crystal ball on a low silver pedestal.

The room is decorated in what I suppose is standard fortune-teller décor. A red scarf is draped over the fringed shade of a floor lamp. A tall glass étagère displays an impressive collection of crystals. At the window, a pair of dusty-gold brocade silk curtains held back with tassels lend the space a certain shabby glamour, as do the throw rugs on the wood floor that are worn in spots, but still elegant.

Several framed and incomprehensible astrological charts adorn the walls, along with a quote from Henry David Thoreau: *"It's not what you look at that matters, it's what you see."*

Next to the Thoreau quote hangs a vaguely disturbing portrait of Jesus with an open chest cavity exposing his bloody, thorn-encrusted heart. His eyes are turned beseechingly heavenward.

I sit at the table, inhaling the heady scent of patchouli while looking around for any sign of my sanity.

Good grief, what was I thinking?

My hostess doesn't give me time to dwell on my regret. She plops herself down opposite me and announces, "I'm Destiny, sugar. And it is my great pleasure to meet you. Now, y'all tell me why you're here."

"I'd like a psychic reading, I guess?"

She crinkles her nose. "Oh, honey, you don't have to draw the pictures on the wall for me. I know you're here for a reading! My question is *why* do you need a reading? Tell me what's goin' on in your life."

"Isn't it supposed to be your job to tell me what's going on?"

"Yes, yes, but I need a question for the Tarot." She points at the deck of cards on the table between us. "You have to approach a reading with intention, you see. There's a process to this. We have to do it proper."

I answer with what I hope is appropriate respect. "Of course. Um. Well, I guess my question would be . . . What am I supposed to do?"

Destiny flutters her false eyelashes accusingly at me. "While I cleanse the cards, you can think about how to narrow that down to somethin' more specific."

She proceeds to conduct an elaborate "cleansing" ritual on the cards that includes first blowing on the deck, then setting various crystals on top of it while muttering unintelligible words. Once that's finished, she shuffles the deck, raps the bottom edge against the tabletop three times to straighten it, then sets the deck in front of me with a theatrical flourish.

I regard the deck of oversized cards warily, expecting to see an eyeball staring up at me from among the scrolls and twisting vines illustrated on the back.

Destiny goes to the window and pulls the drapes closed, plunging the room into a murky semi-gloom while I think about what exactly I want to ask. Then I remember how Aidan said I need clarity, and it crystallizes.

I've been spending so much time grieving, looking back instead of forward, that I neglected to focus on the only thing that will bring me peace.

Letting go.

Destiny takes her seat again. "You have your question, sugar?"

"Yes."

"Ask the Tarot."

"How do I move on from my husband?"

"Good. Cut the deck in half, then put it back together and fan the cards out in a half circle."

Her voice is hushed now. Her level of excitement seems to have risen. Even in the murk, I can see the drops of perspiration gathered on her upper lip.

After I've followed her instructions, she says, "Now, pick three cards and place them in front of you, from left to right, turning them over as they lie on the deck without flipping them upside down as you do."

I have to take a second to work that out in my head because my brain is a wet noodle. But I manage to complete the task to her satisfaction.

At least I *think* she's satisfied. She could also be having a heart attack.

Her only visible reaction is widened eyes, but there's something chilling in her stare. The way she's gone from animated to frozen in the space of only a few seconds is unnerving.

Following her gaze, I glance down at the cards I've drawn.

The one on the left shows a person lying on the ground with a row of swords sticking out of his back. The one in the middle depicts a nude couple holding hands under a tree, but the card faces toward Destiny, not me.

The one on the right is the weirdest. It's an upside-down skeleton in full body armor riding a horse with a scythe in his bony hand, and boy, that is really fucking freaky and not at all helpful to my fragile state of mind.

I look up at Destiny. "So? What does it mean?"

Her voice hushed, she says, "You have two major arcana cards, which in itself is significant." She points to the scary skeleton and the nude couple. "The major arcana represent karmic influences and what's happening on the soul's journey toward enlightenment. These are important lessons you're being called to process. But when reversed, it means you're not paying enough attention. And here, both major arcana are reversed. This is a very complex draw."

I'm already disliking the sound of this. "Complex bad you mean?"

Ignoring that, Destiny points to the card with the guy with all the swords in his back. "The card on your left is your past. This is the Ten of Swords. Swords carry a powerful masculine energy that deals with the mind. As you've drawn it upright, it indicates crisis, loss, deep wounds, painful endings . . ."

She glances up at me. "Betrayal."

The skin on the back of my neck crawls.

She points to the nude couple. "The card in the middle is your present. You've drawn The Lovers, which normally represents a balance of forces, complementary energies, trust in

264 · J.T. GEISSINGER

a relationship, harmony, and strength. But here it's reversed, which indicates disharmony and imbalance. Whatever's happening in your love life will cause you great pain."

Wonderful. Just fucking wonderful. I can't even catch a break from a stupid deck of cards.

Destiny points to the card on my right, the armored skeleton on horseback.

"This card represents your future."

When she doesn't say more, I prompt impatiently, "And? What does it signify?"

She says simply, "Death."

We stare at each other across the table as the clock ticks on the wall and my heartbeat goes haywire.

Desperate for some kernel of positive news, I argue, "But it's upside down. Wouldn't that mean life or something? When it's reversed, doesn't it mean the opposite?"

She shakes her head, making the ornaments in her hair quiver. "Death is a very misunderstood card. It isn't just about life ending. It's about new beginnings, transformation, and change. Metamorphosis from one state to another. When the Death card is reversed, it means you're resisting change. There's been a major upheaval in your life, but you're not letting go of the past. And the longer you refuse to let go, the more painful your situation will become. You must purge yourself of old baggage before it weighs you down permanently."

Purge myself of baggage? Like a psychic enema?

Befuddled, I sit back in my chair and exhale.

Destiny says gently, "Sometimes it's helpful to draw a follow-up card to understand better what the Death card wants you to let go of."

I look at the fanned-out deck of cards and think I'd rather chop off one of my own fingers with a dull knife than hear more depressing news.

"Go ahead," she insists. "It'll be good for you."

I snort. "Good for me like a root canal?"

"Pick one, sugar."

Well, shit. Might as well get my ten bucks' worth.

Hesitating, I hold my hand over the deck, trying to get some kind of karmic signal from it. When nothing happens, I just pick one that's sticking out a little farther than the others and place it face up on the table to the right of the Death card.

"Ah. The Magician."

Destiny sounds pleased, which makes me feel better. "Is that good?"

She shrugs. "Well, it's another major arcana card, and reversed, so it's complicated."

"Of course it is."

Ignoring my defeated tone, she says, "But boiled down, it means that what you need to let go of are your illusions."

I furrow my brow. "Illusions about what?"

Destiny meets my gaze. There's something very sad in her eyes.

"Only you can answer that question, sugar. You asked the Tarot how you can move on from your husband. My advice to you, based on this reading, is to take a hard look at exactly what you're holding on to." She taps a fingernail on the Ten of Swords. "There's a betrayal here. Maybe it's about that."

I shake my head. "No. That doesn't make sense. Michael never betrayed me."

"Are you sure?"

Into my head pops the memory of the time the woman at Michael's holiday work party called him a prick. Sharon or Karen or whatever her name was, the same woman who stood behind me at his funeral and wept.

I push the memory aside and say firmly, "I'm sure. It has to be about something else."

Destiny looks at me as if she knows all my secrets, and they're really bumming her out.

"All right, sugar. You know best. Just sit on it for a spell when you leave. Think it over. And in the meantime, I'll pray for you."

Why the hell do people keep telling me they'll pray for me? Fiona said the same damn thing!

Irritated, I stand. That's when I realize I left my purse in the car. "Sorry, but I have to run out to my car to get your money."

Destiny stands, too, folding her hands at her waist and smiling at me. "Oh, there's no charge, sugar. The reading's on me."

So now I'm getting the pity discount, same as Eddie the handyman gave me. I must be much worse off than I realize if my face inspires such charity. "Thank you. That's very nice of you."

I back up, eager to get out of this house. Destiny doesn't offer to walk me to the door. She simply stands there smiling sadly, making me feel worse than when I walked in.

As I'm closing the front door behind me, she calls out, "Safe travels, sugar!"

Somehow, that strikes me as the most ominous thing she said of all.

30

Dear Dante,

As you can see, my curiosity about you has won. I hope this letter finds you well. I'm not so well, myself. Actually, I think I've blown past unwell and landed squarely in Crazytown, USA, where I'm currently running for mayor.

Have you ever felt like your life is out of your control? Like there are unseen forces pulling the strings, and you're just a puppet dancing around helplessly, getting jerked this way and that?

That's how I feel. Helpless. Lost in a storm.

Also more than a little pathetic because the only person I can talk to about my problems is someone I've never even met. Who is currently incarcerated for reasons unknown to me. Who might be a serial killer for all I know. (That wasn't a dig. I'm just pointing out facts.)

Though it's probably better this way. I doubt I could tell someone I know that a fortune teller named Destiny told me I have psychic baggage, my housekeeper is trying to convince me I'm being haunted, and I'm seriously entertaining the idea of having a séance because nothing "normal" makes sense *anymore. Normal went out the window when my husband died.*

Also . . . I'm falling in love.

It's only happened to me once before, so I'm not much of an expert on the subject. All I know is that I feel incredible when I'm with him and like shit when I'm not. I love making him smile, and I hate making him sad. Which, unfortunately, I seem to have a knack for.

I'm all messed up, Dante. Do you have any words of wisdom for me?

Sincerely,
Kayla

31

Dear Kayla,

You asked if I have words of wisdom for you. The answer is yes. Here they are:

You are not controlling the storm, and you are not lost in it. <u>You are the storm.</u>

I'd love to take credit for that, but it's from a writer by the name of Sam Harris. He was arguing that free will is an illusion, which I'm sure you'll agree is a thoroughly depressing idea. Bypassing the dour philosophical stance, however, I really like the perspective that chaos isn't outside us. It's always within, even if we perceive it to be otherwise.

You're the chaos. You're the storm. You're the one creating the high winds and choppy seas you have to navigate. You're the source of everything that's happening.

In other words, <u>you're the one with the power.</u>

The question then becomes what are you going to do with it?

Sam Harris would tell you I completely wrecked his argument and I have no idea what I'm talking about, but we're not listening to him.

Listen to yourself, Kayla. Stop and really listen.
You're the storm.
What is all your thunder and lightning telling you?

Dante

32

I say crossly to the letter in my hand, "If I knew what all my thunder and lightning were telling me, I wouldn't have asked you for advice!"

Maybe Dante was sent to prison for being criminally irritating.

Why was I compelled to ask him for advice, anyway? The man is the very definition of cryptic. Yes, curiosity plays a big part in why I keep communicating with him, but there's also something else. Some underlying reason I can't quite put my finger on.

Something almost . . . inescapable. Inevitable.

As if our connection is governed by the stars.

With a sigh of frustration, I slap the letter down on my desktop and stare glumly out the window into the rainy afternoon.

More damn rain. It's like the weather is in on some evil plot to drive me even nuttier than I already am.

It's been two weeks since I've had contact with Aidan. Every day that passes is drearier and more depressing than the last. I've developed a severe case of insomnia to go along with all my other problems, and I still haven't found a therapist.

The other day when I visited the building where Eddie said Dr. Letterman has his office, there was no Dr. Letterman listed on the directory.

I don't know why I went to that pothead Eddie for help, anyway. He probably only has a single functioning brain cell left.

Not that I'm in any position to judge. I've been drinking so much wine, I should buy stock in the grape industry.

When I hear the sound of laughter, I lift my head and look toward the window. The laughter comes again, bright and bubbly, though I can't see anyone out in the yard. Curious, I go to the window and peek out.

The little blond boy in the red rain slicker runs across the lawn in front of me.

I gasp and fling myself against the wall, flattening my back against it. My heart pounds. Adrenaline floods my veins, leaving me shaking.

If anyone had told me before this moment that the sight of a cheerful toddler would strike such terror in my soul, I'd have laughed in their face. The guy in the trench coat doesn't even scare me this much.

It's not a ghost. He's too happy to be a ghost. Didn't Fiona say something about spirits trapped in this dimension being sad?

Panicked, I argue with myself that I'm being ridiculous, but it doesn't help.

Then I have such a horrifying thought, it stops my pounding heart cold.

Is that the child I miscarried?

Am I being haunted by the spirit of my dead son?

I know it doesn't make sense. My child hadn't even been born yet, much less grown to a toddler. But what do I know about ghosts? Maybe they continue to develop into the person they would have been if they'd lived?

But where would they get clothing? Did this kid visit some otherworldly kiddie store to pick out his little rain jacket and yellow boots?

I slap a hand over my eyes and groan. "Stop it, Kayla! That is *not* a ghost! Now go outside and find his mother!"

The sound of my voice cuts through some of my panic, enough to galvanize me into action. I straighten my shoulders, take a deep breath, and turn back to the window.

The little blond boy stands a few feet away, looking right at me.

We stare at each other through the glass. My heart feels as if it's about to break my rib cage. It races so fast, I can't catch my breath.

Why is he so scary?

The boy points at me. He lets out a high, bloodcurdling shriek, his mouth stretched open and his blue eyes wide in terror.

Then he turns and bolts, disappearing from sight.

I stand rooted to the spot, hyperventilating, until anger overtakes me. I shout at the window, "Fuck you, too, kid!"

Immediately, I slap a hand over my mouth. I can't be that lady who hollers at children on her lawn. We had one of those on our block when I was growing up, and everyone hated her.

I run through the house to the back door. Barging through that, I launch myself off the porch and look around the yard. There's no sign of the boy. I run left and look around the side of the house, but he's not there either. So I head in the other direction, my breath steaming out in a white cloud in the cold air.

There's no sign of him on the other side of the house. He's

not in the front yard when I search it. He's not hiding in the bushes or running down the street.

He vanished into thin air.

Standing wet and shaking in the driveway, I sense a presence behind me. When I whirl around, I'm alone.

Then I happen to glance up at the second floor.

In the window of my master bedroom, the little blond boy stands staring down at me.

There are no such things as ghosts. There are no such things as ghosts. There are no such things as ghosts.

Rain pelting my upturned face, I shout, "Stay there!"

He backs away from the window and disappears from view.

Gnashing my teeth, I run back inside the house, take the stairs to the second floor two at a time, and storm into the master bedroom.

It's empty.

I search everywhere, every nook and corner of the house, but that little son of a nutcracker is gone.

When I review the camera feed, it shows nothing but static.

Deeply shaken by the encounter, I go around the house obsessively checking locks, drawing drapes closed, and generally acting as paranoid as I feel. I assume the boy came in through the back door after I went through it, but I can't come up with an explanation for how he got out. I should've run right into him coming down the staircase, but didn't.

He literally vanished into thin air.

I'd call Jake and ask him to install more cameras on the inside of the house, but considering how badly our last meeting went, I doubt that's such a good idea.

So I pour myself a vat of wine, lock myself into the bath-room, and draw a bath. Hunkering low in the bubbles, I hold on to the overfilled wineglass with shaking hands and try to pinpoint exactly when it was that I began losing my mind.

Because I can no longer convince myself I have a firm grip on reality. If I'm seriously considering that the ghost of a five-year-old kid is haunting me, I've lost it.

When the lights above the vanity flicker three times, I stifle a sob and guzzle the wine, needing Aidan with an ache that feels terminal.

⤙⤚

That night, I dream that I'm drowning.

It's vivid and horrifying. I wake up sweating, with a scream stuck in my throat.

For the next three nights, I have the same dream. By Saturday morning, I'm a wreck. I haven't been able to work at all. Every little creak of the house scares the bejesus out of me. The burn-ing smell when I run the dryer changes to a stench of something putrid, like sewage.

Only in my heightened nervous state, it smells like rotting flesh.

When I investigate, I can't find the source of it.

If I turn on the television, it turns itself off. Every gust of wind outside sends a cold draft through the house, making the curtains rustle and whisper. At least I *think* that's what's mak-ing that whispering sound, but I'm too scared to go look.

I'm so jumpy and strung out, I scream when a fly lands on my arm.

Desperate for contact, I send Aidan a text.

I miss you.

He doesn't respond for so long, I think he won't at all. But then his text comes through with a little chime that has my heart leaping into my throat.

I miss you, too.

He sends a white rabbit emoji along with it. For some strange reason, that brings tears to my eyes.

Can I come over?

This time his response is instant.

You still wearing that ring?

No.

Did you take it off right before you answered me?

Shit. Why does the man have to be so insufferably intelligent?

Please, Aidan. I need to see you. Please.

Sorry, bunny.

I stare at the screen, biting my lips. He doesn't sound very sorry. Maybe I need to sweeten the offer.

May I please come over . . . master?

My phone remains silent.

I wonder if I should send him a snap of my booty or boobs, but the thought of taking a series of unflattering nude pictures in desperate search for one good enough to entice a man into allowing me to run to see him leaves me even more depressed than I was before.

How did I get to this point in my life? What the hell has happened to me?

When the doorbell rings and I find the step empty when I

open the front door, I decide the only logical thing left to do is get drunk.

If I'm going insane, there's no reason to do it sober.

⸻

"Kayla? Kayla dear, can you hear me?"

I open my eyes to find Fiona bending over me with a concerned expression on her face. It's morning—apparently, Monday morning—and I'm lying on my back on the living room sofa with a splitting headache and a mouth that tastes like ashes.

"My," she says, chuckling. "You look a sight. Had a wee bender over the weekend, did you, dear?"

"It was more than wee." I sit up. The room tilts, and my stomach lurches along with it. I cover my mouth with a hand and produce a loud, unladylike burp.

"Everything all right?"

"Oh, yes, everything is splendiferous. Absolutely top-notch."

She purses her lips and gives me a disapproving look. "I must say, sarcasm is very unbecoming on you."

"You'll have to cut me some slack. I recently realized my brain has gone missing. Even worse, I realized it's probably been gone for quite a while."

"There's not a thing wrong with your brain, my dear. Now, get off that sofa and pull yourself together. I don't like to see you moping about."

"I'm not moping," I mutter, knowing that's exactly what I'm doing.

When Fiona turns to walk away, I say, "Would it be okay if I asked you for some personal advice?"

Surprised, she turns back to me. "Of course. What is it?"

I exhale and drag my hands through my hair. Leaning over, I prop my forearms on my thighs and stare at the carpet while I gather my thoughts. "When someone says they're giving you space, but you don't want the space they're trying to give, how do you handle that?"

"You mean they've closed a door, but you want it to open?"

I nod, liking that imagery.

When I glance up to meet her gaze, hers is soft and sympathetic. She says gently, "My dear girl. You knock."

Just then, the doorbell rings.

Fiona smiles. "Or you ring the bell. I'll get it."

When she turns and walks away, I call after her, "There won't be anybody there!"

"One never knows," she says, chuckling as if she's enjoying some private joke. She leaves the room. A few moments later, she returns, shaking her head.

"Well, you were right. There was nobody there." She pauses, staring at me meaningfully. "That I could see, anyway."

I groan and drop my head into my hands. "Okay. You win. We'll do the séance."

The doorbell rings again. The television turns itself on, volume thunderous. From the hallway comes the distinct *pop* of a light bulb exploding in one of the fixtures.

Fiona says somberly, "I think that's a very good idea."

33

Dear Dante,

Thank you for the advice. I must say, however, it was shitty. "You are the storm. What are your thunder and lightning telling you?" Was that really supposed to be helpful? Because it wasn't.

Please forgive the rudeness, but my life is falling apart. Correction, it already fell apart. I'm just wandering around in all the broken pieces, kicking up dust and cutting my feet on shards of glass.

And by the way, what was that whole thing about the love that turned the stars and the wheels? That was confusing as hell. As a matter of fact, all your letters have been confusing. I still don't know what you want from me or why you decided we should be pen pals or how you even found me in the first place. I hardly know what's real and what isn't anymore. I don't even know if these letters are real. Maybe I'm staring at the wall in my locked room in a mental institution, conjuring all this up in my head? That's what it feels like, anyway. I feel like I let go of the rope that tied me to a dock, and now I'm drifting alone far out at sea in a leaking raft that's being *circled by hungry sharks. And the wind is picking up. And it's starting to rain.*

I'm drowning, Dante. I'm drowning.

What I really need right now is a life jacket.

Kayla

34

Fiona informs me that the full moon is tomorrow night, so we can conduct the séance right away. She tells me I'm lucky we can get it done so quickly.

I don't feel lucky. I feel cursed. I don't say that aloud, however, because I don't want to tempt fate into proving it.

I spend the rest of that day and the next in a state of high anxiety, every so often glancing at my left hand. I'm surprised each time to find my wedding band still there on my ring finger.

Aidan was correct when he guessed that I'd taken it off right before I answered his text. I won't lie to him again, so I had to get creative. But I put it back on when he didn't answer me, and I still can't figure out why.

Though I'd never admit it to him, something felt wrong when I took off that ring.

It felt as if the house itself sucked in a breath of horror. Which is obviously a figment of my overwrought imagination, but that's how it felt. At some point over the past few months, the house has become more than simply a collection of rooms under a leaky roof. It's taken on a presence I can physically feel.

This house has a pulse, and its dark heart beats for me.

I think it wants something.

I think it's trying to send me a message.

Another blue jay committed suicide on my office window. It felt symbolic, so I looked up the meaning of a dead blue jay online. Yes, I'm now so desperate, I'm hitting up the internet for help. Anyway, it turns out those particular birds have strong spiritual associations and were often considered by Native Americans to be messengers from the gods. Seeing one is supposed to bring good luck.

Unless it's dead, in which case it means that you're running away from your problems.

If only I could run faster.

⌒

"Hello, Kayla. It's lovely to meet you. I'm Claire."

I stand in the open doorway looking at Fiona's sister and thinking I must be seeing double. They look exactly alike, right down to the dimples in their cheeks. Same short gray hair, same bright blue eyes, same stout legs and cheerful smile.

They're so similar, it's eerie. If Fiona was sick one day and sent Claire to clean the house in her place, I'd never know it. The only difference is that Claire's carrying a black duffel bag and Fiona has an umbrella.

"Nice to meet you, too. Please, come in."

I stand aside to let the pair enter the foyer, then shut the door against the blustery evening. "You didn't tell me you had a twin, Fiona."

She drops her dripping umbrella into the stand next to the console table and smiles. "We're not twins."

"You could've fooled me."

Claire pats her hair. "Don't be ridiculous. I'm much prettier than she is."

They share a fond glance, then remove their matching blue wool overcoats in moves that look synchronized. While Fiona takes both coats and hangs them in the hall closet, Claire turns to me and looks me curiously up and down.

"What?" I ask nervously, wondering if I have stains on my shirt or spinach in my teeth.

Her smile is kind. "Fiona has told me so much about you, I already feel as if we're old friends."

"Oh. Well, I could use a few friends right now, to be honest. My life is pretty chaotic."

She chuckles. "Don't worry, my dear. You're in good hands. I've been communicating with spirits since I was four years old, so we'll see what this one wants and have her on her way in no time."

Bypassing my shock that this poor woman has been carrying on conversations with dead people her entire life, I say, "Great. Except the spirits haunting me are male." My laugh is nervous. "I can't believe I just said that."

"Ah, yes, excuse me. I have two other séances to perform tonight, and the details get mixed up."

"Two?" I repeat, astonished.

She gestures toward the ceiling. "The full moon is a very busy time for me. And forget about the solstices and the equinoxes! I'm booked a year in advance for those."

When she sees my expression, she explains, "Experienced mediums are in high demand. You wouldn't believe the amount of people who die and refuse to move on to the Other Side."

I don't know how to respond to that, but I feel as if it deserves a polite reply, even if it is nuts. "I'm glad to hear business is booming."

Fiona returns and asks Claire, "Would you like to do a sweep of the house before we begin to see if you sense anything?"

Claire shakes her head. "That won't be necessary. I'm getting very strong energy already." She points toward the hallway. "What's down there?"

"My office. And my husband's."

She and Fiona share a meaningful look.

"You guys can't go all twinny telepathic on me. I'm freaked out enough already. What was that look for?"

Claire says, "I don't want to alarm you, dear, but . . ." She hesitates, making a face as if she needs to run posthaste to the nearest toilet.

Sweet baby Jesus, if this gets any worse, I'll climb up to the roof and throw myself off.

"Go on."

"I think we should conduct the séance in your husband's office."

A distant boom of thunder rattles the windows. Of course it would happen right then, because even the goddamn weather wants to see me go crazy.

"Why?"

She and Fiona share that weird look again. "Because I sense that's where the spirit wants to have it."

We stare at each other. Nobody says anything for a while. Then I say, "Claire, I'm going to ask you something now, and I want you to be completely honest with me."

"Yes?"

"Is this bullshit?"

"Oh, no, my dear," she says vehemently, shaking her head. "I assure you, this is the farthest thing from bullshit."

As more evidence of my crumbling grip on reality, I spend a moment debating with myself about the difference between the words furthest and farthest. Then I sigh and give up.

"Fine. We'll do the séance in Michael's office. But if the Ghost of Christmas Past shows up, I can't be held responsible if I crack and bludgeon it with the nearest heavy object. Let's get this over with."

I turn and walk down the hall, listening to their footsteps behind me and wondering if it would be poor spiritual etiquette to drink wine during a séance.

I have a feeling I'm going to need booze before this is done.

I open the door to the office and switch on the lights. Stepping aside to let Fiona and Claire pass, I notice how cold it is in the room. It feels like a walk-in freezer.

Shivering, I say, "Sorry about the temperature."

Ignoring me, Claire wanders around, looking things over as Fiona and I watch. She sets her bag down on an occasional chair and points to the round table next to it.

"Can we move this into the middle of the room?"

"What do we need that for?"

"A round table is most conducive."

I don't bother asking conducive to what, because we've officially arrived in Loonyville. When in Rome and all that.

While Fiona and I move the table, Claire unpacks her duffel bag. From it, she takes a black cloth and shakes it out, murmuring something over it. I have to assume spells. She drapes it over the table, adjusting it so it's even to the floor all the way around, then goes back to the bag and removes three white candles, which she sets in the center of the table. Next is a small bowl of unwrapped chocolates that she places beside the candles.

"What's the chocolate for?"

"A food offering for the spirit," Claire replies, as if it's obvious.

I can't resist countering this nonsense with a little logic. "How's it going to eat if it doesn't have a real mouth?"

"Ah, but the spirit doesn't *know* it doesn't have a real mouth, now does it?"

When I look at Fiona, she shrugs. "A little suspension of disbelief wouldn't hurt you, dear."

I mutter, "A little gallon of Cabernet wouldn't hurt me, either."

"No eating or drinking during the séance!" reprimands Claire, lighting the candles. She sends me a stern look over the rims of her glasses. "And no jewelry, either. That will have to come off." She jerks her chin toward my wedding ring. "Along with anything else you might be wearing. Also switch off any electronic devices, please. Fiona, will you dim the lights?"

I'm expecting Fiona to shut off the main overhead light and leave the lamps on, but she kills both, plunging the room into darkness broken only by the wavering glow of the candles on the table.

The distant boom of thunder rolls through the sky again, louder this time. A sudden gust of wind howls through the trees outside. Rain patters against the windows, sliding down like silvery tears.

If Claire was going for a spooky vibe, she couldn't have picked a better night for it.

"Everyone pull up a chair," she says, setting a pad of paper and a pencil on the table.

I roll Michael's desk chair over and sit. Fiona drags a side chair from one corner of the room and takes her place to my left. Claire pushes the occasional chair over, removes her duffel bag from the seat, and sets it on the floor. Then she settles herself in the chair and looks at me.

"Dear?"

"Yes?"

"You need to take off your ring."

"Oh, right. Sorry." I slip the ring off my finger and shove it into the back pocket of my jeans.

Claire looks dissatisfied. "It can't be on your body. Perhaps you could put it on the desk?"

I don't know why it should be such a big deal, but I don't want to wreck the possibility of finding out what the ghost who doesn't exist and isn't haunting me wants, so I take my wedding ring from my pocket and put it on Michael's desk blotter.

Right next to the folded newspaper with the article about his death.

His face stares up at me in black and white from beneath that terrible headline.

Local Man Drowns.

My heart palpitating, I carefully move the ring to his picture. Then I nudge it over until it's resting atop his face. I don't know why, but it feels right. As I back up, it seems as if one of his eyes peers out from the circle of gold, following my every move.

Unnerved, I return to the table and take my seat. I wipe my sweating palms on my jeans and try to shake off the gathering sense of foreboding.

"Everyone place your hands flat on the table in front of you, please."

Fiona and I follow Claire's instructions. Then she does the same, looking at each of us in turn, her demeanor somber and her voice low.

"Before we begin, a word of warning. Spirits are unpredictable. Whatever happens, keep your composure. Remain silent. Don't break the circle of energy by standing up. I'll start by stating our intent to make contact and inviting the spirit to join us at the table. If the spirit accepts our invitation, you may hear strange noises such as knocking or taps. I'll ask the spirit yes or no questions to begin, and if they prove amenable, I'll ask them what they want. They might communicate through me, using my hand to draw on this pad or my voice to speak directly to you."

Oh fuck. If I witness a dead guy speak through this nice old woman, I'll never be right in the head again.

Frightened now, I swallow and press my hands more firmly against the tabletop to try to get them to stop shaking. It doesn't work.

"When the séance is over and you have no questions left, I'll thank the spirit for coming. Then we can turn on the lights and discuss what happened. Are you ready, Kayla?"

I nod, though I don't feel ready at all.

"Then let us begin."

Claire closes her eyes. With her face tilted toward the ceiling, she says in a hushed voice, "We gather tonight under the full moon to seek guidance from the spirit world. We welcome the spirit haunting this home to join our circle. Please make your presence known."

The following silent pause is the longest of my entire existence. It might only last sixty seconds, but it seems like lifetimes. My pulse accelerates. My breathing turns shallow. My teeth start to chatter. I feel lightheaded, queasy, and impossibly cold.

When nothing happens, Claire repeats, "We welcome the spirit haunting this home to join our circle. Please make your presence known. Are you with us? Give us a sign."

Michael's framed college diploma slides off the wall and lands with a clatter on the floor.

I gasp. All the hair on my arms stands on end. I sit frozen, my back ramrod straight and my eyes wide and unblinking. My pounding heart is the only muscle in my body able to move.

"Remain calm," says Claire quietly, her eyes still closed.

Calm I am not. Calm I might never be again. Calm is for people on lovely beach vacations with their toes in the sand and a daiquiri in hand, not for people in imminent danger of having proof that their dead husband is reaching out from beyond the grave.

I'm so *not* calm, I'm about to fucking explode.

A clap of thunder makes me jump in my seat. It's followed by a crackle of lightning that burns white fire through the black night sky. The room is briefly illuminated in theatrical brightness, then plunged into disorienting darkness again like a carnival funhouse meant to terrorize kids on Halloween.

"Spirit," says Claire, "thank you for joining us. Are there

more than one of you? Please knock on the table to answer. Once for yes and twice for no."

The wind outside increases. The temperature in the room drops another few degrees. Rain batters the windowpanes with a sound like hail.

And my heart. Jesus, God, my poor fucking heart is screaming bloody murder, because through the room echoes the unmistakable sound of two loud knocks.

"One of you, then," murmurs Claire. "Welcome, spirit. We're honored by your presence."

Her voice has slowed, along with her breathing. She appears to be going into some kind of a trance.

Whatever the opposite of a trance is, that's what's happening to me. I'm about to piss myself. Nerves I never knew I had have woken up and started shrieking. I might puke.

"Michael?" I whisper, my entire body shaking as I look wildly around the room. "Michael, are you here?"

Nothing happens. There are no knocks on the table. No pictures fall off the walls.

Claire says, "Spirit, do you know any of the people in this room?"

Knock.

"Did you know them when you were alive?"

Knock.

"Is it me?"

Knock. Knock.

"Is it Fiona?"

Knock. Knock.

"Is it Kayla?"

The answering single knock is so forceful, I flinch and whimper.

"Do you have a message you want to pass along?"

KNOCK!

The sound of my labored breathing is even louder than the wind. By now, I'm shivering uncontrollably.

Claire reaches out with her eyes closed, blindly hunting for the pad of paper on the tabletop beside her. She grasps it, finds the pencil, and whispers, "Tell us, spirit. What is the message?"

Gripping the pencil so hard her knuckles are white, Claire's hand hovers over the blank page of the pad.

Fiona sits across from me with her eyes closed and her hands flattened on the table. I think if I closed my eyes now, I'd die instantly from a heart attack.

I'm so scared, I'm on the verge of bursting into tears.

"Spirit, what is your message?"

Seconds turn into minutes. The storm rages outside. The three of us sit silently at the table in wavering candlelight, waiting for a response that never comes.

After a long time where nothing happens, Claire says, "Let me rephrase the question. Spirit, what do you want?"

Her hand holding the pencil tenses. Then it twitches. Then it begins to tremble uncontrollably. I watch in fascinated horror as Claire's forearm starts to move, jerking back and forth over the paper in short bursts.

Abruptly, her arm freezes. She presses the pencil to the paper and writes a word in one fast scrawl from start to finish. The word is composed of heavy block letters all in caps, scratched so deeply into the paper, in some places it's torn through to the page beneath.

REVENGE

A sudden freezing draft snuffs out the burning candles. Something cold brushes against my cheek, like a ghostly wind.

Or ghostly fingers.

I scream at the top of my lungs and run from the room.

35

Fiona and Claire find me in the kitchen, huddled on the floor in a corner with my back against the cabinets and my knees drawn up to my chin.

Glancing around, Claire asks, "Why did you open all the cabinets and drawers?"

"They were open when I got here." My laugh sounds unhinged. "The resident ghost thinks it's hilarious to do stuff like that."

The sisters look at each other, then at me. Claire suggests gently, "Why don't we all sit at the table and have a chat?"

"A chat sounds great. So does an exorcism. *There's a fucking ghost in my house!*"

Fiona says, "Yes, but look on the bright side. At least there's only one."

I groan and drop my forehead to my knees.

"Now, now, my dear, don't despair. This is actually quite good news."

"Remind me where, in this unmitigated supernatural disaster, good news can be found?"

She says brightly, "Now we know what the spirit wants!"

I look up and stare at her in disbelief. "From the sound of it, the spirit wants to commit murder. And as I'm the only person who lives here, I'm thinking I'm the prime candidate for its homicidal quest."

"The spirit is angry, but I sensed the anger isn't directed at you," says Claire, pulling up a chair at the kitchen table. She sits, patting her hair and smoothing a hand down the front of her blouse. She looks exhausted.

Being possessed by a dead person must really take the wind out of you.

"But it *knows* me. What does that mean?"

"You're the owner of the home. You've been living here with it. Of course it knows you."

I'm horrified all over again. "Oh God. Has it been watching me when I'm in the shower?"

Fiona says, "I think you're missing the bigger picture here, dear."

Exasperated, I demand, "Which is?"

She pulls up a chair next to her sister and sits down. Folding her hands in her lap and looking at me with kindness in her eyes, she says, "If you can help the spirit get what it wants, it will move on."

I glance at Claire, who nods.

"You're saying you want me to be an accessory to murder?"

"The spirit said nothing about murder. It said revenge, which can take all sorts of forms."

I drop my forehead to my knees again and say miserably, "I can't believe this is happening."

Ever the practical one, Fiona says, "We need to contact the spirit again."

I lift my head and insist, "There's no *way* I'm doing another séance!"

Claire shrugs. "Suit yourself."

Growing more desperate, I demand, "So that's it? We're out of options? Can't you just burn some sage or something to make it go away?"

Claire laughs as if I'm being silly. "Oh, my dear, that's a myth. A spirit isn't a pesky insect one can banish with a little perfumed smoke."

"Great. So I have to sell the place if I ever want peace again?"

"Unless it's not the house your spirit is haunting."

"What do you mean?"

"Perhaps the spirit is haunting *you*. In which case, it doesn't matter where you live. It will always find you."

I stare at her with my mouth hanging open. She shrugs again, as if she hasn't just delivered the worst news yet.

Then something hits me. "Holy shit. Maybe it's one of my parents. Oh God, I never considered that!"

Claire and Fiona share another of their odd looks. Feeling defensive, I say, "There was no answer when I asked if it was Michael, so I have to assume it wasn't him. Right?"

There's something strange in Claire's pause, as if she's carefully choosing her words. "We can't assume anything. How long have your parents been dead?"

"Many years. Both of them."

"Then it's not them."

"How do you know?"

"You would've been contacted before now. Spirits can't cross to the Other Side then return to this dimension. Once they ascend Beyond, this plane of existence is closed to them. The only spirits who can make contact are lingering in limbo. Now, come sit at the table. My legs are getting cramped just looking at you huddled on the floor."

Though my legs are shaky, I manage to stand. I join them, sitting across from Fiona and propping my elbows on the table. I drop my head into my hands and sigh.

After a moment, Claire says gently, "Kayla, please look at me."

I lift my head and meet her gaze.

"I want to help you. We both do."

She glances at Fiona, who nods.

"So if you won't do another séance, here's my suggestion for what you *should* do."

When she pauses, I say, "I'm listening."

"Research the history of this house. Find out who lived here before you did. Perhaps you'll find a clue about the identity of this ghost. If it isn't someone you know, it's someone who lived here before."

"That makes sense. Except you're forgetting that during the séance, the spirit said it knew me *while it was alive*."

She waves a hand dismissively in the air. "I wouldn't take that as canon. Usually, they're very confused."

When I only stare at her, she explains herself.

"Ghosts are a bit like people with psychiatric disorders. They cannot distinguish illusion from reality. When a soul is trapped here, it needs a guide—a spirit guide, if you will—to help lead it to the light."

"Wait. Now you want me to be a *ghost guide*?"

She quirks a brow. "Do you prefer to be haunted for the rest of your life?"

I look at Fiona for help.

She only shrugs. "It's either that or we go back in the office and try again."

"No way. It *touched* me." I shudder in disgust. "God, how am I supposed to sleep here now knowing there's a freaking ghost floating around?"

"It's been floating around for quite some time, dear."

"Is that supposed to make me feel better?"

She chuckles. "Well, it hasn't molested you yet, if that's what you're worried about."

Horrified, I gape at her. "*Yet?*"

"No one is molesting anyone!" interrupts Claire, irritated. "The spirit doesn't want to fondle you, it wants you to help it get revenge."

"On who? For what?"

"Do some research and find out."

I glare at her. She says, "Or we go back in that office right now and put the matter to rest." She looks at her watch. "Either way, I'm already running behind schedule. What's it to be?"

"If I can help it, I'm never going in that room again."

"Well, that's it, then. If you change your mind, give me a call."

She stands. Fiona rises with her. I can't let them leave without thanking them, so I rise and follow Claire into the foyer as Fiona retrieves their coats from the hall closet.

Claire's duffel bag of séance supplies is already sitting next to the door, packed up and ready to go. They must've gathered the things while I was huddled on the kitchen floor in psychic distress.

When Fiona returns, I say, "Thank you for your time, Claire. I appreciate it."

"It's my pleasure, dear."

"You, too, Fiona."

"Be well, Kayla. I'll see you next Monday."

"Right. Unless I'm murdered by a vengeful spirit before then."

She smiles at me, which is in no way helpful. I open the door for them. Claire is about to cross the threshold, but she stops short.

Fiona and I follow her confused gaze.

Lying on the doormat is a bright orange neoprene vest with four black straps sewn across the chest. Plastic buckles dangle at the end of the straps. In the porch light, the reflective patches on the shoulders of the vest are dazzling.

Fiona says, "What on earth is that?"

"A life jacket," I whisper, starting to shake again.

A visibly confused Claire says, "What is it doing on your porch?"

"I asked my pen pal for it."

They look at me and repeat in unison, "Pen pal?"

"Yeah." Gripping the doorframe for support, I laugh breathlessly.

Fiona asks, "Why is that funny?"

"Because I think I figured out who's haunting me."

⁓

Ten minutes later, the three of us are back at the kitchen table looking through Dante's letters that I brought down from my underwear drawer upstairs. Claire called her other two clients to cancel, because my haunting just became too juicy for her to pass up.

Apparently, it's not every day that a ghost delivers mail and a personal floatation device from beyond the grave.

"Remarkable," says Claire, bent over the table as she peers closely at one of the first letters I received. Careful not to touch the paper, she points at the lower right corner. "That looks like it could be blood."

"That's what I thought, too. But how could a ghost bleed?"

"It can't." She glances up at me. "But it could be someone else's blood."

"Or some*thing* else's," chimes in Fiona. "An animal, perhaps."

I grimace. "That's sick. Why the hell would he send a letter smeared with animal blood?"

Claire says, "Maybe it's a clue."

The three of us look at the rust-colored smudge. Outside, the storm continues to batter the house. It's raining so hard now, it no longer sounds like hail, but like a constant barrage of gunfire on the roof. The wind howls like a pack of starving wolves.

Claire picks up the letter by one corner and turns it over, setting it down carefully again. "'I'll wait forever if I have to,'" she reads aloud. "That must be in reference to the revenge he seeks. This ghost is waiting for you to help him get his vengeance."

"But there's all this other nonsense about his feelings," says Fiona, gesturing to another letter. "What could that mean?"

"Maybe he has a crush on me. I am pretty cute."

Fiona and Claire look at me with identical expressions of doubt.

"It was a joke, you guys. Sheesh."

"This is serious," says Claire disapprovingly. "If we can't help this spirit transition to the Other Side, it will be our fault that he's trapped in limbo forever. Let's give this situation the respect it deserves."

I can't believe I'm getting reprimanded by a medium wearing orthopedic shoes about the proper attitude toward my own haunting, but here we are.

"You're right. Sorry." I study the letters spread on the table between us and the stack of envelopes off to one side. "Why are they all postmarked from prison? Do you think that's a clue, too?"

"It's more likely that the spirit believes he's imprisoned. Metaphorically speaking, he is."

"Okay, next question: How the hell can a ghost use a pen?"

"Spirits can manifest their energy in all sorts of ways," says Claire. "Using objects like pens is one of them, but they can also control electrical devices such as telephones and computers."

"Or doorbells," Fiona reminds me.

"Exactly," agrees Claire. "They're remarkably adept at manipulating their environment. If potent enough, they can even affect the weather."

I listen to the storm roaring outside and wonder if Dante has anything to do with that.

"But if he can control energy and objects, why doesn't he go get his revenge himself? What does he need *me* for? Couldn't he just drop a piano on his enemy's head?"

"Well, for one thing, he might not recall who his enemy is."

When I look at her in surprise, Claire says, "Being trapped in limbo is terribly confusing. In fact, this ghost of yours most likely doesn't even know he's dead."

"I already told her that," says Fiona.

"So he needs me to help him remember." I look at the letters again. "Remind me why I can't just *tell* him he's dead?"

"It would only drive him further into denial," answers Claire.

"You risk alienating him altogether. If someone told *you* that you were dead, what would your reaction be?"

I snort. "I'd say sure, pal, and you're an heirloom tomato."

"Precisely. We must gently coax him toward the truth. He has to come to it on his own. It's like the steps a child takes to learn to read. First comes the alphabet. Then they learn short, easy words. Cat. Dog. Tree. Then they put the words together in simple sentences, until eventually, they're devouring Shakespeare. Comprehension is a multistep process. It doesn't happen all at once."

"But how did he even get stuck in limbo in the first place? Why doesn't a soul just automatically move on when the body dies?"

"Normally, they do. But sometimes, they lose sight of where to go. The dense reality of the third dimension combined with the gravity of our planet makes things quite complicated for a nontemporal being. Add to that the emotional distress of whatever unfinished business they're suffering from, and you wind up with a very confused and cranky lost spirit."

I exhale hard and mutter, "Ghosts are high maintenance."

Fiona chuckles as if that was especially insightful. "Indeed."

Sitting back in my chair, I cross my arms over my chest and examine the letters again while sifting through everything in my head. "So, to recap, what I need to do is coax this spirit into accepting that he's no longer alive and that he needs to go to the Other Side."

"Just so," says Claire, beaming.

"How exactly am I supposed to do that if I can't tell him he's dead?"

She and Fiona share a loaded glance, then she says softly, "If you give people light, they'll find their own way."

Irritated by her ambiguity, I say sourly, "Sure. I'll just start shouting, 'Go into the light!' at the ceiling at random intervals, how about that?"

"Trust your instincts," says Fiona soothingly. "You'll think of something. You've got the battle halfway won already just by discovering his identity."

"But I don't know anything about him! I only have his name!"

I point at his signature on one of the letters, that familiar scrawl.

Dante.

Fiona and Claire look at each other again in their weird twin-telepathy silence.

I say flatly, "I swear to God, if you guys don't stop doing that, I'll break something."

"Why don't you start by researching his name?" suggests Fiona.

After a moment, I admit grudgingly, "That's not a bad idea. I was thinking I'd call my detective friend to get some information about Dante." My laugh is small and weak. "That was before I knew he was a ghost, though."

Claire repeats, "Detective friend?"

"The man from the police department who interviewed me after Michael's accident."

The overhead lights flicker. We all look up at the ceiling. A low electrical buzzing sound fills the room, then the lights go out. They come back on within seconds.

Claire murmurs, "Yes. You're definitely headed in the right direction there."

I lean in and whisper, "Is he just floating around eavesdropping on us? *That is so creepy!*"

"Kayla, focus."

"Seriously, though, why did we even need a séance if this ghost can hear every word we speak?"

Gazing at me, Fiona muses, "He does seem rather omnipresent, doesn't he?"

"That's what I'm saying!"

Claire stares with narrowed eyes at the ceiling. I can almost see the gears turning in her head. Before I can ask her what she's thinking, she says loudly, "Spirit, are you still with us?"

Down the hallway, a door slams shut with such force, it sets the open kitchen cabinets gently swinging.

I jump and gasp.

Fiona murmurs, "Oh, my."

Claire grabs Fiona's hand and says urgently, "I think we're close."

"Close to what?" I ask, confused and alarmed.

Claire orders, "Kayla, call that detective."

"What, *now*? It's after eight o'clock!"

"Maybe he works late. If not, leave him a message. Do you have a laptop I can borrow?"

"Well, yes, it's in my office. But—"

Without waiting for me to complete the thought, Claire leaps up and hurries from the kitchen.

Staring after her, I say, "Fiona, what's going on?"

She replies calmly, "I believe Claire thinks we're on the cusp of a breakthrough."

"Breakthrough?"

"In helping the spirit."

I glance warily at the ceiling and the overhead lights, which are now flickering continuously. In a moment, Claire returns, carrying my laptop. She sets it on the table in front of me.

"Oh," she says, pulling something from the pocket of her cardigan. "This was sitting on top of the computer lid. I thought it might be significant."

She sets the object down on the table.

It's Michael's 1937 D-type buffalo nickel. The one I found under the tree where the man in the gray trench coat stood staring at me. The one I then found on the dashboard of my car outside Aidan's.

The one I left tucked safely inside a drawer.

I lose my breath. My heart starts to pound. A savage gust of wind rattles the kitchen windows. Then through the ceiling drops a small metal object that lands with a clatter on the table beside the coin. It spins for a moment before settling into stillness, light glinting off its rounded edge.

It's my wedding ring.

36

I stare wide-eyed at the coin and the ring with my pulse throbbing and a scream trapped inside my chest, knowing that there's something extremely significant here that I'm missing.

When I glance up at Claire, she says calmly, "Call the detective."

I whisper, "How did my ring fall through the ceiling?"

"Call the detective, Kayla. We don't have much time."

"What do you mean? What's happening?"

Outside, the storm is gathering power. Rain lashes the windows and roof. Thunder booms and lightning crackles. It seems as if the house itself sits in the center of a tornado and is about to be ripped right off the ground and launched into space.

From her other pocket, Claire removes my cell phone. She must've picked it up from my desk. She thrusts it at me, insisting, "Make the call!"

Panicked, I grab the phone from her hand. Crossing the kitchen, I rummage through the open drawer next to the stove where I keep all the junk. I find the detective's business card and dial his number with shaking fingers.

A woman answers, her tone clipped. "Seattle PD, how can I assist you?"

"Detective Roman Peters, please."

There's a pause, then she says, "Are you a friend of his, ma'am?"

What a strange question. "What? No. No, he helped me a while back. My husband was in an accident, and he interviewed me and gave me his card. I'd like to speak with him, please. It's urgent."

I glance up to see Claire and Fiona standing beside the kitchen table, encouraging me with smiles and nods.

The woman on the other end of the line says, "I'm sorry, but that's impossible."

"Why?"

"Detective Peters passed on."

I'm in such a state of agitation, I don't understand her meaning. "Passed on? You mean he was promoted to another department?"

"No, ma'am. He died. Sudden cardiac arrest. I'll transfer you to the extension of his replacement, Detective Brown. Please hold."

I hear a click, then brief silence. Then a recording of a man's voice plays, instructing me to leave my number.

I disconnect, feeling strangely numb.

Fiona prompts, "Well, what did they say?"

"He's dead. Detective Peters is dead. He died of a heart attack."

"When?"

"She didn't say. Why does it matter?"

Shaking her head in impatience, Claire opens the laptop and

taps the power button. She pulls up the internet browser and starts to type.

"What are you doing?"

"Looking up the office of the county recorder. We can check the property records for this address to discover who owned the house before you." She clicks around for a minute, then types into a search bar. Then she stands back, frowning.

"What is it?"

"Was the deed to this property recorded in someone else's name?"

"No. It should be listed as Michael and Kayla Reece." I walk closer and peer over her shoulder at the screen. "Who the hell are Sandy and David Wainwright? It says they bought this house in January!"

Somewhere upstairs, another door slams. I hear the sound of running feet, then a child's laughter.

My breath catches.

Looking upward, I say, "Wait. The little boy. We're forgetting about him. If Dante's the ghost in this house . . . who's the kid? And what about the man in the trench coat and hat? How does he fit into all this?"

When I look back at Claire and Fiona, they're wearing identical expressions of sadness, along with another emotion I've seen before. I saw it on Destiny's face, the psychic I visited who wished me safe travels as I was leaving. It's unmistakable.

It's pity.

Unnerved, I demand, "Why are you guys looking at me like that?"

Claire says gently, "It's all right, Kayla. Don't be afraid. There's nothing to be afraid of, my dear."

"What is that supposed to mean?"

"Give me the phone, dear."

"Why?"

"I'm going to call the police station again."

"What for?"

"I think there's something you should know."

"Like what?"

"Give me the phone."

An overwhelming feeling of wrongness overtakes me. I back up a step. My blood turns to ice. All the hair on my arms stands on end, and I begin to hyperventilate.

The storm outside rages.

Claire takes the phone from my stiff hand and hits a few buttons. When a familiar woman's voice fills the room, I realize she hit redial, then switched the audio to the speaker.

"Seattle PD, how can I help you?"

"Yes, good evening, ma'am. Will you please tell me when Detective Peters died?"

There's a pause.

Claire explains, "My friend spoke to you a moment ago and was so surprised by the news, she neglected to ask. She'd like to send flowers to the funeral if it hasn't been held yet."

"Oh. I see. Well, I'm afraid it's much too late for flowers. It's been six months since he passed, almost to the day."

Claire thanks her, then disconnects. Then she and Fiona stand there staring at me with that awful pity in their eyes, waiting.

As if from very far away, I hear my own voice. "That's impossible. She's wrong. He interviewed me after the accident. That was only two months ago. He sat with me out on the dock and interviewed me!"

Claire says sadly, "I have no doubt that he did."

My hands begin to tremble. I find it difficult to draw a full breath. I back up another step. Looking at her for help, I say, "Fiona?"

She says softly, "You have to understand, dear, that there are very few people who can communicate with spirits."

My voice rises. "What are you saying? What does that have to do with anything?"

She goes on in that calm, soothing tone, ignoring my panic. "Mediums, of course. A few psychics, too, though most of them are fakes. Also many geniuses, for reasons we don't really understand, though it probably has something to do with their brain chemistry."

Claire adds, "Cats as well."

"Yes, that's correct. Cats can see ghosts, too." She pauses. "So can some gifted children."

The sound of a child's laughter floating down from upstairs makes my heartbeat stutter.

It falls to a complete standstill when Claire says, "And so can other ghosts. Though they don't recognize each other as such."

I look back and forth between them. "I'm sorry, *what?*"

One of the bulbs in the fluorescent fixture overhead explodes. Another one follows immediately afterward, filling the room with a sharp crackle of shattering glass and the acrid smell of burnt wiring. A cold gust of wind whistles down the chimney in a high-pitched wail that sounds eerily like a banshee screaming.

A line from Dante's last letter flashes into my mind:

You are the storm. You're the source of everything that's happening.

Then I recall something Fiona told me the day she came in and set off the alarm:

"A spirit is energy manifesting itself. Akin to an electrical storm gathering force until it discharges a bolt of lightning. When a spirit is upset, that emotion—that energy—is transformed into a physical outcome. Hence your open cupboards and drawers."

And one other thing that I didn't begin to comprehend until just now:

"I'd say the spirit who lives in this house is bloody furious."

The way she looked at me when she said that, it was almost as if . . .

As if she were talking about *me.*

Like an army of spiders, cold horror crawls over my skin. I whisper hoarsely, "No."

Fiona says quietly, "Yes, my dear. I'm afraid so."

With the explosive force of a bomb, a hundred different memories detonate in my head all at once.

How shocked Fiona was when she saw me the day after Michael's funeral. How she asked in that peculiar tone, *"So you'll be staying in the house?"*

How all the people at the grief group ignored Madison, the woman whose child was abducted years ago. How she sat alone in the circle, as if she were invisible to everyone except me.

How Eddie the handyman who dressed like a hippie didn't have a cell phone and thought David Letterman was only a therapist. How, when I went to find him, that therapist didn't exist.

How all the roofers I called never called back.

How the security camera only recorded static when I went out into the yard.

How Destiny the psychic said mournfully, *"I'll pray for you."*

How when I rang the bell, her mother opened the door, looked around, then closed it, as if there was no one standing there.

The Death card. The Lovers. The reversed Magician, indicating I needed to let go of my illusions.

The upright Ten of Swords that hinted at deep wounds, painful endings . . .

Betrayal.

Fiona saying, *"Reality is simply what we believe it to be. Each of us makes our own truths, even ghosts."*

How, when Claire first came in tonight, she referred to the spirit she came to contact as "her" before correcting herself.

Shaking so hard I can barely stand, I whisper, "If you give people light, they'll find their own way."

When I meet Fiona's gaze, her eyes are shining with tears.

I sob, then slap a hand over my mouth to stifle it. Then I grab the phone from Claire, run back to the junk drawer, and pull things out, frantically tossing pens, Post-it notes, take-out menus, and batteries onto the floor until I find what I'm looking for.

Eddie the handyman's business card.

I didn't notice it before, but the card is fragile and yellowed with age, the ink flaking in places. It looks as if it was printed decades ago.

Which it probably was.

With the sound of the raging storm outside nearly deafening me, I dial his number.

The phone rings twice before a man picks up. "Homefront Handyman, three generations strong. How can I help you?"

Gripping the phone in my shaking hands, I ask, "Is Eddie there, please?"

His short silence seems surprised. "Uh, no. This is Mark. How can I help you?"

"Please, I really, really need to speak with Eddie. Can you put him on the phone? Is he around?"

After another pause, the man on the other end of the line says, "Is this a joke or something?"

I shout, "Just put him on the phone!"

He sighs heavily. "Look, lady. I normally don't pick up this late, but business has been slow, so I did. You've made me regret it. Have yourself a good night."

"Please!" I beg, desperate. "I have to talk to Eddie! I have to talk to him right now!"

He snaps, "Yeah, well, that's gonna be kinda hard, lady, because my grandpa died in 1974."

All the breath leaves my lungs. A sob catches in my throat. Two more fluorescent light bulbs in the ceiling explode with a pop.

"Kayla."

When I whirl around in panic, Fiona is holding out one of Dante's envelopes to me.

"Read the name on the return address," she says gently.

Hyperventilating, I snatch it from her hand. "Dante Alighieri," I cry, shaking my head. "His name is Dante Alighieri! So what?"

"Don't just look at it . . . *see*."

When I return my gaze to the upper left corner of the envelope, all the letters in the return address are now moving, trading places with one another and slowly rearranging themselves into something else.

I blink rapidly, trying to clear my vision. It doesn't help. The letters move sideways, overlapping then straightening out into another name.

A name that rips a hole straight through the fabric of my heart.

Aidan Leighrite.

Dante Alighieri is an anagram for Aidan Leighrite.

Into my mind flashes an image of the framed Thoreau quote on the wall of Destiny's parlor: *"It's not what you look at, it's what you see."*

I've been blind. Refusing to acknowledge the truth.

Looking at everything, but seeing nothing at all.

Tears streaming down my face, I drop the envelope and run from the kitchen. I burst through the door of Michael's office and fall sobbing onto his desk.

I snatch up the newspaper with Michael's picture on the front. With shaking hands, I unfold it all the way. When I see the rest of the headline that was obscured, my heart stops beating.

The headline isn't *Local Man Drowns*, as it appeared when folded.

The full headline is *Local Man Drowns Wife*.

From the other side of the crease, my photo stares back at me.

I see myself standing at Michael's grave the day of the funeral, hearing a woman sob my name, and realize with the sensation of the floor disappearing beneath my feet that the name on the headstone wasn't my husband's.

It was my own.

It all comes back in a rush. A locked iron door inside my mind flings itself open, and an icy black ocean of memory floods in.

I scream.

The windows explode outward into a million razor-sharp glinting shards of glass that are instantly sucked into the storm and carried off into the rainy night. A violent whirlwind rips the newspaper from my hand and sends it flying madly around the room, torn to pieces.

Fiona and Claire stand in the office doorway. A small bare-foot figure in blue pajamas cowers behind them in terror, peeking out from around Fiona's legs.

It's the little blond boy I kept seeing on the lawn.

The boy who took one look at me and screamed in pure terror.

The boy who lives here with his parents, Sandy and David Wainwright, who bought this house a month after my husband ended my life.

Michael didn't die.

Aidan did.

Michael killed him.

Right before he killed me.

II

PURGATORIO

Even in the grave, all is not lost.

~ Edgar Allan Poe

37

FIONA

When I told Kayla that ghosts are simply souls with a story to tell, it was the truth. But the thing about ghosts is that they're unreliable narrators. Especially when they're telling a story to themselves.

Figuring out that you're dead is complicated business.

A shout comes from behind me. I turn to find Sandy running down the hall toward us at top speed, her eyes wide and her face white. Clinging to my leg, Bennett bursts into tears when he sees his mother.

She scoops him up into her arms, hugs him tightly against her chest, and stares in horror into the room. Over the roar of the wind, she hollers, "He snuck out of bed. My God, what's happening?"

"Take him back upstairs!" shouts Claire.

Paper flies past, lifted by the gale, twisting like broken birds in flight. The curtains beside the shattered windows flap and billow. Framed photographs tear themselves from the walls and smash against the floor. Books shoot out of the bookcase as if fired from a gun. A light show erupts from the exploding bulbs in the ceiling and lamps, showering the room in a spray of brilliant white sparks.

It's a pageant of sound and fury. The visible chaos when an invisible heart breaks.

"I know, poor dear," I murmur, watching the madness. "I'm so sorry."

The spot where Kayla stood mere moments ago is now empty.

Sandy runs back the way she came, hurrying down the hall with Bennett in her arms. They'll go back to David upstairs and wait for Claire and me to let them know if the spirit of Kayla Reece has finally left their house.

They might have to wait a while, however.

There's still more of the story left to tell.

38

AIDAN

I knew almost from the beginning that Kayla was it for me. Those eyes, you know? So pretty, but so sad.

It would take a while to find out what she was so sad about. By then, I'd told her about my father, about how abusive he was. About what I did to protect my mother from his violent rages.

About how I'd spent time in prison for it.

The judge was lenient because I was underage. My mother's testimony helped, too, as did all the other witnesses the defense called to prove we were living in hell with that man.

But still. Facts are facts. I was a convicted felon. It isn't pretty when you say it out loud.

The amazing thing? Kayla never judged me for it. She never looked at me differently. She didn't let it come between us, when she had every reason to say, "Peace out," and walk away.

She'd already been through so much. She didn't need all my shit on top of it.

They say her husband was a genius. Brilliant, as if that makes up for anything. Like it's an explanation and an excuse all in one. He was some big-shot mathematics professor at the university, brain like a supercomputer.

A supercomputer with a significant glitch.

You know what happens when you're so smart, everyone treats you like you're God?

You start to believe you are.

Combine that dangerous idea with a personality already lacking in empathy and obsessed with control, and then you've got big problems.

Then shit goes sideways.

Especially for the person closest to you.

Michael and Kayla were married young. Before the outbursts started. Before the beatings started. Before he kicked her so hard in the stomach, she miscarried their child.

I cried when she told me that. I broke down and bawled because it was so fucking tragic.

Then she told me about how he'd been following her since the separation, and those tears dried up real fucking quick.

I wanted her to get a restraining order, but Kayla said it would only provoke him more. She'd been counseled by someone that the best way to handle a narcissist was to starve him of his supply of attention, to go no-contact and wait him out so he'd eventually grow bored and move on.

But Michael was more than a mere narcissist.

He was an arrogant monster who thought he was God.

Kayla paid the price for that arrogance. We both did.

But like I told her in my letter, it's a price I'd gladly pay a million times over. Even if I had to do it every day until the end of eternity, I'd slice open my own veins with a razor blade and happily bleed myself dry.

There was no way I was going to live without her.

So dying for her was the only choice.

My mistake was that I thought my blood alone would satisfy the monster inside her husband's head.

Unfortunately, he was more bloodthirsty than I imagined.

39

KAYLA

Four months ago

As I sit at the kitchen table staring at my wedding ring in the palm of my hand, I sift through all the memories of my marriage to Michael until I realize that the reason I haven't taken off this ring before now is very simple.

I've been honoring the dead.

My dead child.

My dead marriage.

My dead hopes for the life I once thought I'd have.

Now, the only way I can think of to move on from the past is to do what humans do when we mourn that which is no longer living.

Hold a funeral.

I go upstairs to the master bedroom and find an empty shoebox in the closet. In it, I put our marriage license, my wedding ring, and the black-and-white sonogram of the baby from my first ultrasound appointment, along with a few other mementos.

Then I go out to the backyard with a spade I took from the shed and dig a hole beside the vine-covered pergola I told Michael I was pregnant under.

When the hole is deep enough, I set the shoebox in. Then I cover it with dirt, every so often wiping the tears from my eyes with the back of one hand.

My marriage has been over for a while now, but it still hurts. I know it always will. The kind of pain I've lived with for so long leaves indelible scars.

My throat choked with emotion, I sit back on my heels and search for something appropriate to say to the small mound of disturbed earth.

Words elude me, so I simply press a trembling hand to the dirt in a final goodbye.

Then I make the sign of the cross over my chest and go back into the house to change.

If my past is dead and buried, my future still awaits.

*

It takes him a while to open the door after I knock. It's late, and he's not expecting me. I stand on the step with my heart pounding outside my chest and all my nerves on fire with longing until I hear his footsteps approach. The doorknob turns, then there he is.

Though it's been a few weeks and our last meeting at the Harbor House restaurant didn't end well, Aidan looks at me as he always does, like I'm the first sunrise he's ever seen in his entire life.

My voice cracks when I say, "You told me to call you when I got clarity. I thought I'd knock instead."

He glances down at my bare ring finger. "Thank fuck," he says faintly, exhaling. "I haven't been able to breathe without you, bunny."

He grabs me in a bear hug and squeezes me so tight, I can't breathe either.

Then we're kissing. Hot, desperate kisses as he drags me through the door and inside his apartment. He kicks the door shut behind us and hugs me again, pressing his face against my neck.

He holds me, his arms trembling, and I'm thankful for everything that brought me to this moment, because I've never found anything finer than this.

I whisper against his ear, "Thank you."

"For what?"

"Giving me the space I needed, even though I didn't want it. But if you try giving me any more of it, I'll kick your ass."

His laugh is low and breathless. He pulls away and gazes down at me with shining eyes.

"How about if I give you something else you need?"

I lift my brows and say coyly, "Depends on what it is."

His grin turns wolfish, and his voice turns dark. "Oh, I think you know what it is, little rabbit."

He bends down, picks me up, and throws me over his shoulder, then carries me down the hallway to his bedroom, laughing as I feebly pummel my fists on his muscular butt. He kneels on the mattress and takes us down to the bed.

I flinch and wince. "Ow."

"What's wrong?"

"There's something under my back."

Aidan lifts himself up to allow me to roll to the side. From underneath me, he pulls out a book.

"Sorry. I was reading."

He tosses the book aside and kisses me again, but I'm too curious to let this go that easily. "What were you reading?"

"*The Divine Comedy.*"

He tries to take my mouth, but can't as I'm still talking. "What's *The Divine Comedy*? That sounds interesting."

Pausing to glower down at me in disapproval, he says drily, "We're having a book club meeting now?"

I smile and toy with a lock of his dark hair. "We have all the time in the world to do the other stuff, Mr. Lion. Besides, I'm curious about your taste in literature."

"Apparently, my taste in literature is as odd as my taste in women. We haven't seen each other in weeks, you're in my bed, and you're stalling me getting inside you. What's wrong with this picture?"

I give him a peck on the lips, then reach over and pick up the book he tossed aside. It's a black hardback, missing the dust jacket. The title and author name are embossed in gold on the spine.

The Divine Comedy by Dante Alighieri.

I say, "That sounds like a made-up name."

Aidan scoffs. "He's only the greatest poet *ever.*"

"Then how come I've never heard of him?"

"Maybe you're not as smart as you think."

I make a sour face. He grins.

When I ask, "So what's this *Divine Comedy* about?" he sighs and rolls off me, settling on his back.

"It's an epic poem about one man's journey through hell."

I laugh. "Sounds like the perfect light reading before bed."

He gazes at me with smiling eyes, though his face is attempting to look stern. He wants me to think he's disappointed that I'm not naked yet, but I know he's happy just to have me here.

That makes two of us.

I lift up onto an elbow and rest the book on his stomach. "So tell me the story. How does it go? Why is it called a comedy if it's about hell? And why does the author's last name have so many *I*s in it? It's fake, right?"

Trying to stifle a laugh, he reaches up and tucks a lock of hair behind my ear. "I never realized how strange you are before now."

I lightly thump him on the chest with my knuckles. "Like you're so normal. Tell me."

With an exaggerated sigh, he pulls me down, sliding an arm under my neck and tucking me against his side. I snuggle there, closing my eyes and breathing in his warm scent of cedar, musk, and woodsmoke.

Happiness shimmers inside me, as light and airy as soap bubbles.

"Dante was an Italian poet and scholar who was born in the thirteenth century."

"No wonder I've never heard of him!"

Ignoring that, Aidan continues. "The story is about his soul's allegorical journey through the three realms of the dead: hell, purgatory, and heaven. He's accompanied by three spirit guides along the way who help him understand what's happening. At the end, he enters heaven, gains the knowledge of what God truly is, and achieves eternal salvation."

After a moment, I say, "And you're reading it in bed on a Saturday night?"

"It's considered one of the world's greatest works of literature."

"Please refer to my previous question."

Chuckling, he kisses my forehead. "I'm surprised Dante didn't come up in your fancy university education. But I've made an ongoing effort to try to make up for lost time."

I open my eyes and look at him. He gazes back at me with a soft smile. I know he's talking about the time he spent in prison for what he did to his father, but we haven't really discussed that yet, so I'm hesitant to ask for details. Like, for example, how long he was there.

Gently stroking my hair, he murmurs, "Seven years."

Damn. The man can always read my mind.

I whisper, "Was it awful?"

He nods.

My throat closes, but I manage to say, "I'm sorry."

"It's in the past. This is what matters now."

He gives me a squeeze and a smile so tender, it could break my heart in two. Holding back tears, I close my eyes and press my cheek against his chest.

Sensing I'm on the verge of getting overly emotional, he has mercy on me and changes the subject.

"What really blows my mind about Dante—other than his work—is that his name is an anagram for mine."

"Anagram means what? Like it sounds similar?"

After a pause, he says, "You didn't really go to college, did you?"

I thump him on the chest again. He chuckles and says, "An anagram is a word formed using all the letters of another word. Like 'iceman' and 'cinema.' You mix up all the letters and they spell something else."

I think about it for a moment. "Okay, that's freaky."

"What's freaky about it?"

"Your name and some famous thirteenth-century Italian dude's names are the same."

"They're not at all the same."

"Yes, they are, if you mix up all the letters!"

He dissolves into laughter. "Fuck, I've missed you."

"Glad I amuse you, Fight Club."

He takes the book off his stomach and sets it aside on the bed, then rolls on top of me, propping himself up on his forearms. Cradling my head in his hands and gazing down into my eyes, he murmurs, "But already my desire and my will were being turned like a wheel, all at one speed, by the Love that moves the sun and the other stars."

When he doesn't add more and only lies there staring at me with intensity, I say, "Um . . . okay?"

He drops his forehead to my shoulder and laughs again, harder this time, his whole body shaking with it.

I grumble, "I fail to understand what's so hilarious here."

"It's the last line in the final canto of the poem, where Dante ascends to heaven and is engulfed in the divine light and love of God. It's probably the most famous line of poetry in history."

"Pfft. No, the most famous line of poetry in history is 'I do not like green eggs and ham, I do not like them, Sam-I-Am.' That's Dr. Seuss, in case your reading hasn't progressed that far."

He lifts his head and gazes at me, his eyes full of adoration and his grin blinding.

Smiling back at him, I say, "So that's what heaven is, huh? Turning wheels and spinning stars?"

"It was to Dante, anyway."

"What do you think heaven is?"

His smile fades. His energy slowly changes from light to dark, as does his gaze. Looking deep into my eyes, he says softly, "You."

That's the moment I finally let go of my past and my fears and fall—jump—*rush headlong*—in love with him.

I wrap my arms around his neck and put it all into a kiss.

Because he's Aidan, he gives it back to me a thousandfold.

⌒

From that night on, we're inseparable. We spend every waking and sleeping moment together. The next few months are what dreams are made of, a fairy tale come true.

Then New Year's Eve arrives.

And with it, the end.

40

KAYLA

New Year's Eve

In the candlelight, Aidan's face is as beautiful as an angel's.

"How are you so pretty?" I murmur, tracing a finger across the angle of his cheek then down to his jaw. His dark beard is soft and springy under my fingertip.

We're lying in bed at my house, facing each other, the lengths of our nude bodies aligned from chest to thighs. My feet are tucked between his calves. One of his biceps cradles my head. He's using the other arm to keep me bound tight against him.

Gazing at me with soft eyes, he says, "I'm not. You're just drunk with afterglow."

My laugh is low and throaty. "Is that like beer goggles but with sex?"

"Exactly. Your orgasm has made your vision fuzzy. In reality, I look like a warthog."

Smiling, I kiss the tip of his nose. "You do actually bear a striking resemblance to a warthog. I've been trying to spare your feelings by not bringing it up."

Nuzzling my neck, he whispers, "Speaking of bringing things up . . ."

He flexes his hips, pressing his erection against my thigh.

I laugh again, feeling high and reckless, as if I'm standing at the top of a tall cliff, about to tumble over the edge. "Have you never heard of the refractory period?"

"I have, but my dick hasn't."

"Clearly."

He quirks a brow. "Are you complaining?"

That makes me grin. "No, sir. I love it."

He rolls over on top of me. Lowering his head, he kisses me softly, murmuring against my lips, "Say that again, bunny."

"The sir part or the love part?"

"Both." His eyes darken, and his voice drops. "But leave out the 'no' and the 'it.'"

I have to think about that for a moment. When I understand what he wants me to say, my cheeks heat.

But I give him what he wants. Without reservation and without regret, the way he needs it.

Gazing into his eyes, my face hot and my heart pounding, I whisper, "I love sir."

He moistens his lips. His breathing goes erratic. Heavy and warm on top of me, he feels like the anchor that will keep me steady and the harbor that will keep me safe, no matter how strong the storm.

Rubbing his thumb slowly back and forth over the slope of my cheek, he says in a husky voice, "And I love my sweet little rabbit, who made me grateful for every day I walked through hell because that dark path eventually led to her."

I breathe out a soft sob, but he silences it as he kisses me.

I think he's going to push inside me, but he rolls to his back instead, taking me along so I'm lying atop him. Holding my hair back from my face, he says casually, "There's supposed to be fireworks at midnight tonight."

"Wow."

"What?"

"Talk about a disappointing segue. I thought you were about to make love to me again."

He chuckles. "I was, but then I got the genius idea of taking the boat out so there would be fireworks exploding overhead the next time I make you come."

"Ah. Yes, that would be a memorable way to ring in the New Year."

We grin at each other. He says, "I bought chocolate and champagne. Just in case you were up for it."

"In what universe would I *not* be up for you feeding me champagne and chocolate under a fireworks-filled sky after giving me a mind-blowing orgasm?"

"Oh, so I'm feeding you now, too?" He rolls his eyes in mock dismay. "I have to do all the work around here."

I press a kiss to his lips and whisper, "Poor baby."

He tosses me onto my back and growls, "Careful. Warthogs eat bunnies for dinner." Then he nips at my neck and tickles me, making me scream.

Laughing, he rises. I watch, smiling, as he goes into the closet. He emerges clothed soon thereafter.

"Get that sweet behind moving," he says, shooting me a wicked grin as he leaves the room. "I'll meet you downstairs."

I pop up from bed and dress as quickly as I can, pulling on jeans and a thick sweater over a long-sleeved shirt. It's not raining tonight, but with the temperature in the low fifties, it will be cold on the water. I shove my feet into a pair of boots and head downstairs, grinning.

It's strange how light joy makes your body feel. If I concentrated, I bet I could float right off the ground.

I find Aidan in the kitchen loading the champagne, chocolates, and a pair of champagne glasses into a picnic basket. I tease, "Look at you, so domestic."

"I think the word you're looking for is romantic."

I go up behind him and wrap my arms around his waist. Resting my cheek against his broad back, I murmur, "Actually, the word I'm looking for is amazing. No, wonderful. No, that's not it either. Hmm . . ."

"Glorious," he supplies, turning to embrace me. "I'll take spectacular, too."

"Yeah, I bet you would."

He kisses me, cradling my face in his hands. It's a sweet kiss, but it quickly turns heated. I pull out of his arms, laughing.

"Okay, Fight Club, let's get this show on the road, or we'll never make it out of the kitchen."

"So bossy," he says, shaking his head. He's trying to frown, but not quite managing it.

"I'll get a couple blankets. Meet you at the back door."

I leave him in the kitchen and go hunting through the linen closet in the guest bedroom for the throws kept folded in a stack. Choosing two that are thick and soft, I wrap one around my shoulders and carry the other to where Aidan stands waiting at the door with the wicker basket in hand.

When I drape the blanket across his shoulders, he makes a

face. "You realize warthogs don't get cold, right? We're way too tough for that."

I wave him aside. "Be quiet, macho man. You'll thank me when we're on the water."

We head across the lawn and down to the rocky beach toward the *Eurydice* tied at the end of the dock. The air is fresh and cold. It smells strongly of pine sap, wet bark, and moss. Above us, the sky is a bowl of deep sapphire sprinkled with stars. It's still and quiet except for the crickets serenading us with their evening song. Aidan grasps my hand and squeezes it, glancing down to smile at me.

If there is a heaven, I hope it's exactly like this.

Aidan helps me onto the stern of the boat, then hands me the picnic basket. He hops over the edge of the hull and unties the ropes from the cleats on the side while I climb the narrow stairs up to the bridge. Elevated above the main and lower decks, it offers an unrestricted view of the water.

Moonlight shines off the dark, undulating waves. The sound is calm tonight and the skies are clear, which will make for spectacular fireworks viewing.

I run the blower for a minute to clear fumes from the engine compartment, then turn the batteries on and fire up the engines. After checking the gauges to make sure we're good to go, I call down to Aidan, "You ready?"

He doesn't answer.

Walking over to the stairs, I call more loudly, "Aidan?"

Still no response. He must not be able to hear me over the engines.

Because the stairs are so steep, going down the steps is

slightly more awkward than going up. I have to climb down carefully, facing inward and grasping the metal railings on either side. When my feet finally touch the deck, I turn around, expecting to see Aidan in the seating area on the stern.

He's not there. The picnic basket sits alone on the table.

Frowning, I glance inside the main cabin . . . and freeze in horror.

Aidan stands stiffly on one side of the cabin, staring at the man standing across from him, about six feet away.

It's Michael.

Wearing the same gray trench coat and hat I've seen him in several times over the past few months when I've caught glimpses of him following me, he's thin and unkempt, with hollowed cheeks and dark shadows under his wild eyes.

His arms hang by his sides.

In one hand, he grips a silver pistol.

I suck in a breath. My heartbeat slams into overdrive. A cold tremor runs through me, chilling me all the way down to my bones.

My voice high with stress, I say, "Michael, what are you doing?"

Eyes feverish, he replies in a hard voice, "Taking back what's mine. Did you really think you could leave me, Kayla? *Me?* You belong to me. And if I don't get to have you, nobody does."

His laugh is the most evil sound I've ever heard.

Terrified, I swallow and look at Aidan. He stands perfectly still, every muscle in his body tensed.

My mind is a rabid animal, scratching sharp claws at the inside of my skull.

Where did he get a gun? Does he know how to shoot it? Is it even loaded? Oh God, what do I do?

Though I'm panicked and desperate, I try to keep my voice as calm and soothing as I can. "I'm not yours, Michael. It's over."

Spittle flies from his lips when he screams, "You belong to me!"

He jerks his arm up and points the gun at Aidan's chest.

I'm so frightened, I think I might faint.

Aidan remains perfectly still, his face impassive and his breathing shallow. I see wheels turning behind his eyes and am terrified of what might happen next.

Swallowing a sob, I lift my hands and start pleading. "No, please, listen to me. Don't do anything you'll regret. There's no need for this. We can talk it out."

Michael licks his cracked lips. He shifts his weight restlessly from foot to foot. That hand holding the pistol is now shaking hard.

Then he slices his wild gaze in my direction. "*Now* you want to talk, huh? After everything you've put me through? After the way you treated me? Leaving the way you did. Discarding me like trash. You've got some fucking nerve."

I grasp my mistake when Michael turns the gun toward me. I jerk back a step, a scream caught in my throat.

Aidan says firmly, "Michael, listen to me. Put the gun down."

"You don't get to fucking talk to me! You don't get to tell me what to do!"

"Yes, I do. Because I'm the one who started it all."

Michael looks back and forth between us, then jerks the gun back in Aidan's direction.

"Started what?"

"Kayla never wanted to leave you. I'm the one who made her

file for divorce. It was all my fault. I'm the one you should be angry with, not her. Let her go and we can talk."

Aidan looks at me. What I see in his eyes makes me want to scream, it's so stupid. So stupid and reckless and so fucking like him, the self-sacrificing fool.

What he's saying is a lie. I never met him before I ended my marriage. But he's going to try to appease Michael long enough to get me to safety.

Except he's not the one holding the gun. And he doesn't know how unpredictable Michael can be . . . or how fiendishly clever.

No, God, no, this isn't happening, this can't be happening.

Aidan looks back at Michael and repeats calmly, "Let her go. You and I can talk better if she's not here."

"No, Aidan, I won't—"

"Be quiet, Kayla."

"I'm not getting off this boat!"

"You are. Right now. Do it."

Michael's wild gaze darts back and forth between us. In his eyes, I see nothing of the man I married so long ago. The monster has finally swallowed him whole.

My pulse is a roar of thunder in my ears.

How can I distract him? What can I hit him with? The fire extinguisher! It's right over there!

Seeing me looking around in panic, Michael suddenly screams, "What the fuck are you doing?"

"She's just scared," says Aidan. "You're pointing a gun at her. Anyone would be scared."

Panting, Michael hisses, "You're not scared."

"That's because I know you deserve an apology, and I want to give it to you properly. Kayla, get the fuck off this boat."

Goddammit, Aidan, no! No! Stop this!

Tears stream down my face. My vision is blurred by them. My breathing is labored. I take a halting step backward, then another, hysteria gripping me in a cold, crushing hand.

I can call 911. If I can make it to the house and Aidan can keep Michael talking, I can call the police and get them here before anything awful happens.

I stop short when Michael says in the barest of whispers, "No. You're lying. I see it on your face." He looks at me. His voice rises. "You *both* have to die!"

When I sob and clap my hands over my mouth, Aidan says in a commanding voice, "Nobody has to die. Just put the gun down and we can talk about it."

His hand shaking and all the whites of his eyes showing, Michael screams, "*One of you has to die you have to choose right now who dies who dies who dies if you don't choose I have to kill you both!*"

He points the gun at me again. He points it right at my face. The only reason I don't topple over is because terror has turned my muscles to stone.

Aidan says, "If we choose, you'll only shoot one of us?"

My heart stops beating then. It stops dead in my chest, stalled by horror. "No, Aidan, stop it, don't say another word—"

"Michael?"

"Aidan, no! Stop it!"

Michael screams, "*Yes!*" and cocks the hammer of the pistol with his thumb.

Aidan looks at me. His heart shines in his eyes. He says softly, "I love you, bunny. I'll love you until the end of time."

Then he looks back at Michael and says words I'll never be able to unhear. They'll echo in my head for all eternity.

"Shoot me, then."

Time changes. Everything takes on the surreal quality of a dream. I see what happens next unfold in front of me like a movie played in slow motion with the sound warped and the colors blurred, dragging by at half speed.

Michael swings his arm toward Aidan.

Aidan lunges.

A fireball explodes from the end of Michael's gun.

Aidan's head snaps back.

The forward motion of his body stops abruptly, as if he's been slammed against a wall.

A small red hole appears in the center of his forehead.

Blood and chunks of brain matter splatter the window behind him.

He falls back, his eyes open and his mouth slack.

Collapsing onto the sofa, he lies still and silent, gazing sightlessly at the ceiling as a dark stain creeps across the beige cushion under his head.

In the night sky above us, fireworks burst into sprays of color with a crackle and boom.

My scream is a living thing. A creature of horror, disbelief, and heartbreak, clawing its way up my throat. I fly across the space between us with that scream surrounding me everywhere, vibrating in my ears and in my head, inside all the hidden sacred places in my soul that only he has ever touched.

I fall on top of Aidan's lifeless body, screaming and screaming the same thing over and over, the thing every cell in my body screams along with me.

No. No. No. No. No.

He doesn't look at me. He doesn't respond to any of my desperate pleas or the kisses I rain over his cheeks and lips.

He can't.

He's gone.

Sobbing hysterically, I cling to him until something hard and heavy bashes me in the back of the head.

Pain shoots through my skull. I see stars. For a moment, my vision goes black.

When light fills my eyes again, I'm on my back and Michael is dragging me by my wrists across the wood deck toward the swim step at the back of the boat.

My words come out slurred. "Michael. What are you doing?"

I can't make out what he mumbles to himself. It's incoherent, babbling nonsensical words spoken between labored breaths as he drags me away from Aidan's body. I try to pull my wrists from his grip, but don't have the strength.

Hot liquid trickles down my neck. Blood. He must've hit me with something heavy.

The gun. He pistol-whipped me with the gun.

More fireworks explode overhead. I see them above us, starbursts of color painting the midnight sky like the domed roof of a cathedral. Smoke drifts over the water. Somewhere far away, a dog barks.

Michael drags me to the edge of the stern and rolls me off.

The water is a cold black shock, cutting through my stupor like a blade. I go under for a moment before starting to kick and flail. I break the surface, sputtering and gasping, disoriented and panicking, fear as sharp as a knife shoved between my ribs.

I cough and scream. The boat's engines hum and rumble. Michael looms over me on the step, laughing maniacally now, his lips peeled back from his teeth.

I flail at the step, missing it by inches. Michael drops to his knees and reaches out. I grasp his hand, thinking he's offering help, but quickly discover he's not.

He grabs me by the throat and squeezes.

He pushes me down and holds me under.

Even underwater, I can hear his evil laugh.

Something slips out of his shirt pocket. It splashes into the water and tumbles past my face, small and round, silver and glinting.

It's his lucky 1937 buffalo nickel, the one he never leaves home without.

I kick and struggle. My heart hammers against my rib cage. Salt water stings my eyes and burns my lungs. Fireworks illuminate the surface of the water in a shimmering kaleidoscope of colors.

I can't get his fingers off my neck. I claw at his hands, thrashing and coughing, smelling diesel fuel and gunpowder, smoke and sea and blood.

Aidan.

Aidan.

Aidan, I love you. I love you.

My body is heavy. The churning water above me stills. I drift, my hair floating around my head, my eyes turned toward the surface, my hand outstretched for help that doesn't come.

A brilliant bloom of color suffuses the sea above me in shades of red, green, and gold, then the fireworks fade, and everything goes black.

My heart throbs one final time before stopping for good.

III

PARADISO

Death is not extinguishing the light;
it is only putting out the lamp
because the dawn has come.

~ Rabindranath Tagore

41

KAYLA

What we call memory is the intersection between imagination and fact. Memories are the stories we tell ourselves about the important events in our lives. In the telling, some details get lost, others embellished, until truth is closer to fiction.

It's like Fiona said. Each of us makes our own truths, even ghosts.

I suppose I should've figured it out the day she came in the house and disarmed the security alarm without me having told her the code. That was the same day she said she thought something was troubling me and that ghosts need closure. By that time, she'd been working for the Wainwrights for more than a month. They kept her on when they bought the house, never knowing just how helpful she'd turn out to be.

She isn't quite as gifted as her sister, Claire, but the gift does run in the family.

It took months of me sifting through memories and reliving my past to understand what happened. I lived two parallel lives, one past and one present, removed from reality but believing myself in it, utterly blind to the truth.

Everything that happened with Aidan was real. So was everything that happened after New Year's. But it got all jumbled together and mixed up, because being dead and not realizing it is very fucking confusing.

Past. Present. Fact. Memory. Everything interconnected and part of a whole, like individual pages in a book before it's bound.

But now my binding is set. My story is told. The book of my life has been written to its final chapter.

All that's left is to close the cover and put it away.

◦⁓◦

When I open my eyes, nothing looks the same. The walls are painted a different color. The carpet has been replaced by wood. The furnishings are unfamiliar, as are the people in the framed photographs on the walls.

The house is very different from when I lived in it. Different but familiar, like the face of a friend you haven't seen in many years. I never noticed the changes before, but the blinds have been lifted from my eyes now. My vision is finally clear.

The storm outside has ceased raging. Everything is still. Beyond the living room windows, dawn spreads glimmering light over the yard and faraway hills. I hear birds chirping, smell springtime in the air, and marvel at the beauty of it all.

The doorbell rings.

I move toward the front door, compelled by a force as elemental as gravity, as unstoppable as time. I turn the knob, pull the door open, and find Aidan standing on the porch.

He's drenched in golden sunlight, smiling at me as if I'm the first sunrise he's ever seen.

"Hey, bunny," he says softly, his eyes shining with adoration. "Did you miss me?"

I fall into his arms. His embrace is sweeter than a thousand kisses, better than a million wishes, more perfect than any dream could ever be.

"You found me," I whisper, crying tears of joy.

He rubs his cheek against mine, breathing me in as he holds me tight.

"I never lost you. Who do you think has been ringing the doorbell this whole time?"

I bury my face in his neck. "I'm sorry. I didn't know. I couldn't see. I was so confused."

He murmurs against my ear, "It's okay. I told you I'd wait forever if I had to."

When I raise my head and stare at him through watering eyes, he smiles a smile of such beauty, it takes my breath away.

I say, "The life jacket was a nice touch."

"I thought so."

"Was that you during the séance, or was I doing all the knocking and special effects?"

"That was me. But all the other stuff that went on in the house was you. The flickering lights, the open cupboards, the TV going on and off . . . I'm sorry to say, you made it pretty miserable for the Wainwrights."

"Wow. I'm dead *and* melodramatic. You'd think making it to the afterlife would give a person a certain perspective on things."

He says gently, "You were traumatized. Give yourself a break."

"And my wedding ring falling through the ceiling? The coin that kept getting moved? I suppose that was you, too?"

"None of that matters now. What matters is that we're together."

"But wait, how come *I* didn't understand what was happening, but you did?"

He smiles. "Maybe I'm just smarter than you are."

"That isn't even a little bit funny."

All around us, the golden light grows brighter. I feel a pleasant urgency, an upward pull that increases with each incremental lift of light. I want to surrender to the pull, but I have something I need to ask first.

"Why did you postmark all the letters from prison? Was that a clue about your past?"

He smiles. "More like a clue about the future."

"What do you mean?"

"Washington State Penitentiary is where a certain asshole is being held on charges of murder. I've been thinking we should pay him a visit."

I recall how Fiona told me that many geniuses can see ghosts and can't help but laugh. "Oh, Aidan, you're diabolical."

The golden light surrounding us grows brighter. Then he takes my face in his hands and kisses me. In his lips, I taste forever.

That and something almost as sweet:

Revenge.

EPILOGUE

Transcribed from the notes and session recording of March 16 conducted by Dr. Patrick Templeman, forensic psychiatrist, with Michael Reece, currently awaiting trial on charges of first-degree murder.

DR. TEMPLEMAN: Thank you for joining me today, Mr. Reece.

MICHAEL REECE: It's Doctor Reece. And you say that as if I had a choice in the matter. They brought me down here in handcuffs. Have you noticed the handcuffs?

DR. TEMPLEMAN: How are you feeling today?

MICHAEL REECE: I wonder how many times you'll say the word "today" before you get to the point?

DR. TEMPLEMAN: As you're aware, Mr. Reece, my objective is to determine your current mental capacity to stand trial, as ordered by the court.

MICHAEL REECE: The court can kiss my ass, and so can you. And it's *Doctor* Reece.

DR. TEMPLEMAN: Do you understand the charges brought against you?

MICHAEL REECE: Let me tell you something. You're not the only person in this room with a big degree. I've got three of them, all right? Ph.D., master's, etcetera, all from Ivy League schools. Your medical degree doesn't impress me.

Physician's note: Patient is visibly agitated.

DR. TEMPLEMAN: You have had several violent outbursts since your arrest, is that correct? I understand you broke a guard's arm.

MICHAEL REECE: Are you the best they could do? You look about as competent as that public defender they assigned me.

DR. TEMPLEMAN: How is your relationship with the attorney? Do you feel he's adequately described the charges brought against you?

MICHAEL REECE: That idiot couldn't adequately describe the color of a turd. They let anyone pass the bar these days, apparently.

DR. TEMPLEMAN: Can you tell me what the charges against you are, please?

MICHAEL REECE: Seriously?

DR. TEMPLEMAN: I'm trying to evaluate if you understand what's happening to you.

MICHAEL REECE: Yes, I understand what's happening to me. I'm being held for defending myself from an attack.

DR. TEMPLEMAN: We're speaking of the murder of your estranged wife, Kayla, and Aidan Leighrite, is that correct?

MICHAEL REECE: Jesus Christ. This is going to take forever.

DR. TEMPLEMAN: Do you recall the events of December thirty-first last year?

MICHAEL REECE: I'm not an imbecile.

DR. TEMPLEMAN: I'll take that as a yes. Will you please describe for me what you feel your current relationship with your attorney is like?

MICHAEL REECE: *unintelligible*

DR. TEMPLEMAN: What do you think will happen if you're convicted on the charges?

MICHAEL REECE: I won't be convicted. Someone like me shouldn't be in prison.

DR. TEMPLEMAN: Someone like you?

MICHAEL REECE: I'm a highly respected member of the community. My work is incredibly important. I'm not some rapist or drug dealer. Those people should be behind bars, not me.

DR. TEMPLEMAN: You don't believe a double homicide is just cause for a prison sentence?

MICHAEL REECE: I can't be held responsible for that. It was self-defense. *I'm* the victim here, okay? Me!

DR. TEMPLEMAN: Do you regret what happened?

MICHAEL REECE: I regret that you're wasting my time with this ridiculous line of questioning.

Physician's note: Patient displays traits of narcissistic personality disorder.

DR. TEMPLEMAN: What do you understand regarding the stages of the proceedings in a capital murder case? Has that been adequately explained to you?

MICHAEL REECE: I understand that I shouldn't have to stand trial. Which is obvious, because of who I am. Geniuses shouldn't be on trial. Or in jail, for that matter.

I have an IQ of over two hundred points, for Christ's sake.

DR. TEMPLEMAN: Do you also understand that if your case does proceed to trial and you're convicted, you may be facing life in prison with no possibility of parole?

MICHAEL REECE: What? No, that's not right. It was clearly self-defense. What are you talking about?

DR. TEMPLEMAN: The issue is intent. You have a documented history of physical abuse against your wife. The prosecutor will introduce evidence that you were stalking her for months prior to her murder. He will also introduce evidence that you were involved in a long-term affair with a coworker at the university. Sharon, I believe is her name? Or is it Karen? I'm sorry, I don't have those notes in front of me. There's also the matter of the life insurance policy you took out on your wife. Was she aware of that policy?

MICHAEL REECE: Listen, I've had enough of this. I want . . .

DR. TEMPLEMAN: Yes? Go on.

Physician's note: Patient is fixating on a spot on the wall and becoming unresponsive. He appears to be in extreme distress.

DR. TEMPLEMAN: Mr. Reece, are you unwell?

MICHAEL REECE: Oh God. Oh my God!

DR. TEMPLEMAN: Mr. Reece?

Physician's note: Patient is screaming. Attempts to exit the interview room. Pounds on the door in visible panic.

DR. TEMPLEMAN: Mr. Reece, what's wrong? Tell me what's happening.

MICHAEL REECE: It's her! It's her and him both! Oh God! Let me out of here! Let me out of this fucking room!

Physician's note: Patient appears to be experiencing a visual disturbance.

DR. TEMPLEMAN: Mr. Reece, we're alone in the room.

MICHAEL REECE: She's right fucking there, you fucking idiot! Look! *Look!*

DR. TEMPLEMAN: As I said, you and I are the only people in this room.

Physician's note: Patient has crouched in the corner of the room and resumed screaming. I cannot discount the possibility that this behavior is a calculated ploy to introduce an alternate defense to his case, namely mental incompetency.

DR. TEMPLEMAN: Mr. Reece, will you please calm down? I'll have to call for you to be tranquilized if you can't control yourself.

MICHAEL REECE: (*screaming*) Stop saying that! Stop saying that! Stop saying that word!

DR. TEMPLEMAN: What word are you hearing, Michael? Is someone speaking to you? What are they saying?

MICHAEL REECE: BOO!

Physician's note: After being restrained by guards, patient received intramuscular injection of phenobarbital and was transferred to the psychiatric department for further evaluation.

AUTHOR'S NOTE

I've never cried writing a book as much as I did with *Pen Pal,* a sentiment I know a lot of people shared while reading it. So many readers have reached out to me to express their emotions about these characters and request more, especially from Aidan's point of view. This bonus scene overlaps with chapter ten, allowing a glimpse into what Aidan was thinking and feeling the night Kayla showed up soaking wet on his doorstep, seeking solace in his arms.

BONUS CHAPTER

It's long past midnight. The room is dark and still. I'm lying on my back in bed, a thin sheet my only cover as I stare up at the ceiling and listen to the winter storm gather strength outside.

Rain thrums on the roof. Tree branches sound like ghostly fingernails scratching against the windowpanes. Gusts of wind wail eerily like a wolf pack's howls. But above all that noise, a single word repeats over and over inside my mind.

Kayla.

Kayla with her sphinxlike smile, devastating beauty, and soulful, eloquent eyes.

I met her a week ago. I've thought of nothing else since.

She burns in my brain like a fever.

When I went to give her an estimate for roof repairs on her house that first day, I was in a shit mood. Not unusual for me, but the week prior had been worse than most. Jake was on my case again about me spending too much time alone. A big job I was counting on went to a competitor. My truck got a flat, my bike blew another fuse, and I dropped my brand-new cell phone in a damn puddle of water and fried it.

Worst of all, another bank denied me a construction loan.

Money men don't like to take risks on convicted felons.

So the progress on the house I'd been building for myself on the other side of the island would continue to move at a snail's pace, funded only by what I had leftover in my checking account at the end of every month and what I could do in trade with other contractors.

It was frustrating as hell, because working on that house was the only time I was close to being at peace. And I had this hope, this dumb, baseless hope, that when it was all finished and I moved in, I might actually be happy.

Then I knocked on Kayla Reece's door.

She opened up and looked at me, and all the happy I'd been waiting my whole life for hit me at once, detonating into a burning fireball inside my body.

I've heard people talk about joy and rapture before as if they were real things. I always thought those people were fucking idiots, but standing there on Kayla's front porch looking into those bottomless ocean eyes, I felt as if God Himself had tapped me on the shoulder and said, "Here you go, son. Don't fuck it up."

I'm not ashamed to admit that she took my breath away. She sucked all the air right out of my lungs.

Then she smiled, and I felt like I could breathe for the first time in a hundred years.

I could breathe, but not talk. The power of speech had deserted me. I stood staring at her in awe like some kind of starstruck lunatic until she said, "Can I help you?"

The only response I could manage was my name.

Which I barely remembered.

Then she invited me inside and I proceeded to irritate the shit out of her, because not only are my people skills about as smooth as a porcupine's ass, I was having a hell of a time fighting an almost overpowering desire to take her into my arms and hold her until that strange sadness in her eyes disappeared.

I'm not normally a huggy kind of guy. Scratch that—I'm *never* huggy. But something about Kayla Reece made me want to wrap myself around her and protect her from harm.

So she hired me to fix her roof, but she fired me the very next day. Like I said, I irritated the shit out of her.

But I had the strangest feeling that wasn't the end of it. A few moments in her presence quieted all the demons in my head, and I knew that couldn't be for nothing.

Five days went by. Then, tonight, I decided to go to the bar downstairs for a drink. Don't know why, I haven't been there in weeks, but all of a sudden I needed a beer on tap like I needed oxygen. Ten seconds after the bartender set the IPA in front of me, I got a sharp zap out of nowhere like a charge of static electricity. I glanced over at the door, and there she was.

Our eyes met.

The hair on my arms stood on end.

The clock on the wall stopped ticking.

Maybe I'm being melodramatic, but it felt preordained that Kayla walked through the door at that moment. It felt like something bigger than us had decided to bring us together again, as if Fate were weaving its dark magic around us.

That strange sense of destiny caused me to be more obnoxious than usual.

The look on her face when I asked her if she found me attractive will be burned into my memory forever. She wanted me, that much was obvious, but more importantly, I could tell she felt safe with me. She felt so safe, she let me kiss her.

There isn't language for what I felt when my lips met hers. I won't even attempt it.

I also won't attempt to describe my feelings when she eventually left the bar after we spent half an hour having the most intense conversation of my life. Both of our lives, if I had to judge by her dazed expression.

She said goodbye. I said good night, because goodbye was much too final. With everything inside me, I wanted that to be a word we never spoke.

When she'd gone, I sat in the booth alone and let my atoms slowly rearrange themselves into a beautiful new reality, one with Kayla Reece at the center of it.

Tough but fragile. Smart but lost. She's a woman I suspect has as many secrets as I do, but the only thing I care about now is seeing her again and getting another chance to make her smile.

Lying here in bed awake and electrified, listening to the storm rage outside, I long for that chance. I want her so badly, I ache.

Frantic pounding on the front door pulls me abruptly from my reverie.

I jump from bed, drag on the pair of jeans I left on the floor, and jog through the apartment, flicking on lights. When I pull open the door, my heart stops dead.

Kayla stands on my doorstep. She's shivering, barefoot, and dripping wet.

She's not wearing a bra. Her perfect breasts are clearly visible beneath the fabric of her T-shirt. Her nipples are hard.

The whole world disappears. Somewhere off in the distance, thunder booms, echoing the sound inside my heart.

Eyes wide, she looks me up and down. Then she glances behind me into the living room, and a look of dismay crosses her face. She blurts, "I'm so sorry to disturb you. I'm going now."

She turns to run away, but I grasp her arm before she can and pull her inside.

Closing the door, I say, "What's wrong? What happened?"

Teeth chattering, she crosses her arms over her chest and hugs herself. "I th-thought s-someone broke into my h-house."

"So you came here?"

I didn't mean for it to sound accusatory. It's just that I'm stunned by the sight of her. Stunned and thrilled by the knowledge that she thought of me when she needed help. But I can tell by her expression that it didn't come out right, so I clarify. "That wasn't a reproach."

She's silent. Pensive. I can't help but notice how goddamn beautiful she is. Her face, her body, even her bare toes, every part of her is pretty. The urge to pull her into my arms and kiss her is so strong, it's crossing all the wires in my brain. Which must be why the next thing out of my mouth is so ridiculous.

"You're wet."

Idiot! Pull yourself together! She's upset, and she needs your help!

I manage to string together two coherent sentences. "Let's get you warm. Then you can tell me what happened."

I lead her inside by the elbow and sit her down at the kitchen table. Then I head into the bathroom for a towel, wondering if maybe I've got a cardiac condition I didn't know about because my heart is thudding painfully hard.

Kayla Reece is in my home. She's wet and in distress and she's fucking *here*.

My hands shake as I grab a clean towel from the bathroom shelf.

When I return to the kitchen, she looks miserable. Like she's regretting this already. Like she's worried about what I'll think of her for showing up here this way. My thudding heart decides it's time for a change of pace and melts.

"Stand up."

Emotion makes my voice brusque, bordering on rude. But if she's annoyed by my shit manners, she doesn't show it. She obeys me without hesitation. I wrap the towel around her back and shoulders and start to rub her arms with it.

She stands there with her cheeks burning, looking like she'd like to kick her own ass.

"Don't be embarrassed."

"Easy for you to say. You're not the wet idiot standing in a stranger's kitchen at one o'clock in the morning."

"I'm not a stranger, remember? And you're not an idiot."

You're an angel. A sweet, perfect angel. Let me take care of you forever, beautiful girl.

My hands are shaking again. Trying to hide it, I pull the towel up over her head and start blotting the rain from her hair.

Her face flaming, she says miserably, "I think I might be dying of humiliation."

"You're not dying of anything. Be quiet and let me do this."

Again, she obeys me without protest. I love that. I love that she's allowing me to do this without running away as she so obviously wants to. I also love that she keeps looking at my mouth but doesn't realize it.

My dick loves that, too. I'm getting hard.

My mind wanders into a fantasy of pulling up her wet T-shirt and touching her, feeling the weight of her breast in my hand. I imagine her clinging to my shoulders and arching into me as I suck one hard nipple into my mouth. Then I imagine pulling off her wet jeans and sinking my hard dick deep inside her, and I have to swallow a groan of need.

I take a moment to make sure that when I speak, my voice comes out steady. "We're gonna have a discussion later about why you chose me to come to when you were scared, but in the meantime, walk me through what happened."

Eyes closed, she tells me everything that happened at her house. The creaking floorboards, the oppressive atmosphere, the terrifying sense of being watched. When she's done, I say, "You don't have a security alarm?"

"No."

"We'll fix that tomorrow."

She glances up at me, her look tentative. I can tell by the way she's eyeing my beard that she wants to stroke it, which of course makes my dick even harder. I concentrate on rubbing her wet hair with the towel and hope she doesn't notice the bulge straining the zipper of my jeans.

She says, "What do you mean?"

"You know what I mean. And you're still shivering."

"I can't help it. I'm freezing."

I stop rubbing her head and meet her eyes. "I'm gonna say something now. Don't freak out."

She makes a face. "You should've just said it. Now I have to freak out."

"You need to change into dry clothes."

She frowns. "Why would that freak me out?"

"Because the dry clothes you're gonna change into are mine."

"I doubt you have anything that would fit me," she says drily.

Goddamn, this woman is adorable. "Look at you, not freaking out at all."

"Oh, I am. But I've done enough weird things for one night, so I'm keeping it on the inside."

"Come with me."

I drape the towel around her shoulders and lead her by the hand out of the kitchen and down the hallway into my bedroom, then go into the closet and turn on the light. I grab one of my sweatshirts. When I come back out, I find Kayla looking around my bedroom as if she's thinking I must've been robbed.

I look at it through her eyes—mattress on the floor, simple wood dresser on one wall, bookcase on the other, nothing else—and vow to myself that if I get the chance, I'll give her the best of everything.

"Yeah, I know. Super deluxe. Here."

She takes the sweatshirt and clutches it to her chest like a security blanket. She's still shaking with cold. With every second that passes, it's getting harder and harder to resist the urge to touch her.

"Aidan?"

"Yes, Kayla?"

"I'm really sorry about this. I promise I'm not a giant basket case. I'm just a little one."

She looks so lost. So sad and lost that my self-control snaps. Without realizing I'm going to do it, I reach out and stroke a strand of damp hair off her cheek.

Dazzled by the feel of her smooth skin under my fingertip, I murmur, "You're not anything but beautiful."

Fuck. You sound like a pervert. Do better.

"You don't have to freak out about that, either. I don't try to seduce traumatized women who run in from the rain."

"Okay. Thanks for that. Um . . . do you possibly have a pair of sweatpants I could wear with this?"

"You'd be swimming in them."

"I know, but . . ."

"But what?"

She draws a deep breath. "I'll be extremely self-conscious if my coochie is hanging out."

Her coochie?

"I don't have any underwear on."

"Oh. *Oh.*"

"Yes. So."

"Wait. You came over here with no underwear on?"

"I promise it wasn't premeditated. I got dressed in a panic. I didn't have time for panties."

"Or a bra, either," I say, my voice lower.

She winces. "You noticed."

"Are you fucking kidding me? Of course I noticed." I pause. "I also noticed that your cheeks get really red when you're embarrassed."

Her tone turns sarcastic. "Thanks for the info. Are you giving me sweats or not?"

"I don't own a pair of sweatpants."

"Oh."

"I can put your jeans in the dryer, though."

When she doesn't say anything, I add, "Or we can just stand here and stare at each other. I'm good with that, too."

"Why?"

My voice quiet, I admit, "I like looking at you."

She stares up at me with her lips parted and the vein in the side of her neck throbbing, and from one moment to the next, the air turns to fire.

She shrugs her shoulders. The towel drops to the floor. Then she pulls her wet shirt over her head and stands naked from the waist up in front of me.

She whispers, "I want you to do more than look."

My voice gruff, I reply, "Whatever you say, boss," and pull her into my arms.

Need makes me greedy. I crush my mouth to hers. She shivers against me, skin on skin, her hands in my hair and her heart pounding hard against mine.

Gravity ceases to exist. The floor drops out from under me. I'm stunned by the force of how much I want from her, how much more than this, more than whatever we could feel and share in one night.

I want more than tonight.

I want forever.

With a silent plea and a promise, I take her down to the bed.

Give me the rest of your life, Kayla. I won't let you down.

I promise I'll take care of you until the end of time.

BOOK CLUB
DISCUSSION QUESTIONS

1. Do you think *Pen Pal* has a happily ever after? Why or why not?
2. What were your theories about what was happening in the house at the beginning of the book? Did they change as you moved further into the story?
3. Did you guess the ending before you got there?
4. When you reached the end of the book, was there anything that happened earlier that you reconsidered in light of your new knowledge?
5. What do you think the wedding ring and the Buffalo coin symbolize in the thematic context of the novel?
6. Now that you know the ending, will you reread the book looking for clues that you missed?
7. Which scene from the book did you find most memorable?
8. At what point did you realize what was really happening to Kayla? How did that affect you?
9. What connections can be drawn between *The Divine Comedy* by Dante Alighieri and this story?
10. Do you believe in ghosts? Have you ever had a supernatural experience?
11. How do you know for sure that you are alive at this moment?

ACKNOWLEDGMENTS

The idea for this novel came from one of my characters. If you're familiar with the Queens & Monsters series, in book three, *Savage Hearts*, Riley is kidnapped by Malek, a Russian assassin. As one does when one is recovering from a bullet wound and being held hostage in the middle of a remote Russian forest, she starts to write a book during her captivity to pass the time. It's about a woman who doesn't know she's dead. I really liked that idea.

So thank you for that, Riley.

There are also several other sources of inspiration for this novel that I'd be remiss if I didn't mention. In no particular order, they are the movies *Ghost, Poltergeist, The Sixth Sense, The Others, Pan's Labyrinth,* and especially *Jacob's Ladder,* which I saw when I was twenty years old and never emotionally recovered from. Also the brilliant novels *Leaving Time* by Jodi Picoult and *We Were Liars* by E. Lockhart, the novella *The Turn of the Screw* by Henry James, the play *Hamlet* by Shakespeare, and the narrative poem *The Divine Comedy* by Dante. And finally, the ancient Greek legend of Eurydice and Orpheus, which served as both an influence on the story and a name for Kayla's boat.

There's one other major influence that's much more personal in nature: my father's death.

My father was in hospice care at home for three weeks before he died. I sat with him at his bedside in the house I grew up in and watched him deteriorate until finally, he was no longer there. I'll spare you the details, but it was heartbreaking. I'm still not over it, and it's been eight years.

But two significant things happened in those weeks that I will tell you about, because they permanently altered me.

The first thing is that before Dad got to the point where he could no longer speak, he asked me to bring him his address book. He kept it in a big wood rolltop desk in his office, under the framed posters of Amelia Earhart and WWII fighter planes. The book contained the names and phone numbers of all his lifelong friends and extended family members. (He'd put a line through a name if the person had died, but never removed the listing.) Because he was too weak to do it, I dialed the numbers from the book and held the phone to his ear as he called everyone he loved to say goodbye.

Listening to those conversations is one of the most meaningful experiences of my life.

It is also one of the most painful.

To know you're dying is not an easy thing. To face your imminent death with courage isn't easy, either. But my father didn't make a fuss. He simply went about dying as he went about living. With competence and quiet dignity, doing what needed to be done despite whatever he might have been feeling about the situation.

He wasn't what you'd call an emotionally demonstrative guy. He grew up in Brooklyn in the 1940s. His own father died when he was a child. His mother, my grandma Ella, was about as cuddly as a cactus. He went to college on an engineering scholarship and eventually became an aerospace engineer. I never once saw him cry, get drunk, or lose his temper. He was the poster child of the Greatest Generation's ethics: personal responsibility, self-sacrifice, humility, frugality, integrity.

I could go on, but my point is that the man was more stoic than the Stoics. He'd never be accused of being whimsical.

Which is why it came as such a shock when he matter-of-factly declared that his mother had visited him.

My grandmother had been dead at that point for thirty-two years.

Then he told me about the angels.

"They're right there," he said, gesturing to the ceiling above his bed. So were all his old friends who'd already passed on. Everybody was just patiently waiting for him there in the beautiful white light.

I cannot express how overwhelming it was to hear him talk like that. He wasn't on morphine. He wasn't drugged in any way. He was weak, yes, and very tired, but indisputably lucid.

And he was seeing angels and dead people.

When I spoke to the hospice nurse later to find out if that was unusual, she told me that visions of the afterlife are one of the most common experiences among the dying. They see loved ones. They see angels. They see brilliant white light. The closer they are to death, the clearer the visions become.

I was dubious, to say the least.

"But couldn't these hallucinations simply be oxygen deprivation to the brain?" I asked. "Chemical imbalances? A side effect of the body's systems shutting down?"

That hospice nurse smiled at me as if I were a sweet but very silly child.

She never gave me an answer.

That silence haunts me, as do my father's visions.

I don't claim to have any answers, but I'll leave you with something Helen Keller once said: "Death is no more than passing from one room to another." I suppose we'll all eventually find out.

Thank you to my parents, for everything.

Thank you to Jay, for everything else.

Thank you to my readers, who give me much more than I could ever give them.

Thank you to my sensitivity reader for her thoughtful insights on abuse survivors and helpful feedback on the manuscript.

Thank you to Letitia Hasser of RBA Designs, Sarah Ferguson of Social Butterfly PR, Linda Ingmanson, Wander Aguiar Photography, the amazing members of Geissinger's Gang, and Mrs. Prouse, my sixth-grade English teacher, who thought I wasn't listening.

I was.

ABOUT THE AUTHOR

J.T. GEISSINGER is a #1 international bestselling author of thirty novels. Ranging from funny, feisty rom-coms to intense erotic thrillers, her books have sold over fifteen million copies and been translated into more than twenty languages.

She is a three-time finalist in both contemporary and paranormal romance for the RITA Award, the highest distinction in romance fiction from the Romance Writers of America. She is also a recipient of the PRISM Award for Best First Book, the Golden Quill Award for Best Paranormal/Urban Fantasy, and the HOLT Medallion for Best Erotic Romance.

Connect with her online in her Facebook reader group, Geissinger's Gang.